THE GOLDEN RUSH

The Golden Rush

ARIELLA TALIX

Ringmaster Publishing

Dear Reader,

Thank you for choosing my book for your entertainment. It means the world to me.

I want to make it clear before you begin that while I understand that in today's vernacular, we refer to the indigenous people of North America as Native Americans, during the nineteenth century, they were almost exclusively called "Indians." I have made every attempt in this book to be true to the language and slang of the times, so I have used the term "Indians" in some places. You will also see the terms "Gypsy" and "Negro" used. Both terms are meant with respect and used with adherence to the terms that were common during this historical time period.

My great-grandfather was Osage, and my great-grandmother was Cherokee and Blackfoot. It was important to her that we take pride in our Indian (as she called it) heritage. Her influence has always struck a chord in how I looked at life. As a typical American whose family has been here for many generations, I can also claim several other ethnic groups in my heritage, so I don't pretend to belong to any particular tribe, or to speak for its people. However, indigenous people are part of my family. I use the terminology in this book with an understanding of its history.

On another topic, it is interesting to note that the word "homosexual" was not used until 1868; "heterosexual" did not appear in print until far later in 1924. You won't see either term in this book as a result.

And one other very small thing that you may notice is the total lack of the well-known term "gold nugget." While that seems as normal as anything to us, the term was not used in California until it was introduced *after* the Gold Rush by Australian miners. This is not to say the Gold Rush miners didn't find them, for they certainly did. They just called them chunks or lumps of gold.

    -Ariella Talix

Sex is a hallowed ancient tradition that we humans have been performing since the dawn of time. It should not come with baggage or rules for what is allowed and not allowed. Besides, just because something is not allowed doesn't mean people aren't doing it.

-Anonymous

We are all, all of us fragile and flawed, yet we can reach for the stars and do tremendous good. That astonishing combination of weakness and courage is part of what defines the human condition.

Opening Exercises 2021, "Millimeters"
-Christopher L. Eisgruber, President Princeton University

Chapter One

San Francisco, California, 1850

Royal Dawson clapped his best friend on the back, a grin split his handsome face in two. "It's going to be a fine hotel, Jasper. All we need to do is help Isaac build some more furniture, outfit the kitchen properly, and hire one of the cooks we've spoken to. People will start lining up to stay here."

Together they admired the fine brick building. It was sturdy and substantial looking compared to the many tents and ramshackle buildings around the city.

"I hope so," answered Jasper Langley. "I can't wait to lay my head on something softer than the floor or the hard ground finally." He smiled at Royal and added, "We've earned it!"

Laughing, Royal replied, "I seem to remember you using *me* for a pillow more than once. Don't tell me you're turning soft."

"Well, there's nothing soft about you. I may have ended up with my head on your chest a time or two, but it's as hard as a rock. I probably just drifted over because I was cold."

Royal snorted good-naturedly. "I never minded."

Smiling, Jasper turned away from the freshly painted sign over the hotel entry and faced the harbor. His eyes lit up as he exclaimed, "Look, Royal, a ship is arriving! This one looks like a cargo ship! Let's grab the wagon and see if we can purchase anything important for the hotel."

They were off in a flash.

As the two friends made their way down the pier that jutted a long way out into the harbor, they could tell by the hoard of men crowding the rail of the ship that the Wind Gypsy had to be a cargo ship as they'd hoped. There were no families or obvious passengers aboard—just some rough-looking sailors who wanted to disembark in the worst way. They shoved and cursed at each other to get to the gangway first.

Royal chuckled and said, "These rascals certainly look like they've traded sea sickness for gold fever. So many hopeful arrivals every day, and they don't even know they're still over a hundred miles from any mining sites."

Instead of agreeing, Jasper suddenly grabbed Royal's arm and asked, "Do you hear that?"

Through the cacophony of the cheering and cursing men, they could barely hear the voice of a woman pleading for help. It was coming from the Wind Gypsy.

"What is the matter with these fools?" hollered Royal as the two men fought their way through the riot of men thundering down the gangway and spilling into the pier. The dock was so overcrowded it creaked precariously beneath their feet. Finally, the mob thinned enough for them to climb up and board the ship. What they saw took their breath away.

Chapter Two

Getting There, 1847

Royal and Jasper both grew up in New York, but they didn't meet until adulthood.

Royal Dawson was an adventure-craving young man who needed to make something of himself on his own. His father owned a dairy farm that Royal's six younger brothers all seemed content with, but Royal had dreams of something different—and decidedly less bovine. He had dreams of marrying his sweetheart and making a name for himself with her by his side.

Unfortunately for him, his beloved's father saw only that she was spending too much time with a kid who milked cows. The young lady Royal had had his eye on for five years was married off to an older, wealthy man—much to her tragic dismay. She'd professed to love Royal as much as he'd loved her, but her father's word was law. "My daughter will *not* marry a simple dairy farmer!" he'd fumed at her once he'd discovered the depth of their affection and attraction for each other. Despite the fact that Royal had a brilliant mind and read anything and everything he could get his hands on, he was still just a simple farm boy.

This was more than Royal could stand, so at the age of eighteen, he packed up his few belongings and set out for the West on his own. He vowed to himself to purge his mind of the narrow-minded father's decision and her disappointing acceptance of being treated like property.

Royal's family barely felt it when he left. He knew he would be leaving the farm in good hands; his brothers all worked hard and never spoke of anything other than animal husbandry and selling milk.

Royal loved them all, but he simply *had* to leave. *If I never milk another cow in my life, it will be too soon*, he thought as he rode away to begin his new life. *I don't even like milk. Cheese is pretty good, though*, he remembered, *and there's nothing like butter melting into a hot biscuit.* He longed for one of his mother's delicious meals and sighed. *I can't think about that now; I've made my decision to leave. And I certainly cannot think of what and whom I've lost. No. Just no.*

It took him four long years of working odd jobs and traveling from town to town until he found what he was looking for. All along the way to Missouri, as Royal completed one strenuous job after another, his body matured from a lanky boy into a tall, handsome young man. He radiated a golden glow of happiness, and he surely broke many hearts as he left bereft young ladies behind in his wake.

Finally in 1847, Royal met a former fur trapper who planned to head up a wagon train bound for the New West, and Royal signed on to be his assistant. The wagon master was happy to have someone young and strong with him who knew a lot about taking care of large animals, as he was well aware that the trip would be grueling.

Jasper Langley came from a well-to-do, city-dwelling family. He'd received a fine education and tied the knot with Isabella Carrington—a lovely young woman whose social status his parents praised—shortly after he finished school and went to work managing one of his father's textile factories.

Jasper's mother looked forward to spoiling many grandchildren and often doled out unsolicited advice about how to raise them. Isabella was polite and understanding to her new mother-in-law and privately ignored most of what the woman said. The opinions kept coming at such an alarming and escalating degree, however, that one day, Isabella exclaimed, "Perhaps, Mother Langley, you would do me the honor and write all of this down. I doubt I'll have the presence of mind to remember it all when the time comes, but your words are so important, I'd like to keep them close."

This had the temporary effect of quieting Mrs. Langley as she spent a few days writing down her copious lists. But then it got even worse when she presented Isabella with the stack of papers and insisted on reading all of them aloud to Isabella. She did so with much extraneous dialogue and painstaking elucidation.

Isabella had a hard time keeping her eyes open.

"Izzy, I think my job is going to kill me," Jasper grumbled a few weeks after their wedding. "I swear my brain is atrophying and I feel so stifled being cooped up indoors, some days I can't even catch my breath." The day-to-day sameness of his factory job made Jasper antsy, and most days he'd sit at his desk muttering and cursing the pile of paperwork he had to plow through. The cacophony of the factory hurt his head, so he took to stuffing cotton in his ears, but that just made him feel more claustrophobic. He longed to take Isabella in a carriage and head out for a romantic ride in the country where they could have a lazy picnic and listen to the songs of birds.

Often, Jasper couldn't sleep at night because he was so frustrated with what felt like a dead-end existence. He would pace the floor and then finally settle his nerves with a glass of brandy before heading back to bed. His only solace was sweet Isabella, who sated his manly needs in the most delicious ways and cooked scrumptious meals for him. Even with that, however, Jasper's insides burned for something better for the two of them.

Isabella loved her husband so dearly she often told him, "I'll go anywhere with you that pleases you." She encouraged him to think of what might one day quench his yearning.

About three months after they married, Jasper received a middling inheritance from his grandfather. The young couple shocked their families by making plans to seek an exciting life in the New West.

"What do you mean you're leaving?" Jasper's mother nearly shrieked.

Patiently, Jasper explained, "I've bought passage to head up the Erie Canal and to begin the trek westward. Piece by piece, we'll make the trip by boat, rail, and sometimes by wagon until we finally reach Independence, Missouri. In Independence, we'll find a wagon train heading west."

"A wagon train?" she demanded. "What do you mean?"

"I plan to buy the finest Prairie Schooner I can find as well as six sturdy oxen to pull it. Independence is where they start out on the California and Oregon Trails heading west. We might travel with as many as eighty to a hundred other wagons, but some groups are smaller. We'll just have to see when we get to Missouri."

"But why don't you buy a lovely team of horses, Jasper? Don't you want to make a good first impression on your new neighbors when you arrive?"

Ignoring how ridiculous that sounded to his ears, Jasper explained politely, "Horses aren't even as sturdy as mules,

Mother. And mules may be faster than oxen, I've been told, but they are not as reliable over the long trip, and we would have needed more of them. The oxen can also live on poor-quality grass when good grazing isn't readily available. So, oxen it will be."

"You're very clever, Husband," Isabella interjected with a doting smile.

"I want to get us there safely, Izzy," he reasoned to his wife. "And even if mules are quicker, we can't go any faster than the other travelers in the wagon train."

Isabella praised her handsome husband, "You are so wise and practical in these matters. I'm sure you know best." She regarded him fondly as she squeezed his hand. She was just as anxious for exciting new experiences as Jasper.

To her friends, Jasper's mother often wondered, "Did that silly girl Isabella put this ridiculous notion of leaving me into my poor son's head? Can you imagine, leaving everything we have in New York and traveling across the continent with a team of filthy oxen? Jasper would never have thought of such a thing on his own. She must be the culprit."

Mrs. Langley's opinion of the young woman plummeted. She held Isabella responsible for depriving her of the joy of seeing her future grandchildren grow up properly. What chance would these children have out west in the wilds of...? She didn't know what. She repeated again and again that she had no parting advice to give for this asinine plan, while also continuously voicing her opinion that oxen were horrible sounding beasts that were surely too lowly and humble for her lovely son—no matter what he thought about their supposed reliability.

Jasper had tried and tried to get his father to understand his need for adventure. But the man was furious with his son and frequently bellowed at him, "I've spent a lifetime grooming you to be my business successor! This is how you thank me?" He refused to see them off. This made his mother uncomfortable, so she only watched out the front window, crying and waving her lace handkerchief at them.

Isabella's parents, quite unlike Jasper's, were excited for them. "You must promise to write to us often and tell us all about your adventures," they ordered.

"I shall surely do that just as soon as I find a post office in the wilds of the west," she replied with a laugh.

After what felt like ages of tearful hugs and well-wishes, the young couple climbed aboard the wagon that would transport them to the Erie Canal.

The journey began.

Weeks later, Jasper and Isabella reached Missouri. As they made their necessary purchases for the trip west, Jasper couldn't help seething on behalf of his impressive new team of oxen. He fumed at Izzy, "What does my mother think I need? Six matching black stallions or some silly thing? I'm not exactly royalty, you know? 'Make a good first impression on the neighbors,' indeed!" He shook his head while Isabella stifled a giggle.

Along with Jasper and Isabella on the wagon train, there were several families and a few unattached men. People tended to gravitate to the young couple because of their delightful personalities, good looks, and generosity.

Isabella was a talented, big-hearted cook and often fed the single men, who lacked female companionship and sorely missed the typical feminine skills along the journey. It took no time at all for the wagon train to fall in love with the young lady. Each day, the lonely men would present her with a dressed rabbit, a few game birds, or a sack of beans, and she would cheerfully work miracles with these offerings to feed their new friends. One of these men was Royal Dawson.

One wretched day, six weeks west of Independence, they all stopped their animals and wagons for the evening. A blood-curdling feminine scream rent the air followed by Jasper's voice crying, "Izzy? Isabella? Can you hear me, my love?" Then hearts broke everywhere along their ranks as Jasper began to sob. "No! Wake up, Izzy! Oh, no! Please, God!"

Isabella had caught her foot in her long skirt as she was climbing out of the wagon. After a second of struggling with it, she lost her balance. In a freak accident, she tumbled out of the wagon and broke her neck.

It was not uncommon for travelers to lose their lives along the California Trail, but the death of a kind and pretty young woman cast a pall over the entire wagon train. Jasper was devastated. And to make matters worse, Isabella had just an-nounced to him the week before that she was pregnant. She'd complained about feeling nauseous and lightheaded at times, so Jasper was sure that he'd somehow contributed to her fall. Typically, Isabella was so graceful; she had to have been feeling poorly.

Berating himself over and over, he thought, *I should have gotten to her like a gentleman and helped her out of the wagon. What is wrong with me that I thought first to check on the ox that seemed a little sluggish, and I left my own wife to fall out of the wagon like that?!*

Jasper was inconsolable. After burying his beloved Isabella, he couldn't eat and did not speak to anyone for several days. Everyone cringed when they heard his plaintive sobs at night.

As miserable as Jasper was, however, he never considered quitting or returning to New York. He and Izzy had a dream, and he planned to see it out—even though he felt like his heart had been ripped out by buzzards.

Royal, who'd had many a supper with the young couple and thoroughly enjoyed their company, tried his best to keep

Jasper from wallowing too deeply in his depression. When he wasn't busy with the wagon master, Royal rode or walked his mule alongside the Prairie Schooner and once in a while took Isabella's place on the seat next to his friend. At first, Jasper said nothing and barely even seemed aware of either the companionship or the landscape around him, letting the oxen follow the wagon in front of them. But gradually he seemed to pay more attention, and Royal would point out interesting scenery or ask simple questions that brought Jasper back to himself more and more each day.

The trip that loomed ahead of them seemed as though it might take forever. They only averaged about ten miles a day since there were no real roads to follow. Broken wheels, broken livestock, and broken hearts seemed to be a daily occurrence.

Royal and Jasper's friendship grew as they traveled through treacherous country. More and more, as Jasper sloughed off his grief and tried to be more practical, they spent their long days discussing their plans for what they hoped to do once they reached California. At this point, it was an unspoken yet totally accepted fact that whatever they did, it would be together.

Taking pity on Royal for sleeping on the ground, Jasper invited him into the relative opulence of his four-foot-wide bed at night. Royal felt like a king the first time he lay down on the thin mattress. He thought he'd do just about anything for his friend at that point for offering him such luxury and comfort. Royal had a tent, but this was better by far. In the name of sharing the wealth as far as he could, he turned his tent over to two Irish friends who accompanied them. The young men were only equipped with the barest of essentials.

Jasper was immediately comforted by the presence of another person in his bed. He found that, with Royal present, he slept easily for the first time since Isabella's accident. In his need for companionship and the warmth of another body, Jasper often woke up to find his arm draped over Royal. Royal never seemed to mind and took it in stride. Gradually, he too would wrap an arm around Jasper even before they went to sleep. Neither ever complained nor even discussed it—it felt so natural.

Although their friendship was already strong, one event solidified it to an unbreakable degree.

It was not uncommon to see discarded items left by previous travelers along the trail. This far into the journey, many oxen teams became fatigued, and the people sought a quick way to ease the burden. Heavy furniture was cast out when sentimentality gave way to a deeper sense of practicality.

Jasper and Royal's wagon train passed by bulky, weighty wooden pieces that had once felt so important to the travelers, abandoned when they realized they would never reach the west if they taxed their animals too badly.

On one day, they were moving particularly slowly. The ground was scorched and rocky, and the hot, dusty air choked their lungs. Royal was walking beside the Prairie Schooner to give the oxen and his mule a lighter load when he spied an interesting item that he recognized from his dairy farming days.

Bounding away from the wagon, Royal exclaimed, "Jasper! Look at this, will you? It's a modern ice cream churn—the very one that Nancy M. Johnson invented!" He had nearly reached the cylindrical item when Jasper looked up. The churn didn't spark any sense of recognition in Jasper's mind, but as soon as he looked at Royal, his blood ran cold.

"Roy! *Don't move!*" he cried.

Royal's spine stiffened, and he stopped breathing. He knew Jasper meant business. Out of the corner of his eye, he saw Jasper racing toward him, brandishing his rifle. Jasper grabbed the churn and pulled it to the side before aiming at something on the ground. The gun blast nearly burst his eardrums, and Royal was peppered with fragments of rock, dirt, and...slimy whatnot from his left side. Slowly, he turned toward the source of the spray and saw the shattered remains of a rattlesnake. All of his breath whooshed out, and he thought he might be sick.

"Jasper, are you *insane?* That rattler could've just as easily bitten you when you grabbed the churn! You almost got yourself killed!"

Jasper's chest heaved with emotion. He swayed on his feet and plunked down onto the rocky earth. With pain etched into his features, he explained, "I had to move it away so I didn't shoot *you.* No one else is going to die around me because I'm not vigilant. I couldn't let it happen, Royal. Not to you too."

Royal didn't know whether he wanted to pound Jasper into the ground the way he and his rowdy brothers used to settle their disputes—or whether he wanted to kiss his friend senseless. He wasn't sure where *that* idea came from, so he went to Jasper to help him up and engulfed him in a bear hug. "Thank you," he whispered into Jasper's ear.

Royal knew that from that day forward, he would do *anything* for Jasper Langley.

Chapter Three

As they traveled westward, the ranks of fellow adventurers inevitably shrank. Some just wore out and gave up along the treacherous trail across the country. They usually decided to make do where they found a small settlement. Some reached their chosen destinations and hoped to meet up with friends and family who had already ventured forth before them. Some stopped in the territories that the wagon train passed through where they were delighted with breathtaking landscape and plentiful game.

Death sadly visited all too often due to disease and accidents. One entire family drowned when their wagon tipped over while fording a river. A few people died from heart attacks or exhaustion. And there was one man who'd driven everyone crazy with his bitter complaints and pugnacious nature. Several times, people had to restrain him when he'd put up his fists and charged forward, threatening to clobber any man who disagreed with him. He died due to an "accidental shooting" while hunting. This was not investigated or questioned by anyone.

Fortunately, there were four other men with whom Royal and Jasper bonded during their journey. They were all honest, hard-working sorts who had strong visions of success for themselves.

Two of them were the Irishmen who'd been gifted Royal's tent, Séamus Flynn and Timothy Duffy. Not brothers, but as close to it as they could be. At the age of seventeen, they'd been sent to America together to live with Duffy's relatives in Boston. Their parents had managed to scrape together enough to send their cherished boys away from the desperate lives they lived during the potato famine.

Séamus had coppery red hair, and Timothy's was as black as coal. They had heavy Irish brogues, and they made a pledge to each other to honor their parents' sacrifice and make them proud. However, they quickly grew tired of feeling like a burden to Timothy's distant relatives, and the promise of a new life in the frontier sounded exciting to them. They voiced their desires to head west.

Timothy's mother's second cousin's husband was so relieved to hear the boys would be moving on that he generously offered them both a pair of strong mules and gifted them with a Hawken rifle, telling them, "With a bit of luck, this will keep you alive. If you can shoot, you can eat." Before they left, he also unearthed an old blunderbuss that he'd found in the barn. "If you plan to hunt anything with this, you better hope it's blind and deaf because you'll practically have to be on top of them to make your shot. Still, it's better than nothing."

A year later, when they reached Independence, the wagon master signed them on with the condition that they would provide their own transportation—so the mules were a fortunate asset—and they would obey his commands without question. The wagon master was pleased to note that they were both excellent shots and had their own guns. "This will be important both for hunting and in case of Indian attacks," he told the boys.

They looked at each other nervously, and Séamus silently mouthed, "Attacks?"

Throughout the trip, they were quiet and congenial until they had a snort or two of whiskey. Then they would both sing and carry on until someone shoved them toward their bedrolls, insisting that they shut up for the night and let everyone sleep.

Walter James, a bespectacled twenty-seven-year-old fellow traveler and something of a Renaissance man, left his stifling architectural position to go on a personal quest. His employer never allowed him to design anything more elaborate than the simplest dwelling. Fascinated by railroad travel, he'd gone up and down the eastern states for a while observing—and once in a while riding—this newest innovation in travel and drawing inspiration for structures he longed to build. He needed a place where he could create something original and groundbreaking.

He decided to make the enormous trek all the way to the west coast. He too made a halting, pieced-together trip to Independence where he sought out a wagon train pilot. Rather impractically, he'd brought along a collection of books on a variety of topics that he thought might come in handy. Some of them would eventually do nothing more than help start a cooking fire, but he wasn't to know that for many months.

He had a rudimentary knowledge of cooking, and, after their loss of Isabella, he would invite them to sit around his nightly cookfire. As they had with Isabella, the men provided whatever ingredients for a meal they could come up with, and Walter would prepare the food while he entertained them with endless, ridiculously embellished stories of his family and friends back home in Philadelphia. It sounded to all who listened as if Walter was set on having an adventure of his own that would outdo anything he'd heard of so far, and he planned to return east eventually to tell his tale and maybe even write a book about it.

"Not a bad ambition," Jasper told Royal with a laugh. Walter's meals filled their bellies, though nothing even close to the way their beloved Isabella had done, but Walter did his best, and for that, they cherished him as well.

It was during one of Walter's meals that Séamus talked about Timothy's colossal cooking failure. Apparently, once they'd hit the trail and after not finding any game to roast, he'd taken a sack of unsoaked beans and tossed some into a pot over the fire—hoping to end up with baked beans. With no culinary skills whatsoever, he was dismayed to find the beans ended up even harder than they started out. The men all got a good laugh at Timothy's red face and protests that, "I have plenty of other more important skills than cooking damned beans."

Night after night, Walter spun tales and kept everyone's homesickness at bay by making his new friends laugh and laugh. He told them stories about his eccentric relatives, what it was like working in a big city firm, and then he would postulate about the wonders of the railroad. "One day soon," he told them, "Folks will be able to travel by train all the way to the west coast. That will be something!"

The last man in their party was Isaac Stark, a cheerful young chap of 21, whose heart of gold and artistry were matched by his enormous height and muscled physique. He had met Walter passing through Pittsburgh. They immediately struck up a friendship and recognized a profound desire for adventure in each other. Making the spur-of-the-moment decision to join Walter, Isaac brought along his prized fiddle. He'd crafted the instrument himself, much to everyone's admiration and delight. The fiddle had a special case, but Jasper encouraged Isaac to stow it in the more watertight Prairie Schooner to keep it safe.

Walter and Isaac walked alongside their open mule-driven wagon most days and slept together in Walter's tent at night. Isaac had left Pittsburgh with nothing more than the clothes on his back, his fiddle, a camp knife, and his precious packet of woodworking tools. These proved to be a godsend as the trip progressed and wagons broke down.

The younger man's skills with wood were only outshone by the music he played, outdoing the Irishmen's singing by far. Many of the travelers would dance around their nightly campfires to Isaac's cheerful songs. As their ranks decreased with each mile they journeyed, the happy music was a balm to their souls. Everyone was worried about safety and just how much *promise* the promised land would have for them once they arrived.

"It has to be better than contending with rattlesnakes and tornados," Royal reasoned. They were, at that moment, hunkered down waiting out a hailstorm—soaked to the bone and completely miserable. Jasper had made his Prairie Schooner available to his five friends, and they were packed in uncomfortably tight. At least the oiled, double-thick canvas top kept any more rain and hail off of them.

As they made their slow progress west, their fellow travelers, like those before them, tossed more and more unimportant items out of their wagons, desperately trying to make it easier on the animals that pulled the weight. Survival was reduced to the bare essentials, and creature comforts were largely abandoned. Still, animals—and people—died of malnutrition, cholera, and accidents.

Chapter Four

After journeying over two thousand scorching, dusty, freezing, wet, and windy miles from Independence, the wagon train reached the fur trading post of Fort Hall, situated on the Snake River in eastern Oregon Country—an area that later became part of the state of Idaho. From here, the itinerants had to choose whether to continue northwest on the Oregon Trail or try their luck crossing the treacherous Sierra Nevada by way of the California Trail.

Most went northwest, expecting an easier trip, but the wagon master took the rest via the more southerly route. Some simply went along because their trusted leader seemed certain they could make it. He alluded to possible employment opportunities in San Francisco, a newly named town that had previously been known as Yerba Buena.

To reach the coast, they still had nearly eight hundred miles to go. Even though they'd had to contend with hunger, tornados, broken bones, and broken wagons, in some ways, the worst was yet to come. It was getting late in the year, and they had to somehow make it through the mountain range before heavy winter snowfall made the route impassable. They heard gruesome stories of failures, including the Donner Party, a wagon train that had been stuck in the Sierras over the winter. Horror stories of what they endured scared their party into making good time—as far as they could.

Sadly, Jasper and Walter had to give up their wagons before trying to make their way through the Sierras. They had known ahead of this that there would be no roads in this part of the journey, and the mountains were far too steep to drive through. Jasper resigned himself and made what he knew was a one-sided trade with a fur trapper. He exchanged his team of still-healthy oxen and his wonderful Prairie Schooner for two mules. He took what he could, strapped the burdens onto their backs, and proceeded from there on foot. He'd also managed to get some large fur pelts and a decent tent thrown into the deal, so he wasn't terribly upset. As in everything on this trek, practicality won without question.

Luckily for them, the wagon master had heard of a particular route that was less horrible than most that had been attempted. Nevertheless, the cold weather closed in on them as they reached the western side of the mountain range, and conditions could hardly have been worse. A blizzard kept them stationary for a few days, and it still was not even the dead of winter yet. Jasper squeezed so many of his friends into his tent at night they all had to sleep sitting up. Having the pelts to protect them from the frigid ground and the combined body heat of so many men probably saved their lives.

It was at this point that one of Walter's books helped him light a small fire. He'd stuffed as many tomes as he could into his pockets and his underclothes, then laughed about how the extra padding had kept him from freezing.

The beaten down group was even smaller now; a few more travelers had frozen to death while making the treacherous Sierra Nevada crossing. However, the milder weather that greeted them in the foothills on the west side of the mountain range was a tremendous comfort to their worn-out bodies.

Finally, with many weary shouts of excitement, they reached the end of the trail near Sutter's Fort and the small settlement of Sacramento. After enduring unspeakable tragedies and extreme conditions for six unforgettable months, the travelers finally disbanded, even though they were still nearly one hundred miles from the Pacific coast. Anyone who wanted to continue did so on their own as the passage was less treacherous from here on out. They would still be challenged daily, but they would not freeze.

The six friends stuck together, agreeing to tough out the trip to the coast as a unit. Roads were nonexistent, but many of the threats that had previously plagued them were thankfully gone. There was no snow, though the muddy trails still made their travel as slow as molasses. It was the rainy season, and they were all filthy, starving, and exhausted. Buoyed by their success, however, the six men were jubilant. They'd made it! They had crossed North America.

Jasper, Royal, and their four companions stopped short of reaching San Francisco, and they easily found jobs in Coloma with a businessman named John Sutter. Sutter had plans to build a sawmill on the American River and was fairly desperate for men. Besides the proposed mill, he also ran a tannery business and had fields of crops, so there was no shortage of work to be done. The six friends worked alongside at least fifty Indians and roughly the same number of men from the Mormon Battalion. The latter were fresh from the Mexican-American War and were sent from the military fort in Sacramento to earn some fast money before heading back to Salt Lake City.

The newcomers from the east knew very little about military life or Indian customs, so they expected to stick together more or less on their own. The Mormons, however, were adept in many disciplines and helped the new arrivals with their working skills. They forged many new friendships as they all worked together, and the Mormons, who believed strongly in teamwork, welcomed them wholeheartedly into their fold. It was a congenial way to work, and Royal finally announced, "I'm glad to be in one place for a while."

Jasper and Royal planned to work hard and earn enough money to buy some property somewhere. They also hoped someday to start their families, although they hadn't laid eyes on a single available woman in months.

Fate, however, had a different plan for them, and they never received a cent from John Sutter.

Chapter Five

The Discovery, 1848

Not long after they began working on the mill, on January 24, 1848, Sutter's partner James Marshall discovered some flakes of gold at the mill site. Despite trying to keep the find quiet—because they foresaw the repercussions of word getting out—the news still managed to create quite a stir amongst the workers. The camp fizzed with excitement as word passed from man to man. Sutter's worry came to fruition right away as men came down with gold fever.

It took from January to June to officially certify the gold, though the locals all understood its value and authenticity. Once the shiny metal was verified as truly gold, President Polk realized the great potential of this discovery. He immediately put the steps into motion for California to become a state and ordered news companies to send word around the world that gold had been discovered in California.

Thus began the mad rush from all corners of the earth. Hopefuls swarmed in by ship, wagon, horse, mule, and foot to grab their share of the vast riches that California promised. Over the next seven years, 300,000 people—mostly men— dropped everything and raced to California looking to make an easy living off of either gold prospecting or supplying people with what they needed.

The only workers at Sutter's Mill who were initially unaffected by the discovery of gold were the Indians. At first, they saw no value in the shiny flakes and were bemused by the furor it caused. They had seen it in the ground for generations. Quickly, however, the indigenous residents began to appreciate the trade value of the gold that was so highly prized by the new arrivals, and they became extremely adept at finding it.

Jasper, Royal, and their friends had the great fortune to already be in the middle of the hot spot when those first bits of gold were recognized. The earliest prospectors had an extreme advantage over those who came after—news took a while to spread across the globe. Gold sounded to the uninitiated like a quick way to get ahead, but the supply of easy pickings would prove to be limited.

Walter had read a few books on mining prior to his departure from Philadelphia and was now hellbent on making his fortune. Thanks to his advice, the six friends immediately recognized the potential, scrounged up some gold pans and shovels, and took off, abandoning the mill project. They found a place nearby that looked to be a likely spot for some panning and worked all day until they were too exhausted to lift anything. Before their first full week of prospecting was completed, they collectively found eight pounds of precious gold.

Fortunately for the team, Jasper quickly hatched a business plan that would set them up well for their futures. He left the others to their prospecting, took his mules and a sack of gold dust, and scoured the area settlements for every pick, shovel, pan, and anything that could be used to mine gold with. Ten days later, he returned to the mining areas to discover that hordes of men had swarmed in with nothing but their bare hands to work with. He sold out everything he had at a ridiculous profit. Then he got back to work alongside his friends.

Unfortunately for John Sutter, the property at his mill site was both ransacked and then deserted, leaving him with no mill, no workers, and ultimately with no money. His crops remained unharvested, and his tannery business flopped when hides were left to rot in various stages of processing.

At first, all of the newly-minted prospectors were a congenial bunch. The six friends and the Mormons felt no competition with each other. They shared ideas and tools and worked alongside each other's claims like the best of comrades. No one needed to mark off their territory by doing anything more than sticking a pick or a shovel into the ground to signify that that area was spoken for. Each man worked with honor and respect for his fellow. As the weeks and months passed, however, and more and more greedy fortune-seekers arrived on the scene, protection and secrecy became important.

The six men banded together with a tight bond, deciding to form a company and protect each other carefully. Guns sadly became important for survival—and not just for hunting for food. Thievery was rampant in the mining camps, and more than one miner was murdered over gold findings. Each of the six partners had their specialized skill sets, and they would take turns mining, guarding their holdings at gunpoint, or traveling to nearby towns for food and supplies. By pooling all of their gold, each had an equally vested interest in their collective success.

A man's word was law in an area that had no laws, no government... and no women.

"Jasper, I feel like it's a miracle that we ended up here, don't you agree?" Royal asked one day in a hushed tone. They had learned not to make a big deal out of what they found for fear of robbery.

Jasper smiled warmly at Royal, nodding his head.

Miners and their makeshift dwellings crowded all around them, turning the area into a full-on mining camp. As soon as the obvious gold that was found on the surface of the ground became depleted, many of their neighbors left to find easy pickings elsewhere, but new miners quickly claimed the abandoned sites.

Many were frustrated by the amount of effort they needed to find their riches. Stories had been circulating that led them to believe the gold was there for the taking, and all one needed to do was pick it up effortlessly. Jasper and Royal's crew, however, continued to labor on. They learned that they needed to dig down to bedrock to get to the good stuff. It was miserable, backbreaking work, but they persisted. To ease some of the manual hardship, Walter remembered reading about using a shaker to separate the gold from the rocks and dirt, so Isaac built them an effective one that used the running river water and agitation to do some of the work for them.

Because much of their work consisted of digging in the dirt in horribly hot weather, the men also became filthy. Walter and Isaac finally put their heads together and designed a shower of sorts that worked by recycling water. The bather had to stand on two foot pedals and alternate steps to run a pump. The pump ran icy water up into a rusty old kerosene can with holes poked in the bottom. The rusty water sprayed over them and was collected in the bottom of the shower where it went back into a buried barrel filter filled with sand and rocks. The bather never stayed in the spray very long due to the shivering it caused, but nevertheless they all felt a lot better after soaping up and rinsing off. When word got out that there was a way to bathe in the area, the six partners discovered another source of steady income. Their only expense was the soap.

Chapter Six

Men were everywhere in the mining camps. Tempers were short, and emotions ran high when someone struck it rich or ran completely out of funds. During all of this, men longed for the wives they'd left behind or fiancées who awaited their return with mountains of gold. They missed their mothers and their sisters and just the softness of having women around, period. They longed for homecooked meals and a pretty smile to lighten their burdened minds and soothe their exhausted bodies. Once in a while, a few prostitutes might show up at the camp and leave with plenty of gold in their purses. Unfortunately, they left behind several raging cases of syphilis. Scurvy also plagued many of the miners who lived on salted meat and ignored the need for fruits and vegetables. It was not uncommon for miners to die of disease or serious injury, and the numbers of deaths easily rivaled those of the California-bound travelers.

Given the lack of women, it was customary—though not often discussed in the history books—for men to form "bachelor marriages." In the early part of the immigration to the gold fields of California, women only made up four to five percent of the state's entire population, and men had their physical needs in spite of these odds. It was common for men to dance, live, and have sex with each other.

Being young, virile men with normal desires, Royal and Jasper fell into this practice willingly. They saw and heard what was happening around them, and it seemed like a logical way to take the edge off after a long, frustrating day or to celebrate a great one. Accepting their normal craving to be touched by someone, they'd slept spooned together in their tent, warding off the cold at night. A true affection for one another developed, and this grew along with their physical relationship.

It began when one night, Royal reached around Jasper's waist and snaked his hand under Jasper's shirt where he felt a warm, naked belly. Royal's hand ventured lower and wrapped around a cock that wasn't his own.

"Is this alright with you?" he whispered to Jasper, who groaned his affirmative reply. It had been so long since Jasper had felt aroused this way, and there was no way in hell he'd have stopped Royal. In fact, Jasper rolled over and kissed his friend deeply. They stroked each other until they both roared with release that had been pent up seemingly forever.

"I think I've wanted to do that for a long, long time," Royal admitted.

Jasper smiled and answered, "I'm glad you did finally. I've wanted it too."

Now that their attraction for one another was acknowledged, this became a nightly occurrence for them. Eventually, they began stripping as soon as the tent flap was closed, and their naked bodies would come together with hungry abandon, seeking friction and comfort from the expected release. They had seen men fellate and fuck each other in broad daylight, so they were well aware of how things worked. Jasper especially enjoyed rubbing his cock against the crack of Royal's ass, and they almost lost their minds with excitement the first time he spit into his hand several times and wet his willy so that he could slide it into Royal's tight channel.

Gasping and shaking, Royal grabbed himself roughly and began to stroke. When Jasper sunk deeply into Royal's backside and reached a sensitive spot, he cried out, "Oh, my god!"

Lowering his voice, he whispered, "You just wait until I do that to you, Jas. You won't believe what it feels like."

"What I'm doing feels pretty incredible too, Roy," Jasper answered in a strained voice. Gradually, he began thrusting in and out, picking up speed. He gripped Royal's body and kissed his neck and shoulders as they both began to sweat. Jasper pounded Royal, and Royal had a chokehold on his own cock as he squeezed and stroked himself faster and faster. After just minutes, they both roared in ecstasy.

At the very least, kissing and fondling happened each night, as they were often dog tired when they made it to bed, but fucking each other became a favorite pastime when they had the energy.

Still, they wanted families.

Chapter Seven

Adeline Hart's Journal October 10, 1849

Day one:

Today Father and I finally boarded the Wind Gypsy, and I pray that this vessel is seaworthy as it has not sailed before. Prior to this journey, the only vessel I'd ever been on was a tiny rowboat on the pond near our home. Our former home, actually. How does something so large and full of people and heavy cargo stay afloat? I am told the Wind Gypsy is a Brigantine, which is an old design but newly adapted to carrying plenty of freight. We are considered a merchant ship rather than a passenger steamer. I'm afraid I know nothing about sailing, and this will be quite the adventure for me.

The shipyard area is crammed with men who are building so many vessels, it's a wonder there is any wood left in the country. I keep referring to them as "boats," but Father has corrected me good-naturedly. "Ships," he says.

Countless men are just as hellbent as Father to reach San Francisco and make their fortunes by prospecting for gold. It's as if a fever has taken hold of everyone and is propelling them westward.

We made the trip by wagon from Philadelphia up to Boston. Father secured our passage by having the shipping company hire me to be the ship's cook and by paying them what sounded to me like a king's ransom to ferry our goods around Cape Horn all the way to the California coast. Believing he needs his cargo to set up a hotel in San Francisco, Father sold our house and all of the contents except for what he deemed necessary for the trip.

The shipping company was most delighted to have us outfit the ship's galley with our own stove and cooking utensils. I personally think Father made a poor investment, and the shipping company should have let us travel by paying in trade rather than taking our money. I shall never say that to Father, however. I know he is doing his best. I hope when we start the new hotel, he shows a better aptitude for business. He has had much on his mind of late. The truth is, he has always been a bit of a dreamer.

The trip will take anywhere from four to six months. I shall pray each day for calm seas and favorable winds to get us to our destination quickly. It is my understanding that our winter months are the best time to be traveling around Cape Horn. How strange that it will be summer down there.

Our overland trip to Boston was tiresome, though it pales, I'm sure, to the arduous trip some determined souls are taking by wagon train to get to the West. Still, I'm sorry we couldn't have gone half the distance to New York. Sadly, however, the only ships leaving that harbor were passengers only. I might also have liked meeting other families making the trip as I am the only woman aboard this vessel. I will not complain, however. I look forward to helping Father achieve his goal in the West. How enterprising of him to not want the quick money of finding the shiny gold we read about in the newspapers each day.

Day two:

My duties last night and this morning were simple and light, considering half the crew was too sick to partake in supper. Many of the men aboard are not experienced seamen at all, and they seem to be men the skipper hired in haste to get on his way. Father and I share a small cabin with two berths, but the rest of the ship, save for the captain's quarters, has open bunks attached wherever they will fit. Many do not look safe to me, and there was a lot of equipment sliding around as the ship pitched and rolled with each swell. I hope we do not run into harsher weather. The more experienced sailors showed the others how to fasten their belongings to something stationary with ropes. I'm surprised no one was seriously injured before the personal effects were secured.

Writing in this journal is a particular challenge with the motion of the waves buffeting us. I will no doubt need to choose the times carefully when I can put pen to paper.

I am somewhat embarrassed to add this part of my situation to this journal, but since it has a significant impact on my life, I shall write about it. Back in Philadelphia we had a housemaid who assisted me in getting dressed each day- primarily to lace up my corset. Now that I have no female companionship aboard the Wind Gypsy (and I certainly would not embarrass my father into assisting me), I have had to dispense with that particular under-garment. It is so liberating! I also ascertained that extra petticoats were impractical in the galley, for I feared I may catch my skirt on fire. I am glad my dear mother does not have to look upon me in this state, but I am certainly more comfortable.

Day three:

Most of the men are still ill with mal de mer. I fixed light meals for those who wanted to eat. Father and I must have strong constitutions because I enjoy the roll-ing waves and the wind each time I go up on the deck. I could not stay above deck for very long, however, be-cause it was too cold and windy. Captain Greely assures us we will soon long for these chilly days. I have a hard time imagining that as I quickly grew chilled from the icy spray.

Father seems excited by each new day, and I find my-self comforted by the positive change. He desperately needed to start a new life after losing Mother to a long illness. I briefly considered remaining and possibly find-ing employment as a tutor somewhere, but the thought of being alone was not appealing, and I know Father will need my help. Such an isolated job as a private tutor would also not be conducive to my future dream to marry one day. I do not see myself remaining a spinster well into my dotage.

Being a tutor had its appeal from an intellectual point of view, for I have enjoyed a fine education from those employed on my behalf. My father made certain that I had nothing but the finest in both academics and music. I have an academic curiosity in many things, but my favorite pastime is still my piano. Alas, it was a sad day when Father admitted to me that he had to sell my instrument to pay for the newest healing scheme for poor, sick Mother. In the long run, the cure did nothing but drain Father's coffers and deprive me of my music.

I am ashamed to admit that I cried to see workmen carry the instrument out of the house. I hid in my room to keep my tears secret, but it did nothing to dull my disgust with myself. How could I compare the importance of Mother's health to my enjoyment? I felt like a terribly ungrateful daughter, for I'd been given the gift of music for many years. How could I cry such selfish tears when my dear mother lay dying? In fact, she told me so many times that hearing me play gave her great comfort and eased her pain. I wish the lack of my playing had given her more than that, but it was not to be. I hope the piano went to a good home, at least, for it was my greatest pleasure.

I've spent so many months caring for my ill mother, cooped up in her sickroom; being out in the fresh air on the ship is a relief to my troubled spirit. That is not to say that we are callous to have lost dear Mother. We miss her cheerful, gentle presence terribly.

I just hope and pray that Father finds what he's looking for. He is a headstrong man.

Day four:

I have had to completely dispense with female attire. Even though I have very little contact with them, the sailors' attention to me has been terribly unsettling. We determined that the most intelligent course of action for me would be to borrow some trousers and a man's shirt. I find myself most comfortably attired thus. My hair is often hidden now under a hat, and my body appears shapeless in these clothes. Father and Captain Greely think it best for my safety. I do not disagree.

Day fifteen:

Most of the crewmen seem to have learned to cope with their seasickness, so my duties have increased tremendously. I have to contend with feeding everyone, and the ingredients provided to me are far from ideal. The weather, as predicted, has warmed up as we travel south, and now I crave being above deck just to be able to breathe fresh air. But as we approach the Caribbean, the air grows stifling and wet.

A couple of laggards did not appear to be pulling their weight as crewmen, and I overheard the captain threatening that he'd toss them overboard if they did not sharpen up. One poor fellow seemed to be overtaken by a great pain in his chest and died in front of me. He was unceremoniously tossed over the side of the ship. I hope that does not happen often.

Day thirty:

The days have a monotonous sameness to them. Therefore, there has been little to report.

Although we've passed by some islands, Captain told Father that we will not be landing and taking on supplies until we get to Rio de Janeiro. That sounds like a long way off.

It is still terribly hot, and it's impossible to stay in the galley for very long when the stove is lit. I have to climb up to the deck and take short breaks so I do not expire. I am so glad to have dispensed with all of my petticoats and heavy layers. When I go up to take the air, I try to stay as far away from the sailors as possible.

Father and Captain Greely seem to have forged a strong friendship. I am happy for Father, despite the fact that I do not think much of Captain Greely. I'm sure he's at least someone with whom Father can hold a decent conversation. I just don't like the way he looks at me when Father's attention is engaged elsewhere, and he seems rather conceited.

Father still tosses and turns and moans in his sleep at night, however, so I think Mother's passing weighs heavily on him. I miss her most grievously, but I am happy that she is free from pain.

Day ? I have lost count of the number of days now:

We have lost several men to a sickness that swept through the ranks of the crew. Our food supplies are barely enough to keep us all alive, so I hope that we reach Rio de Janeiro before too many more days have passed. Greely avoids me when he thinks I might be ready to ask him once again if he thinks we'll arrive soon. I fear the food is close to running out completely.

The hottest, most miserable day yet:

I have never felt such hunger in my life. And it is up to me to apportion what few resources we have left.

The sea has been fearsomely rough, and I am covered in bruises and small burns from losing my balance and running into things.

Father is beginning to look terribly haggard. I pray he doesn't succumb to the illness that so many of the sailors already have.

At night, it is so miserable in our berths, I can scarcely sleep. The incessant noises, the perpetual movement, and the overpowering stink of the ship conspire to make me wretched. So that I do not go mad from frustration and boredom, I have lately tried to recreate in my memory the sounds and sights of the magnificent concerts we used to attend in Philadelphia at the wonderful Musical

Fund Hall. It was a treat beyond measure when a talented pianist or violinist would play my favorite composer's music—Beethoven. I know some of the newer music is popular now, but I feel Beethoven in my heart. My music teacher, who often performs at the hall himself, seemed to think I had a special talent and often reported to my father that I ought to be on stage. Father always smiled politely and made some disparaging remark that made me feel insignificant. I should not dwell on that, for he was kind enough to employ a fine music master for me—until he lost a significant amount of his savings trying in vain to cure poor Mother.

One of the most memorable recitals we attended at the Musical Fund Hall is one that shall stay with me forever. Even though we were treated to fabulous operas and symphonies, I shall remember with fondness the time we witnessed a ten-year-old boy named Louis Moreau Gottschalk play with such skill and aptitude, he robbed me of my breath.

He only played a couple of pieces by Liszt, but I know that young man will have a shining career. I understand he left for Europe to study there. How wonderful to be able to study and perform that way. My recitals have been limited to the late-night entertainment of my parents' dinner guests now and then. I must admit, however, that although I admire the skill it takes to pay Liszt, I still prefer my Beethoven. I understand from the playbill that Louis Gottschalk admires the music of Henri Herz, and that says a lot about his skill, for that man's music is barely playable.

Arriving in Rio de Janeiro:

The coastline here is like nothing I've seen before. It's quite dramatic and beautiful. However, the people speak

Portuguese here, so it's a pity that I have no idea what they're saying. I was told to remain in the company of my father at all times while we were on land, and the captain oversaw all of the foodstuffs we took aboard. I gave him a list of what I needed, but we shall see if it made a difference to him. He will probably return with barrels of rum and forget all about food.

Day one after leaving Rio De Janeiro:

It seems we had a few sailors jump ship. I don't know if they were tired of the sea or loved it in Brazil so much. I hope no one was lost or attacked. There were many rumblings about that possibility amongst the remaining crewmembers. The men were all so anxious to reach California, it's a mystery to me that they'd quit now. Father alluded to the possibility that some ended up in shady establishments and missed the ship's departure.

We also took on a few new crewmen. Perhaps they are leftovers from the last ship that stopped in for provisions as they seem to speak English. They don't look impressive to me. One in particular is a frightfully large man. Greely seemed quite taken with the man's strength, but I do not like the way he looks at me. It gives me a chill. He has a most aggressive, malicious nature with several missing teeth and strangely disfigured and puffy ears that Father says come from being on the receiving end of too many fists. He also has many scars on his arms and hands and is missing part of a finger.

We have a supply of food again, and I am back to cooking regularly for the men. It's still very low quality, however, so I don't think Greely did his best. I shall have to make do once again. At least we have plenty of salt pork and many bags of rice. He did procure plenty of rum.

The day of The Argument:

I wish I could keep the dates straight, but I do not wish to bother Captain with trifling matters—especially now.

The large man who boarded in Brazil got into a fearsome argument with our skipper. He told Captain Greely that he would be wasting precious time by not staying close to the land and rounding the Horn by way of the Strait of Magellan Route. Greely told him (and very loudly I must add) that he would not jeopardize the safety of his ship and those aboard by taking unnecessary risks in so narrow a passage.

Apparently, the currents through that route, as well as the winds, make travel extraordinarily dangerous, and many ships have been lost there. The large man (I will hereafter call him LM for brevity's sake, for I have never troubled myself to learn his name) turned beet red and got right up into Greely's person, yelling at him that he was a coward and ought to be able to sail his ship better than that. Two of LM's cohorts grabbed his arms before he could swing at the skipper.

Captain doesn't seem as taken with LM any longer. He raged at LM, saying he would see him in chains if that argument did not cease immediately. Then he stomped away, leaving LM muttering curses with vile language. Later, Captain Greely confided in Father that we will be taking the far safer Drake Passage around the Horn. He said that it offered a much wider passage where we were less likely to be tossed into rocks or become icebound. I suppose it's better to sail via the longer, safer route, for I certainly have no desire to become shipwrecked.

LM is rude to everyone and continues to make me feel most uncomfortable whenever he is near.

Sailing around the Horn:

Our weather has grown colder and colder again, despite what they call summer in this area of the world. We have seen some icebergs as well, and I fear that we may crash into one. They are frightening and beautiful in their own way. Captain Greely seems to hold a strong respect for them.

Our crossing around the Horn was a chilling experience. If this was the safest route, I fear grievously for anyone who tried a more expedient passage. The waves were terrifying and the wind most ferocious.

I never want to sail on another ship as long as I live.

The most exciting day of the voyage:

Today the rough seas, the cold, the heat, the boredom, and the lack of decent food were forgotten for a while.

I was preparing our rations as usual when I heard several crewmen bellowing something above me on the deck. Curiosity overtook, and I climbed up to see why they were making such a cry. They did not sound distressed but rather happy!

Much to my wondrous astonishment, we were surrounded by what I heard was a "pod" of humpback whales! I laughed to myself when I compared this sight to a peapod filled with such tiny things. As they gesticulated wildly, the sailors laughed and shouted, "Thar she blows!" I did not know why they thought all of the whales were female or if that is just what they say, but the enormous creatures seemed to be blowing steam out of their bodies like gigantic tea kettles. It was an incredible sight as they arched their backs—seeming to roll up out of the water, blowing their spray, and then sinking back in again. Several of them would flip their huge tails, which was a thrilling sight. But the most exciting of all was when some of those incredible creatures shot straight up in the air and then splashed down again creating a large explosion of seawater. Was this playing? They looked happy—if a whale is able to express an emotion.

This is a day I shall not soon forget. I felt so small at that moment in the vast ocean, surrounded by incredible sea monsters. I wonder if they were as astonished at the sight of us. Were they jumping out of the water to get a closer look?

I also wondered at some of the seemingly ribald comments the sailors made about the bursts of spray coming from the whales' bodies. I did not care to ask any of them, but they jabbed at each other and laughed heartily. LM bellowed loudly that he'd be able to show the whales a thing or two about blowing, at which point I headed quickly back toward the galley. I'm not sure what he meant, but the sideways look he gave me made me shiver.

I will choose to think only about the magnificent whales from here on.

I learned later from Captain Greely that the cry "Thar she blows" is what the lookout on a whaling ship calls out from his high perch—called the crow's nest—when he sees the tell-tale spray. I still wonder why the creatures are characterized as female. He had no answer for that question. He did also tell me, however, that the whales' strange behavior of jumping out of the water and splashing back down is called "breaching." I call it marvelous. I wonder if anything I am learning about sailing will ever come in handy in my future in California. Probably not.

The worst day of the voyage:

My life may never be the same again, for I fear I may have set something terrible into motion. In truth, I know I did.

The weather is finally calm now, so I am able to write, but a storm had been plaguing us all day, and it made the seas particularly rough. This fact may help convince some folks that an accident took place, for the ship was pitching and rolling far more than usual. That is if anyone should even care.

LM has been ornerier than ever after nearly coming to blows with Greely. He has also been worse and worse about the way he looks at and speaks to me. He has tried to brush up against my body more times than I care to count, and when Father saw it, he stepped in and ordered LM to keep his filthy hands to himself. I feared for Father's safety, but nothing happened at that point.

This afternoon, however, Father and Greely were in the captain's quarters, and LM took that advantage to hector me in the galley. I told him I was busy and politely asked him to leave. Unfortunately, I smelled rum on his foul breath when he crowded up behind me. I was cooking at the stove when I felt his enormous hands snake around my body, one squeezing my bosom and the other shoving roughly between my legs as he laughed in my ear, speaking words I do not care to repeat.

Seething with anger that he would treat me in such a dishonorable manner, I snatched up the heavy skillet from the stove and swung around with all my might as I wrenched out of his grasp. He screamed when the hot iron smashed him in the face, and sizzling grease spilled down his body. Lunging backward, he lost his footing with the ship's shuddering motion, tripped over a barrel of salt pork, and flailed his arms uselessly as he hit the back of his head with a resounding crash on my sturdy worktable. He crumpled to the galley floor—or deck, I suppose it's called—and did not move again.

I immediately ran to the captain's quarters to summon my father and the skipper, but I lost my balance a few times in my haste, and that slowed me down considerably. Upon our return and seeing LM's possibly lifeless form again, I covered my face in Father's chest and looked away while Captain studied the man. He did ask me why the skin on the side of LM's face was blistered with a burn and why the man smelled like pork grease. I then had to recount LM's attack on my person and my subsequent response. I got the distinct impression that the captain did not particularly care once he heard my account. He just looked at us and announced in a flat voice, "I'll go find some men to handle this."

Grim-faced, Captain Greely threw a rag over LM's face and quickly left the galley. Father and I did not speak, for we did not know what to think, so I busied myself with retrieving the skillet and trying to wipe up the spilled mess. I also discovered a burn on my wrist that I had not felt at the time. A few moments later, Greely returned with two men who were nearly as large as LM himself. He ordered them, "Take him up and throw him overboard."

During this exchange, the ship continued to pitch and roll and, as one man grabbed LM's arms and the other his feet, Greely spun a quick tale about how LM had lost his footing while he was pestering me with the most malicious intent. If either man noticed the burned side of LM's face, neither chose to comment.

I will never know if he went to a watery grave still alive or not.

I wonder if I shall burn in hell one day for my sins. Father says to put it out of my mind, but I cannot. I find my hatred for LM is as strong, however, as my guilt. There is something in my heart that feels... proud?

satisfied? I know not—other than it's a pleasant thought that I stood up for myself in the face of a monster and did not become a shrinking victim at his hands.

Chapter Eight

Watisé Isjaro, Sierra Nevada Foothills, 1849 to 1850

When the original site the men mined seemed to be tapped out for good, the six partners struck out finally for the southeast and headed deeper into the foothills of the Sierra Nevada mountains. They found a secluded area next to a large, swift stream. Still ahead of the major influx of hopeful prospectors, they found this to be an incredibly rich site. They carefully staked out their claim this time with markers, and Isaac carved a beautiful sign with the name Watisé Isjaro on it.

Walter, who had come up with the name, had a wonderful time on any day that a newcomer ventured by and asked about the peculiar words. He would pronounce it for them in a deep voice with a dramatic flair, "WuhTEEshay IzJARoh!" and then spun stories that grew and grew in complexity. Then Walter would shoo them away before they could ask any more questions and point out some vague area south of there that was "known" to be filled with gold-rich caves just ready to be mined by an industrious prospector.

"You're probably just sending them to a cave full of bat guano, you know," snorted Isaac. "Are there truly any promising caves that way?"

Walter shrugged and winked at the young man.

Although the name Watisé Isjaro fascinated the hopeful miners who poured into the area after them, in truth, the title was just a compilation of the first two letters of each of their names.

After it was reported (truthfully) that Séamus found a four-pound gold lump, word spread even more, and people flocked to California at an alarming pace.

It was now 1850, and hopefuls continued to arrive in droves. The extravagant stories that flew around the world about fifty-pound gold lumps were greatly exaggerated, but they stirred people's emotions and got them to drop everything and rush to San Francisco—only to discover they were still over one hundred miles from the mining sites. One such bogus claim turned out to be a large chunk of quartz with a streak of gold running through it that probably weighed less than an ounce. But President Polk was happy. California was a terrific attraction, and a little bit of hyped-up marketing went a long way.

After the story got out about Séamus finding the huge piece of solid gold, the men didn't like some of the attention they were attracting. They became more careful than ever taking turns being the armed guard of their site as the others worked or slept. As hard as they worked, the night shift was a tough one to take, so they did that in pairs in order to keep each other awake.

One night, Séamus stood leaning against a large boulder while the others slept, and his companion had stepped away to relieve himself in the bushes. Séamus rubbed his tired eyes, stretched, and gave a colossal yawn when he felt the tip of a pistol poke him in the back.

"Give it to me if you want to live, Ginger," a rough voice rasped in his ear. "I want a nice, fat sack of gold, and I want it now, or you'll never live to see the morning."

Séamus' body went rigid with fright. He'd stupidly lain the blunderbuss down at his feet and was unarmed. "I don't know where the gold is, mister. They keep it hidden from me," he lied. Then he heard the gun cock.

"Don't tell me stupid stories, sonny. Get in that tent where your partners are and bring it to me now!" He shoved Séamus with the narrow barrel of his Colt Paterson Revolver. "And if you speak up to anyone, I'll kill all of you fools."

A new voice declared calmly, "No, you won't. You'll step away from my friend and get the hell off our claim. If you ever show up and threaten us again, you'll leave with a bullet in you."

Séamus felt the gun barrel leave his back and slowly turned to see Timothy with the Hawken rifle trained on the stranger's face from a few feet away.

"Just kiddin'," the intruder mumbled and slithered away back into the night.

"Got any whiskey?" asked Séamus. His legs seemed to give out then, and he plopped onto the ground. "Thanks, Timothy."

"Séamus? I think we have to make sure none of us sets down their weapon while on watch from now on. I'm afraid there could be many more scoundrels out there who are hungry, lazy, and desperate."

Chapter Nine

After months of tedious, grueling labor and nervous tension about being robbed or killed, the partners had had enough. Replete with more gold than they could imagine, the six men finally decided they were ready to quit mining, living rough, and slaving through awful weather. Game was also becoming scarce with the influx of hungry men, and starvation claimed lives every day around them.

When they'd first begun work at this site, they came up with a few pounds of gold per week. Gradually, however, it took them all working together for an entire week to produce what they'd started out finding in one day.

Finally, Walter announced, "There is still gold to be had in the area, but at this point, we'll need to dynamite the rock away to get it." It was backbreaking enough to collect the gold dust they found in the stream and under piles of rocks they'd moved around by hand, and not one of them wanted to play around with explosives.

Each time Jasper left for supplies, he'd report back that prices were reaching ridiculous heights, and their gold was becoming less and less valuable. The law of diminishing returns drove them all to consider other options.

Jasper made the trek to San Francisco a few times, and each time he returned with the news that the population explosion was staggering. The sleepy little settlement was becoming a full-blown city.

So, with no regrets, they sold the rights to Watisé Isjaro to a large mining company that was skilled in explosive techniques —making an even larger fortune for themselves—and made plans to relocate in San Francisco. It was time for a change and some civilization, they all agreed.

"How about we build ourselves a fancy hotel and cater to the folks in the city?" Jasper suggested. "We could have a nice restaurant and a saloon, and upstairs we can have some fancy rooms for our guests. They have some hotels in San Francisco, but they'll always need more at the rate folks are arriving from all over the world. And the places they have so far are pretty rough. Most have dirt floors and are full of bugs."

Walter, who loved the idea, had the perfect vision in his mind for how their establishment could look. He explained it, drawing pictures in the dirt of some of his notions. Practically vibrating with eagerness, he announced, "I visited a hotel in Boston a few years back. It's called The Tremont, and that place is so modern, they have indoor plumbing. I think we need to figure out how to implement that in ours. They did it in the White House, so why not in our hotel?"

"I think we ought to build it out of brick because the city has already had several fires. We can stay safer with bricks, I believe," Jasper added.

Walter nodded with understanding. "We should definitely do that."

They all enthusiastically agreed that Walter would be the best one to oversee the general construction, while they all planned to pitch in their building skills to get the job done. They also assumed they'd be able to hire more workers once they got to the city.

Timothy immediately saw the appeal of working as a bartender, and Séamus admitted modestly that he'd always had a good head for figures. He offered to manage the company's finances.

Isaac announced enthusiastically, "I can entertain with my fiddle in the saloon at night, but that'll be after I've finished crafting the woodwork we'll want."

Jasper said he and Royal could manage the hotel property and restaurant. So, it was settled. They were now in the hotel/restaurant/saloon business.

"Just as long as I don't have to milk cows and shovel manure, I'm happy," Royal said with a laugh.

It was interesting, upon reflection, that everyone assumed they would each continue to work hard, despite the fortunes they'd already amassed.

"What shall we call the hotel?" asked Séamus. "The Pay Dirt?"

"Nah," complained Timothy with a shake of his head. "We need something with more sophistication."

"We could reuse the name Watisé Isjaro; that one was always lucky for us. Or how about the Yerba Buena Hotel? Or the San Franciscan?" offered Isaac.

"Let's keep it in the spirit of gold mining and call it The Discovery," Jasper offered with a proud smile. "I have a good feeling about that." They all agreed happily with many claps on the back.

Timothy produced a whiskey bottle from somewhere, and they drank a toast to their new venture. "The Discovery!" they cheered.

Jasper, the best finagler of the bunch, sold off their mining equipment at a ridiculous premium to some desperate new arrivals who'd shown up with nothing. He bought more mules and a couple of sturdy wagons to get them to San Francisco.

On the day of their departure, the men regarded the dramatic backdrop of the Sierra Nevada range and gulped in the aroma of the pine trees and the fresh air. They washed and filled their canteens with the clean mountain stream water and bade it all goodbye. After one last look at the magnificent land they'd be leaving behind, they struck out finally for the Pacific coast.

The trip lasted several days longer than they'd hoped because the rain made passage nearly impossible. Their heavily laden wagons sank into the mud so deeply they had to completely unload their cargo several times, dig the wheels out of the muck, and reload again when they were clear. This was just as laborious and far less exciting than their prospecting had been.

"Everyone always talks about how the weather is so much *better* in California," Timothy groused one day after receiving a huge bruise after tripping over a submerged tree root and smacking into a rock. "We've nearly frozen to death, been scorched by the sun so much my nose has peeled off several times, and now we're swimming through a sea of mud! I sure hope it's better once we reach the city."

Jasper kept his opinions on that matter to himself. He knew that the muddy city streets were also going to be a challenge.

Eventually, the travel-worn men pulled into San Francisco and headed straight to the Assay Office, where they put their gold into an account for The Discovery. Then they went to look for property to buy. Prices were skyrocketing with the increased demand, and Jasper was glad they hadn't waited any longer.

The plot of land they chose was on a bluff overlooking San Francisco. It had a splendid view of the bay and the city, so being forward-thinking men, they bought up several acres.

They pitched their tents on their new land and began the arduous task of building. The work fell mostly on them to do because, even though they'd expected to find men who were eager to work, they had not counted on the vast numbers of them who still vacated San Francisco on a daily basis. Even though the partners recognized that the gold rush heyday was diminishing, the newcomers hadn't yet accepted the news.

The hopefuls had dropped everything to get to San Francisco to make their fortune, and they weren't going to stop without making a decent stab at it.

Chapter Ten

San Francisco teemed with men on a mission. Men, men, and more men were everywhere, speaking several languages, all ages and personalities. They were ready for an easy payoff for their efforts and believed that soon they could return to their families with gold in their pockets just by scooping up handfuls of the stuff that lay around in great quantity.

This plan worked for a few. Sadly, very few, for the stores of gold by this point were nothing like they had been in 1848. Some had become multimillionaires, but they were the minority, and the boom was over. This hadn't deterred the hopeful arrivals yet, however. They still flocked in.

For many, it was a road to failure, starvation, and sometimes murder. Many would perish or leave completely poverty-stricken. Some stayed because they couldn't afford to leave.

The abundance of gold created chaos in the local economy as gold dust became accepted currency in the area. Food and clothing prices were exorbitant, and housing was nearly nonexistent. Abandoned ships—as many as six hundred at one point—floated in the harbor after the crews fled their posts in favor of mining. These vessels became a source for lumber and building supplies as wood could not be brought into the city quickly enough to keep up with the demand. Some of the ships became housing, and some were turned into businesses if they were close enough to the shore. One was a bank, another a general store. There were boarding houses and a hospital, and one became a jail and a place to house the insane. The residents erected piers that provided access to these strange boat-buildings, and the city grew around them.

Fires routinely decimated the rickety structures that sprouted up almost overnight, but they were quickly rebuilt—usually within just a few short days. The city grew to meet the demands of the tremendous influx of hopefuls.

"Doesn't it feel strange," Royal asked in wonderment, "to see so few women? I didn't expect to see many in the mining camp, but now that we're in a city..." They looked around them and couldn't spy a single female.

In fact, there were only *four* women to every *thousand* men in California in 1849, and though the numbers grew in 1850, the ratio was still far from normal. Jasper and Royal would see women if they wandered into a saloon. Prostitutes made up the bulk of the females in town, but there were also a number of otherwise resourceful ladies who made a very good living without prostituting themselves.

Men longed for their wives and their beloved mothers and sisters back home, so paying a lady with gold dust to sit and talk for a while wasn't much of a hardship. Saloons sprang up all over San Francisco, where a significant number of the women grew rich by being friendly to these lonely men.

Well-dressed and polite women who chose prostitution also earned good money—usually working in a nice brothel run by an enterprising madam. Though their lives were sometimes difficult, the American and European prostitutes were often respected members of society as their contribution was so appreciated. This attitude only lasted for a few years, however. Eventually, they were not highly regarded in the least, but in 1850, they were part of the essential fabric of society.

Unfortunately, the immigrant Chinese women who poured into San Francisco on a steady basis were so economically distressed, they were often forced into prostitution, but they were regarded as the bottom of society and were not particularly sought after. Prejudice against the Chinese was vicious in 1850, stemming from their desperate practice of undercutting the going rate of labor and service charges. Also, they didn't speak English or dress like the other women, and potential customers often wanted more than just a quick coupling. The plight of the young, unmarried Chinese women who became prostitutes was grim as they tried to eke out a living, pay back loans, send money to their families, and live under the thumbs of the criminal groups of Chinese men who exploited them.

No matter who they were or what they did, the rare American and European women in San Francisco were stared at, and often followed around through the streets by men who just wanted a glimpse of something pretty.

Jasper took all of this in over the next weeks while the hotel was being built. He told Royal, "We'll need to employ some women to make the business special. Just look around us. There are hundreds of saloons, and more of them open each day. We need to set ours apart with better entertainment than just whiskey."

They took it upon themselves to scour the city for the prettiest ladies and offer them jobs at better than the going rate. "We need to meet all of the ships as soon as they dock," announced Royal. "We'll get the best arrivals that way." He laughed with Jasper at the thought. "I see more and more families arriving by boat each day. Maybe some of them have pretty daughters."

"We need to offer them more than any other hotel or saloon in the city so we can be sure to have loyal employees," Jasper told his partners. "I think we should build housing for them on-site where they can live if they want to."

This arrangement was extremely well-received, and many of the newly hired workers moved into the dormitory adjacent to the hotel. It provided them a bed and a sturdy roof over their heads. Up until this point, most had been living in drafty, muddy tents, or they came straight from the ship they sailed in on.

If they didn't want to dance and flirt or become a prostitute, some women cashed in on their cooking and baking skills or did laundry—although that industry was largely handled by the Chinese immigrants. Opportunities for women abounded, and they were respected and valued in a way they'd never experienced before. This was a new era for women. They weren't controlled by the social mores they were used to in the east, the south, or their native countries. These women dressed as they wished, lived as they wished, and made their own rules for the first time ever.

At night, those men who eschewed the prostitutes routinely sought out each other for sexual release. Even in the growing city, "bachelor marriages" continued.

Chapter Eleven

Adeline Hart's Journal

Mid-March, 1850

With the exception of the storm we encountered off of the coast of Chile, the Pacific Ocean has been more agreeable than the Atlantic. Captain Greely was more amenable to stopping and taking on supplies as we traveled north. It was Father this time who pressed Greely to rush northward, citing the loss of revenue for each day that we spent traveling. Father looks worse than ever, I am sad to say. His poor diet and constant fretting about missed opportunity both conspire to ruin his health. Some of the crew members have frightful coughs, and Father is showing the early signs of coming down with whatever ailment plagues the men.

Now that we are off the coast of Mexico, we often sail in the company of steamships heading north from Panama to the same destination. I find myself wondering about the people aboard those ships and imagine making friends with some of them. I would not let myself think until now about just how lonely I feel. Even now, I cannot dwell on this and lose my good spirits. I miss my gentle mother so terribly and also long for the company of my female friends and cousins whom we left behind.

Father forbade me to strike up any conversations with the crewmen. I can understand. He probably fears I might "accidentally" kill another one if he should get too close.

At least we continue to see many more species of whales and dolphins. I enjoy their company. They always look so happy; it gives me hope that this journey of ours will be worth it.

April 1, 1850

The day I shall never forget:

It's actually been several days since all of this happened. I needed to gather my courage and my wits in order to put any of this in writing. Everything has changed.

Father took to his berth when that horrible cough felled him. He was pasty-faced and had a wretched time catching his breath. I had nothing to offer him in the way of comfort other than hot tea, though our supply of honey was used up long ago. He also seemed to be suffering from a fever that would not abate.

Despite his illness, on the first day of April the mood on the ship was jubilant and excited. Captain Greely had announced the day prior that he expected us to pull into the San Francisco Port the next day. Privately, he told me that we would be entering what was named The Golden Gate. I thought that was fitting because of all the gold people were finding in the area, but he dispelled that notion by explaining that the name was given to the port in 1846 by Captain John C. Fremont, who visualized many riches flowing into this harbor with traders who sailed here from the Orient. He said that Fremont compared the port with the Golden Horn of the Bosporus in Constantinople—another beautiful landlocked harbor that he had admired—and gave this one the Greek name *Chrysopylae*, which means Golden Gate in English. Apparently, the residents liked the name, for they use it often.

But I digress. Even now, I am avoiding the story I must tell.

Attired once again in my own female clothing, I packed our valises with our personal items and made certain that I had this journal in my pocket. Father did his best to make himself presentable—despite his cough and general weakness. He told me that he would see our arrival out on the deck. He had a bit more color to his cheeks and a brighter look in his eye than he'd had in many a day, and I was fooled into thinking he might be on the mend. Now as I look back, I wonder if it was just the fever making him burn more brightly.

Sadly, he was not on the mend at all. As we took in the odd sight of the port completely filled with ships that had the look of being abandoned and stripped of timbers, we focused on the shore and the city of San Francisco. Odd ramshackle buildings seemed to be holding each other up—some made from wood and others made from what appeared to be the canvas of sails. So strange they were! And the dock was densely populated by men who stared and waved at our arriving vessel. They had an air of expectance about them, and they seemed to be as happy as we were to be arriving. No doubt this was because we were a cargo ship, and they had need of supplies.

Just as our captain expertly pulled the ship alongside the dock that stretched way out into the harbor, I grasped Father's arm in excitement. I looked at him and saw that his color was very bad, and he could not catch his breath. Then he toppled over. I screamed for assistance. Unfortunately, the crewmen were either occupied with ropes and whatnot, or they were too busy crowding the rail and gawking at San Francisco while they surely dreamed of the fortune they would soon realize. I was terrified that my dear father was going to perish on the ship without even setting foot on California soil after this grueling journey of ours. I continued to scream for help and tried to make sure Father did not hurt himself as I sat him up and propped him upright. The crew continued to ignore my plight, and the captain was busy piloting the vessel, so he was unaware as well. I truly did not know what to do, so I loosened Father's collar to facilitate his breathing. That did not seem to help.

The gangplank was lowered, and the previously idle seamen immediately clogged it with their departing bodies. They looked like a herd of wild animals, shoving and pushing each other to get to the dock first. They truly could not be quit of the ship quickly enough. As they hit the dock, most of them took off running, and I heard many garbled shouts from them as they sped off. The only word that stood out over and over was, "Gold!"

As soon as the gangplank was safely clear, two young gentlemen ran up from the dock and straight to Father and me, letting me know they had heard my screaming from below. I was so happy to have their assistance, I could have embraced them. Without even conferring, they ever so carefully hoisted Father off the deck and worked together to convey Father to their wagon. At first, they attempted to get Father to walk between them, but his legs seemed unable to bear his own weight. So then one of the men put his arms around Father's chest from behind, and the other lifted his legs. They seemed to work efficiently together without much discussion, making me curious about their association with one another.

The darker-haired man, who politely introduced himself to me as Jasper Langley, said to follow them closely and not to stop to chat with anyone—as if I entertained such a notion! They made their way down the gangway and along the dock, where people kindly stepped out of the way for them. I, however, had a more difficult time as many men tried to stop me. They would tip their hats and introduce themselves, and I do believe at least three of them proposed marriage to me right then! I did not wish to be impolite, but I could not let the two gentlemen carry Father out of my sight. So, I pressed onward and ignored the questions with no more than a brief smile.

The dock went on and on and on; it was *so* long! Ship after ship seemed to be tied alongside it, and it had the appearance of having been added onto over and over as it stretched into the harbor. The sight was so strange with all of those ships sitting idle, and I can see the need for such length. Gradually, we reached their wagon, and I saw that Mr. Langley and his friend, whom he introduced as Royal Dawson, were not the least bit winded after carrying Father the distance to their conveyance and placing him as gently as possible on a pile of blankets. Mr. Langley said that Royal would be happy to take Father and me to the nearest doctor, and he would meet us there after making some arrangements with the ship's captain. Then he muttered something about hoping he wasn't too late and that he desperately needed a stove for the hotel.

I spoke up then and told them, "There may be others in cargo, but the large stove in the galley belongs to Father. We brought it to start a hotel here in San Francisco, and they didn't charge us to ship it if I served as the ship's cook. Actually, we brought several chests filled with supplies."

You could have heard a pin drop at that point, so silent were the two men as they regarded me with surprise, and then their faces broke out into matching—and I must add very handsome—smiles. They looked at one another, and it was as if they acknowledged each other's thoughts clearly and yet without words. With a quick nod, Royal Dawson—the taller of the two by a small margin—spoke up for the first time then and announced, "We're nearly done building a fine hotel. Do you think you'd like to invest your equipment and become partners with us?"

I blinked a couple of times, and then Father waved a feeble hand at me, croaking barely audibly, "Accept, Adeline. You'll need their help." Then he closed his eyes and let out a hideous wheeze. At this point, Royal hastened to help me up onto the seat of the wagon and mounted it next to me. We took off immediately and with great alacrity.

I do not wish to dwell too deeply on what happened next, for I fear my heart shall shatter into a million pieces. We got Father to the doctor's establishment just in time for the man to pronounce my dearest father dead.

Now I sit in what is gradually becoming a lovely room in Mr. Dawson and Mr. Langley's hotel they call The Discovery. They have four other partners in business with them, and they all seem like honest gentlemen. For some reason, they laughed when they told me they'd considered calling the establishment Watisé Isjaro, but that name was already taken. They certainly have some odd names here in California, if that is so. They had to spell it for me.

The Discovery was crafted with care—that I can tell— and the wooden furnishings have a very new smell. I hear the sounds of building in the rooms beside and beneath mine, so apparently, there is still plenty to do. My room overlooks the harbor as we are on a bluff above the town proper they call the Plaza. This structure is made of much sturdier supplies than some of the small businesses closer to the water. There are no sails for walls or roofs on this structure.

If I think about it too much, I fear I will become frightened to death about my future, and I have never felt so sad in my life, but I have a place to live and suddenly a one-seventh share in a lovely new hotel with wonderful modern conveniences—and more to come, I'm told. I shall allow myself only a short time to grieve, however, because I need to get on with things.

Father's stove was brought up to the hotel and installed in the kitchen immediately. This was my entree into the business. Apparently, they hired a talented cook yesterday who came all the way from Paris! I am extremely relieved that cooking was not added to my responsibilities in order to become one of the hotel's proprietors, but if it had, I would have taken on the role to the best of my ability.

Royal and Jasper, for that is what they insist I call them, assisted me in burying my dearest father, and for that alone I shall always be grateful. It was even worse than when Father and I lay Mother to her final rest. Both Jasper and Royal offered their deepest sympathy as well as strong arms to hold onto when I needed it.

It's strange, but in Jasper I see a certain depth of sorrow that makes me feel a profound kinship with him. I wonder if he has experienced great loss as well. He is an exceptionally fine-looking man with dark hair, broad shoulders, and clear blue eyes, but those eyes have seen hard times. Of that, I am convinced. I would be pleased to take some of that sorrow away if I could.

Royal is a delightful person. He seems to look out for Jasper in kind ways that surprise me in a man. I feel a strong bond has formed between the two of them. Royal is tall and rangy with lovely hazel eyes and dark blond hair. He has large, capable hands that look strong but gentle, and he uses them expressively when he speaks. Hearing him laugh is the high point of my day as he does it with joy and abandon.

As I mentioned, they have four other men who are part of their—now *our*—company. I've met two charming young Irishmen named Timothy and Séamus. They seem to like to joke around, and they sing quite often. Royal told me they even sang while they were panning for gold, but he says sometimes they get so loud they could wake snakes. It sounds as if they enjoy their whiskey.

Then there is Isaac, a talented musician who played a beautiful hymn on his violin when Father was buried. He seems to be the artistic one who designs and crafts much of the fine furnishings here at The Discovery. His workmanship is impressive—especially given how quickly he turns out his lovely pieces. He is such a wonderful addition to the company. His great size is almost incongruous with his gentle nature. How such large hands produce such achingly beautiful music is remarkable.

And the final member of the group is a man named Walter. He seems to be a few years older than the others. He has a professorial demeanor and has the gift for telling a story in most colorful and descriptive language. Walter apparently crossed the continent with a small but important collection of books, and he has let me borrow what he thought would keep me entertained while I recuperate from my journey and get my bearings.

I have done a fair amount of reading, and of course I enjoy my writing. I wonder if I can ever find a piano, for it's been so terribly long since I've touched the ivories. I hope I have not forgotten how to play.

They have all been perfect gentlemen toward me, and for that I am relieved and grateful.

Even while there are six gentlemen with whom I am affiliated now in business, I find myself most closely drawn to Jasper and Royal. I don't know if it stems from a sense of hero worship because of the selfless way they jumped to my aid or something more personal. I don't favor one over the other, however, so any romantic notions on my part would no doubt be silly. Neither has shown a stronger interest in me, so there is no tipping of the scales because of that. They are both most aware of my grief and seem to be very solicitous.

I have felt strangely weak after being on a ship for so many months. My sea legs continued on dry land, and I found myself wobbly for the first three days after landing. I feel stronger each day. I am so relieved to have the voyage behind me.

With regards to sailing here, it was an honor to see Captain Greely appear when we lay dear Father to rest. He spoke so very kindly about Father, but he said something to me later that shocked me to my very core. Apparently, he is contemplating settling here in California now that his crew has abandoned him and his pockets are full of money. He let me know that he would like me to consider a proposal of marriage. He is a fine enough man, I suppose, but he is far older than I and not someone I find particularly intriguing. We had some interesting conversations now and then on the Wind Gypsy, but I cannot fathom why he thought I might wish to marry him. At least he knows what a sinner I am, but that in itself is no reason to marry the man. He did not press for an answer when I hesitated but said I would be seeing him again after I'd settled in. Just the fact that he should bring up the topic of marriage while I was seeing to the internment of my beloved parent was enough to turn my heart away from him permanently. I realize that even if he thinks for some reason he needs to rescue me from my dire straits of being alone in the world, I do not need to be rescued by Captain Greely in so callous a manner. Already I have prospects and means that I never had before in my life.

Time will tell what kind of contribution I can make beyond the trunks of blankets, linens, featherbeds and pillows, dishes, cutlery, and of course the stove and accompanying pots and pans for the kitchen that Father and I brought. I also brought along a large supply of fine candles and soaps, and that made the men all quite pleased. My trunk of dresses was probably a waste of space, for I doubt I'll have any need to dress up in this strange city.

The six men who built this establishment are all people worth my admiration, as I have said, and I plan to strive to help make a success of this business with them. Even in my present grief, there is a freedom of spirit that I have never felt before.

Chapter Twelve

The Discovery, San Francisco, 1850

As soon as they met Adeline and offered her a partnership in The Discovery, Royal and Jasper agreed to be gentlemen and give up their nearly finished room to her. They took one of the smaller, empty rooms and never told her their plan.

"She is too much of a lady to expect her to sleep on the floor until we can outfit her with a bed," Jasper announced.

"Absolutely," agreed Royal. "We're so used to living rough, what's another few days? At least we have a sturdy roof over our heads that won't leak."

So, once again, they were back to sleeping in their bedrolls, even though they were very wealthy men. They could have moved into another hotel in town, but the idea of leaving The Discovery for even a night wasn't palatable. And they didn't want to be too far from Adeline Hart.

At night, as they lay down naked on their blankets, Royal asked Jasper, "Do you find Miss Adeline... especially attractive?"

Jasper snorted, "You'd have to be blind to miss her beauty, Royal. That shiny mahogany hair and those brown eyes of hers that... well, they're unsurpassed. She has a beautiful... uh... shape as well."

"Do you want to court her?" Royal pressed on.

"Not if you do."

"Me? Why?"

"I see the way she looks at you, Roy. She smiles at you like you created sunshine."

"Jasper, you could make a stuffed bird laugh. That's preposterous. I see her looking at *you*. She thinks you're a fresh glass of water on a scorching day. And believe me, she's thirsty."

Jasper thought for a moment and dragged his hand over his face. "Maybe we haven't been around enough women lately to figure out what she wants. She's nothing like Isabella, that's for sure."

"Meaning?"

"I just think Adeline will figure out what she wants to do with herself in her own way. Izzy was more interested in being the perfect wife and doing everything that I wanted." Jasper's voice cracked as he added, "I probably caused her death with my selfishness, dragging her away from her family and making her take that long, difficult trek across the country."

Royal wasn't shocked by Jasper's opinion, but it tore at his heart nevertheless. He put his arm around his friend and drew him close. "Never think that, Jas. It was a tragedy and the worst possible loss, but it wasn't your fault." As they did on many a night, he kissed Jasper deeply, tasting the man's sorrow.

Coming up for a breath, Jasper grumbled, "What would Adeline do with me anyway, Roy? I obviously made a terrible husband."

"Don't be ridiculous. You're the best man I've ever known. She would be lucky to have you. *I'm* lucky to have you. Want me to make you feel better?" Royal whispered. When Jasper nodded and sighed, Royal slid down and engulfed Jasper in his hot mouth. Pulling back, he grasped Jasper's cock firmly and licked the head until it was as hard as steel and then swallowed him once again. Smiling to himself to hear Jasper's moans, Royal bobbed up and down several times, keeping pressure on him with his mouth and hand. He briefly pulled back, then and raised Jasper's legs. Royal licked his fingers and bent back over Jasper's rigid cock, worshiping it with his mouth as he maneuvered his large finger into Jasper's anus.

Jasper writhed in ecstasy and found he couldn't stay still. "Holy blazes, Roy, don't stop! That's it, ohhh."

Royal was so excited by Jasper's exuberance he let go of Jasper and grabbed his own cock. He kept pumping his finger in and out of Jasper's backside as he sucked. He began to beat his own shaft with such speed and enthusiasm that within a very short time, he was shooting ropes of cum all over Jasper at the same time that Jasper erupted in Royal's mouth.

Panting slightly, Royal slid back up Jasper's body and nuzzled his neck affectionately. His hand lay across Jasper's chest where he could feel the pounding of his friend's heart. They lay in comfortable silence for a few minutes until Royal finally broke away and headed to the wash basin that had a fragrant bar of soap next to it.

As they cleaned up, Jasper looked deeply into Royal's eyes and announced sincerely, "I love you, and I don't know how I could bear a life without you."

"Then I guess you're in luck," Royal answered. "Because I love you too, and I'm not going anywhere. But if you want to marry Miss Adeline, I'll be fine with that."

Jasper blinked at him and said, "It's way too early to talk about anyone marrying her, but if either of us were to do it, I think she'd prefer you."

They lay back down on their makeshift bed, and Royal laid his head on Jasper's chest. "She'd be wrong, and you are too. She clearly prefers you."

Jasper chuckled. "Go to sleep, Roy."

Ten days after Adeline's arrival, the construction was nearly complete. Jasper and Royal determined the time was right, so they sat her down with a business proposition they wanted to share with her.

"Miss Adeline," began Jasper in a formal tone, "We wanted to give you time to settle before bringing this up, but now we would like to ask you something." Adeline regarded him with curiosity and smiled, so he lost his formality and blurted out, "We think you would be a wonderful asset to our company if you were to become an entertainer in the saloon."

With a horrified expression, she gaped at him and was mortified to feel herself tearing up. "You want me to...?" She couldn't even finish the statement as her hand flew to her mouth.

Grasping her misunderstanding immediately, Royal spoke up. "Please, Miss Adeline, don't think we're suggesting *anything* other than being friendly and smiling at our customers. What they call entertainers here in San Francisco is nothing shameful. You're so beautiful, men will flock in just to get a glimpse of you. Most of the saloons down in the main part of the city are nothing but a tent with a plank of wood inside supported between a couple of old barrels, and they serve the cheapest liquor you can find. They make plenty of money that way. But our vision for The Discovery is that we want a high-class establishment. No prostitutes." He saw her blanch. "Sorry, ma'am. No ladies of the evening for us. We'll have gambling tables and an attractive bar. There will be music and a place for dancing. The entertainers we've hired are all respectable ladies who can show you how to do the job. They'll charge for a dance and for spending time talking to men for a little while. Encouraging the men to buy drinks is another way we'll make money, and our ladies will all make a good wage for themselves. There is nothing shameful in this job, and everyone will love you."

"You want me to earn my keep by getting men to buy alcohol and dance with me?" she squeaked.

"Not completely," insisted Jasper. "We want you to be friendly and... well, you're already beautiful, so you can just stay that way." He smiled to see her color return as she blinked at him. "But you'll be making money right along with us. You're a business partner, after all. The other women will, in essence, be working for you, and another one of your responsibilities will be to see that none of the men try to monopolize a particular entertainer for too long. Encourage the ladies to move along. We'll help you with that, of course. And you won't have to drink alcohol unless you want to. The bartender will keep special bottles filled with tea to fill the glasses of the ladies who want to keep their wits about them. We don't care if the men get drunk. They've worked hard, and now they'll want to spend some gold."

Adeline blinked at his earnest expression. "Well, I suppose I could give it a try."

Jasper spoke up happily, "Wonderful! The saloon is ready to open tonight, and the restaurant will open in a few days. Soon we'll have the hotel going. This is going to rival anything in the whole city!" He looked into her big brown eyes and blurted out, "I could kiss you; I'm so excited."

Adeline's mouth dropped open at that confession, and her cheeks flamed a beautiful shade of pink once again. Gathering herself, she asked, "Why do you want the women to move along and not spend too much time with any particular man?"

Chuckling, Royal responded, "We hear that the reason most of the employed ladies quit their jobs is because they meet someone and get married. And while we're not opposed to marriage for any reason, we hope to keep our employees longer than a few days."

"A few days?" Adeline gave him an incredulous look.

"Haven't you received a few proposals yourself so far? And you've barely been out in public."

"True. I surely don't wish to jump into anything rash, however."

The two men regarded her carefully, and Royal spoke up, "Do you wish to marry?"

"Well, yes, of course. One day."

That seemed to satisfy them.

"Do I need to dress up tonight?" she wondered.

Royal grinned at her and said, "You would look beautiful in anything, but if you have a fine gown to wear, it would be wonderful for you to get yourself gussied up. Just remember that a lot of these men will be coming straight from the mining sites, and they'll look pretty rough. They'll no doubt want to pay you with gold dust, too—so be aware of that. We'll make sure Séamus or Walter will be part of any monetary transaction so we can keep the records straight."

Jasper suddenly had an uncomfortable look on his face and blurted out, "Don't let any of these men get too forward with you. If you have any trouble, we'll be right there watching out, but you'll still want to discourage any untoward behavior or language."

Royal smiled to himself. *Jasper is feeling protective*, he thought. *And I understand. She's exquisite, and if anyone so much as looks at her impolitely, I'll rip his head off. Listen to yourself, Royal! You sound like a mad man. Mad for Miss Adeline anyway...*

Chapter Thirteen

After supper that night, the doors to the saloon were officially opened for business, and people were so curious to see The Discovery, hordes of thirsty customers rushed in immediately. Word was out that the women were the prettiest in the city, and the men were ready for some serious drinking and entertainment. Walter and Royal had set up gambling tables in one area, and the hired faro and monte dealers were ready with their cards. A dance floor took up the center of the room, and over at one side, Isaac was tearing it up already with his rousing fiddle music. Timothy was immediately swamped for business behind the bar, so Séamus and Walter jumped to his rescue to help keep glasses filled and pinches of gold dust collected for payment.

Within moments, the women found themselves grabbed by the hand or arm and swung into the dancing area by exuberant men who had huge smiles on their faces. Monetary transactions were carried out at a breakneck speed, and the room was filled with laughter, stomping feet, and fiddle music. It was obvious to everyone that the hype had not lied. This was a great place to have some fun.

About twenty minutes or so into the frivolities, Isaac had to take a break to down some water. During the lack of music, there was an odd hush and faces turned to the staircase from the hotel rooms above the saloon.

Royal's jaw dropped, and he poked Jasper in the ribs. Jasper's eyes fairly popped out of his face as the entire population of the room gaped at the vision descending the stairs. No one had ever seen a woman of such exquisite beauty; they were all certain. Dressed in a silken gown of sky blue, her shiny hair was plaited and coiled into a chignon and held in place with silver clasps. There was nothing flashy or overdone about her appearance, for she wore a perfectly respectable neckline and sleeves, but she had an ethereal grace that made her seem to flow down the stairs like a waterfall.

Smiling shyly, Adeline made her way directly to Royal and Jasper, who had positioned themselves at the base of the stairway as they awaited her arrival. Men started coming toward her with eager expressions that made her uneasy, so she quickly attached herself to Jasper's arm on one side and Royal's on the other. Both men could feel her trembling.

"Ma'am?" one of the fleet-footed individuals boldly ventured. "Would you honor me with a dance, please?"

Adeline blinked and sucked in a fortifying breath, realizing that the man was actually both clean and polite—nothing like that vile monster on the ship. She looked at Jasper and Royal, who smiled encouragingly at her and demurred, "Yes, thank you, sir."

The music began again, and as quick as lightning, the man disengaged her hand from Royal's arm and swept her out into the middle of the strangest assortment of dancers she'd ever seen in her life. Men danced with women, men danced with men, and the outfits ran the gamut from business suits to filthy work clothes. Adeline plastered on a smile and began to follow the man's lead around and around in a lively... polka? She wasn't even sure what it was, but Isaac was playing his heart out, and people loved it. As soon as there was a pause, another man cut in, and this pattern played over and over for dance after dance after *dance* until she finally announced to her newest would-be partner that she needed a few moments off of her feet and suggested the woman next to her needed someone to partner with. The man did not appear to be very happy, but he made no protest.

Seeing her look around futilely for a table where she might sit and rest a moment, Royal rushed to her side. He adroitly took her by the arm and led her into the back office. She was getting comfortable as Jasper entered the room with a cool drink for her. "Lemonade, Miss Adeline?" he asked with an amused grin. "You're looking a little tuckered out."

"Oh, thank you, Jasper," she sighed. "I haven't danced like that in my entire life. It's a wonder my feet are still attached." She laughed softly and took a fortifying swallow of her refreshing drink. She closed her eyes for a moment and then let out a long exhalation. Rousing herself again, she drank and then asked, "Why are some of the men out there wearing arm bands?"

Jasper chuckled and answered, "They're the gentlemen who have agreed to dance the part of the lady when another man needs a partner and can't find a woman. There's such a shortage of females; men take on all sorts of typical female roles around here. No one thinks a thing of it. It doesn't make them any less of a man, but when the odds are something like fifty to one..."

Adeline looked thoughtful for a moment as she chewed the inside of her cheek. Then she blurted out, "I saw two of the men kissing each other. Does that also happen frequently?"

Royal burst out laughing as Jasper grinned at her, saying, "Oh, yes, ma'am. Indeed, it does. That, and plenty more, if you don't mind my forwardness. Again, no one in this area gives a doggone about it. It's just the way it's done here. Men have *needs,* and they take care of them any way they can." He gave Royal a look she found odd as he continued softly, "Sometimes it's more than that, however."

Adeline's jaw dropped a little until she composed herself, and then she blurted out, "Isn't sodomy against the law?" Her face went scarlet to the roots of her hair, and she found she couldn't look at Jasper in the eye. *What just came over me to ask such an impertinent and unladylike question?* she asked herself. Worse still, she did not understand how thinking about such a thing suddenly made her feel all hot and bothered. A strange, slithery sensation poured through her body, and she found she needed to concentrate on what the men had to say to keep herself focused.

Royal snorted and asked, "What law? This place doesn't have a sheriff or a mayor or a chief of police. It's vigilante justice here, and that's it. Maybe it'll change if California becomes a state, but for now, pretty much anything goes. No one is going to get scandalized about two men who want to keep company. It's not hurting anyone, it's quite prevalent, and the men are most often hardworking members of the community. You'll be surprised to see just what goes on, Miss Adeline. Madams and their whores are escorted out in polite company, and everyone respects them. It's not like it was back home."

Adeline cleared her throat and tried to sound matter-of-fact as she said, "I see." She paused a moment and added, "Apparently, I will need to open my eyes and my heart and see the good in everyone." She laughed softly, "Madams and prostitutes included. For I'm sure some of them are just fine people after all."

"That's a good way to look at it," laughed Royal. "So, Miss Addie, how many men proposed to you so far tonight? I heard Walter and Isaac have a wager going on the number."

Adeline blinked at his familiarity and then decided she liked it. She burst out laughing and answered, "Four! That brings the total up to eight since I arrived, but I truly believe only one of those was sincere." She shook her head and looked down.

Jasper narrowed his eyes at her and asked, "Who did you think was sincere, and what did you say to him?" He didn't like the sound of this one bit.

She waved her hand and answered, "It was just Captain Greely from the Wind Gypsy. He might be planning to settle here and wanted me to marry him—probably out of some sense of loyalty to my father because the two of them were as thick as thieves on the voyage here. He probably thinks I need a protector or... I don't know." She gave a tiny shudder and blurted out, "He told me once that he has a daughter a little older than I! The last thing I want for myself is to become widowed at a young age, so I have no interest whatsoever in an older man, and definitely not in him."

"Doesn't that also mean he has a wife somewhere?" asked Royal.

"No. She died." Adeline noticed how the haunted look suddenly returned to Jasper's eyes as he turned away from her. It gave her a thought as to what melancholy may be hanging over his handsome head, and she wondered...

"Are you ready to go back out there and charm the men of San Francisco, Miss Addie?" Royal gallantly offered her his arm as he looked at Jasper with concern. She stood, and he escorted her out of the office, but she didn't miss that Royal gave Jasper's shoulder a comforting squeeze as the man sat slumped in his chair. Jasper didn't say a word as they left him.

Back in the saloon, the dancing, gaming, and definitely the drinking were all going strong. It was a raucous calamity of semi-organized chaos with a thick layer of bluish smoke that hovered over the gamblers' heads. It was unbearably warm with all of the oil lamps, candles, and crowded, sweaty bodies. Adeline squared her shoulders and braced herself to face a group of men who jostled for position as they thundered her way. One man roughly shouldered another out of the way, saying,

"She's *mine,* Delmer. I done asked her to marry me 'afore that fancy-dressed man took her off an' she disappeared on me. So, git outta the way!"

Delmer, who didn't take kindly to his associate's remark—or his shoving—gave him a hard push and hollered into his face, "Well, for your information, so did I, you drunken fool!" Unfortunately, this man thrust Delmer into another man's way, causing him to fall backward into someone else, and the chain of events immediately evolved into a mêlée of swinging fists and flying curses.

Within seconds, Séamus and Timothy jumped into the fray and stopped the fight. Delmer and the man who shoved him were shown the door. "Come back when you can act in a civilized manner. There are ladies present here!" Timothy shouted at them.

Clutching Royal's arm like a lifeline, Adeline whispered hoarsely to him, "I think I'm done for the evening. I believe I'll retire to my room now."

"I'll walk you up. And be sure to lock your door, Miss Addie. I'll find someone to guard your room as soon as you're safely inside. We can't have this."

As they ascended the staircase, she asked, "Royal?" He looked at her, and she continued, "I'm not sure I can do this night in and night out. As much as I want to pull my own weight, I'm fairly convinced that... *entertaining* is not at all what I'm meant to do."

Looking at her seriously, he answered, "I can see that. It has to be strange to watch grown men make fools of themselves over you."

"It's not just that. I'm just not particularly fond of dancing. Never have been, which is odd because I love music, and I adore playing the piano."

Royal's eyes lit up. "You do? Do you think you could play piano with Isaac and his violin?"

A wide grin made her face glow with happiness, and she answered, "Absolutely. I am more partial to the classics, but I can play anything. I just need a piano. If I hear it once, I can usually play it again almost perfectly. That made for some amusing parlor tricks back in Philadelphia." She looked down and then back up into his sparkling eyes. "I hope that doesn't sound conceited of me."

"Not at all. Miss Addie, you leave it to me. I have the perfect solution." Royal seemed to be trembling with excitement, and out of the blue, he gave her a smacking kiss right on the lips. He spun away and left her gaping at him as he dashed back down the stairs to let Jasper know about his brilliant plan.

Adeline stood in her doorway for a minute with her hand to her mouth and her eyes as wide as saucers. Then she smiled to herself and retired for the night with plenty to think about. At least she remembered to lock her door.

Chapter Fourteen

Royal burst into the office again and found Jasper sipping a whiskey with a far-off look on his face.

"Jasper! We need a piano! Miss Adeline *plays*. She doesn't like dancing at all, but she loves music, and she can play anything she puts her mind to." The words tumbled out of his mouth so quickly he was barely taking a breath. "She doesn't have to put up with men pawing her all night. They'll still come to *appreciate* her and to enjoy her music, but she won't have to be on her feet and in the arms of who-knows-what. Do you see?"

Jasper did, in fact, see, and the prospect of having her near and at the same time away from all of the ogling, groping men of San Francisco did a lot to ease his mind. His face relaxed, and he finally smiled at his best friend. He stroked his chin thoughtfully. "We'll build a stage and have the piano and Isaac on it, away from the crowd. It's perfect, Roy. Now we just have to scour the city for a piano, and the sooner, the better."

"Let's go right now," laughed Royal. "Oh, wait. As soon as I post someone to guard Miss Addie's room. There was a big ruckus when she went back out there, and a fight broke out over her. I guess we might have to expect that."

After posting a sentry at her door, the two of them had a quick conference with Walter. He agreed that it was a splendid idea and suggested the area of town where they ought to start looking for an instrument. The main commercial district was called the Plaza, so that was where they began the hunt.

Hours later and several thousand dollars poorer, Royal and Jasper led a heavily burdened group of tired men into their saloon. The Discovery's crowd had disbursed by then as it was nearly dawn, so maneuvering the piano into the saloon wasn't terrible—just awkward.

Isaac was beside himself with excitement when he saw the gleaming wood of a well-built piano. He rushed up the stairs to pound on Adeline's door, shouting, "Miss Adeline! Come see this. You have to get up!"

Wrapped in a modest dressing gown with her plaited hair falling down her back, a sleepy-looking Adeline descended the stairs once again behind a beaming Isaac. His enthusiasm was infectious, but she had no idea what she would see. All trace of slumber left her, however, when she spied the lovely instrument. "How? Where? Did you...?" she spluttered, looking from man to man.

All six men stood and watched with delight as she rushed to the piano and lifted its fallboard. She stroked the keys as Séamus slipped the piano bench behind her. Thanking him breathlessly, Adeline sat and adjusted her position. She played a chord or two, appreciating the sound as she made happy little gasps of pleasure. Then she limbered up with some scales as the men all grinned at her. She finally broke into a Bach prelude with tears of joy pouring down her cheeks, causing a few wet eyes among the gentlemen as well. It was obvious to all that the piano transported Adeline into a different world where she was happy and content.

When Adeline finally let the final chords die away, she stood and faced the men. With tears pouring down her face, she exclaimed, "Thank you for this incredible gift. And thank you all for hauling it in here for me because I know it wasn't easy. You have no idea how much this means to me to have a piano again, but one as wonderful as this? I have no words to express my elation and gratitude. I was afraid," her voice cracked a little, "that I would never be able to play again. This replaces a part of me I thought I had lost for good."

Royal explained to her, "The owner said this Steinway was shipped here all the way from Germany. He promised that all the keys worked, and it would sound good, but you're the one who's brought the music to life, Addie. This is going to be a wonderful addition to The Discovery. We're thrilled to have found it for you."

The men built a sturdy stage and hoisted the instrument up onto it. Now Adeline and Isaac's music could fill the hall, and they would both be safe from the jostling crowd. It made life especially more pleasant for Isaac—a very energetic fiddler who rarely stood still to play. Between his energy and virtuosity, and Adeline's beauty and brilliance, they were quite the performers.

Word spread around San Francisco that The Discovery not only had the most beautiful women to dance with but also the finest music in the city. It also didn't hurt that their floors were all made of real wood—unlike the rest of the commercial establishments around San Francisco, most of which had dirt floors that became muddy when it rained.

Business tripled within two days of the piano's installation, and men crowded in to listen and gaze upon Adeline while they danced, gambled away their hard-earned money, and drank away their worries. Some jubilant men came to celebrate their success now and then, but mostly it was just to blow off steam. Sundays were the busiest days of all as many of the miners would toil away all week and take Sunday off to relax.

Adeline and Isaac worked out a repertoire that could change with nothing but a quick word and a glance at one another. They controlled the gaiety and general volume of the patrons by speeding up or slowing down the pace of their music. Séamus and Timothy often sang along from behind the bar with their deep, soulful voices, and that was always a treat, especially to the other Irishmen in the crowd. Walter also chimed in with his rich tenor voice now and then. He often encouraged the other patrons to sing with him, and that sometimes led to tears flowing in tracks down their dusty faces. There was nothing like music to remind the men of what and whom they left behind. And all of this caused them to spend their hard-earned gold.

Now and then, a man would show up with a flute or a banjo and ask to play along with them, and these musicians were always welcomed. The men who played with them often seemed transported into a place of extreme delight, for they had missed the comradery of playing with others for so long. The music was often rough when strangers joined in—due to lack of rehearsal—but the crowd was receptive and appreciative, nonetheless.

The liquor, the music, the dancing, and the gambling became the great equalizer as men from all walks of life and all races showed up to enjoy life together. No one cared what anyone wore or how supposedly influential they were in the community. They were all there together to let loose and have fun.

The Discovery became the most sought-after place for entertainment and relaxation in San Francisco. Other entrepreneurs tried to buy up the property around them so they could cash in on the traffic overflow, but the partners weren't selling. They still had plans for expansion. Often, they had to get rid of squatters who attempted to build ramshackle shelters in the shadow of the hotel, but no one lasted more than a couple of hours.

The owners of The Discovery soon realized they needed full-time security so that they could concentrate on business rather than their own protection, so they hired a carefully selected team of knife- and gun-toting men who took their jobs seriously. Such was the life of the successful in a lawless city.

The partners also soon agreed that they needed to build onto the saloon. They needed the existing space for dancing as it was an enormous success. But the real money they made was from the gambling. It seemed that many gold prospectors had gambling spirits, and the men couldn't get enough of it.

Walter drew up plans, and construction began on an annex that would become their designated gambling hall. Jasper hired more dealers, and this time some of them were women, much to the continued delight of the men who frequented the establishment.

Chapter Fifteen

Adeline Hart's Journal

April 30, 1850

I have been here for a month, and I hardly recognize myself any longer.

Men bring me gifts of flowers, jewelry, and even sometimes love poems, and I am not even acquainted with these individuals. They seem disabused with the notion that they are more familiar with me than they could possibly be, for they hear me play the piano, and they watch and listen. It is strange to go from complete obscurity to a bit of local fame just for doing what I love so much.

I have tried to politely refuse a few of the more extravagant gifts that have been pressed upon me. The men are persistent, however, and I have had no luck returning gifts. Isaac laughs and says I just need to get used to it. I wish I could somehow share more of the gifts with him, but he does not seem to have an appreciation for flowers and love poems. At least I can share the gold.

I do not understand myself because I still feel such a strong fondness and attraction to Jasper and Royal. It's a completely different feeling from the comradery I have with dear, talented Isaac. I should at least feel conflicted, but I find myself equally happy with their attentions, and my feelings continue to grow in that vein, no matter what I tell myself. I am thus far a stranger to romantic love, but I wonder if this is the beginning of it for me. If so, I may be in for some heartache, for I cannot imagine how to separate them in my affections.

The three of us take our meals together and spend much of our time together when we're not working or sleeping. I think they actually share a room, but of that, I am not certain. They always politely walk me to my door and bid me a warm goodnight before making sure I'm securely locked in for the night.

There have been no more exuberant kisses from Royal, and I must admit a bit of disappointment in that, for I certainly enjoyed the feeling it awakened in me. I think of that kiss often, and the feeling returns as though it were happening again.

Jasper is generally more reserved than Royal around me, but he looks at me with those beautiful, penetrating blue eyes of his, and I feel myself growing warm. The sensation is not all that different from what I feel when thinking about Royal's kiss. As I said, I barely recognize myself.

May 1, 1850

Something which pleases me beyond measure is the way the six men listen to me and consult me as an equal in all business matters the same way they do each other. My opinions never counted for much at all back in Philadelphia, and I find this new development most stimulating. I thought I would crave the company of women far more than I actually do, for I am so well attended to by the men. The other ladies who work at The Discovery are lovely, however, and I have been able to strike up a particularly pleasing friendship with one of the entertainers. Her name is Olivia, and she is from Charleston. She is also twenty-five, the same as I, and we have similar backgrounds. She arrived here a few months prior to when our ship landed. I hope she and I can forge out some time to spend together.

Olivia has shared with me some of the adventures and misadventures from her journey here with her family. They took the more expedient route, sailing through the Gulf and crossing over to the Pacific Ocean via the Isthmus of Panama. Her parents both tragically died of cholera making that horrible passage, but Olivia and her two older brothers managed to make their way—with guides, of course—through the crossing by way of mules and rickety dugout canoes. They finally reached a steamship on the Pacific side. She shared her opinion of the hideous discomfort of the mosquitos and sweltering heat in Panama. I do not think I could have endured that trek through the jungle, so I am relieved Father and I took the longer route around Cape Horn.

Olivia was frightened that she might be forced to support herself by working in a dreadful bed house after her brothers abandoned her in San Francisco. They naïvely left her at a boarding house with what money they thought she needed to house and feed herself and headed to the gold fields—not realizing the prices in this city are extremely inflated.

She laughed about the "opportunities" she passed up by way of the numerous marriage proposals from complete strangers. Who knows how she'd have fared if she'd agreed to any of them? She is most grateful to the men of The Discovery for being gentlemen to her and providing her with a living wage and decent employment. She has yet to hear from her brothers. I know that makes her nervous.

We have discovered that a wonderful dressmaker has arrived here in the city. Madame Beaufort knows about all of the best French fashions and brought with her many wonderful silk and satin fabrics. The Discovery is going to pay for all of the female employees to have a new collection of ensembles to wear, and the ladies are all very pleased with this. I believe Madame and her three assistants will be moving into The Discovery as part of her payment for the clothing. I think possibly tomorrow an assembly of men will be dispatched to their ship to move them here.

On the subject of clothing, I have continued my scandalous practice of not wearing a corset. There is still no one around who can assist me. We have a chambermaid, but she is terribly overworked already and hardly needs to assist me in getting myself dressed and undressed each day. I have added my petticoats back into my ensemble, but that has been my only concession to propriety. More clothing is simply too impractical for me. I wonder how the other ladies in town handle this. It is not something we have discussed.

Chapter Sixteen

A few weeks after The Discovery was completely open for business, Captain Greely came to call once again. He knew to seek out Adeline before the night's festivities got into full swing—as he was well aware that she was one of the main attractions. News traveled quickly, and her name was uttered reverently by many San Franciscans.

It was a sunny afternoon, and she was sitting out in front of the building sipping lemonade with Jasper and Royal, enjoying the relative quiet and the fine weather. They were laughing and telling amusing stories about things that had been happening in The Discovery when Jasper saw Adeline's face fall and the sparkle in her eyes dim. She seemed to recover quickly and plastered on a fake smile as Jasper heard approaching foot-steps. He turned and was just as dismayed as Adeline to see Captain Greely trudging purposefully toward them. The man looked worn out and grim.

"Miss Hart, gentlemen," he said in a stuffy tone as he nodded in greeting. "May I have a word, please?"

"Sure, Cap'n, pull up a chair," answered Royal for all of them. He indicated some furniture a few feet away on the wide porch. He did not get up to rearrange the seating himself, however.

Greely cleared his throat and narrowed his eyes. "I'd like a word with Adeline. *Alone.*"

Not wanting to seem intimidated or overly interested in the man, Adeline demurred and answered in a soft voice, "Jasper and Royal are fine where they are, sir. My business is their business, so if you would care to join us, I'll ask them to remain." Greely scowled at her, and she merely straightened her spine. She would not back down or be bullied, so she said, "Furthermore, I am not certain it is appropriate for a lady to be alone with a single man without an escort, sir."

Squinting at her, he answered nastily, "Do you suddenly imagine you're some fancy blue-blood or something? You work in a dance hall, Adeline. Since when are you concerned with social protocol?"

"I am a *serious musician*, Captain Greely, and no one to be sneered at because of where I choose to entertain patrons of the arts."

"Call it what you want. I'm not here to argue with you." He realized his tone was getting him nowhere and immediately tried to soften his words. "I apologize, Adeline. I just worry that your father might not approve."

Her eyes flashed with suppressed anger. "My father isn't here to approve or disapprove of my actions—not that there is anything shameful in them, sir. Were he still alive, he would probably be thrilled to be in the position of having me help further his business success in whatever reputable ways I can, and I am certainly more suited to this form of employment than I ever was to be a *cook* aboard a sailing vessel that wasn't even supplied with adequate rations for its crew." Her voice shook. "It's no wonder my poor father died."

"You need to go home, Adeline."

Her jaw dropped, and she looked at Jasper and then at Royal, who were both as astonished as she was. "Home? This is my home. Whatever do you mean?"

"I mean this city is a godforsaken den of debauchery hell-bent on separating a man from his fortune wherever he turns, and I hate it here! I've seen men murdered in the streets over the damned gold that's made everyone go mad. There are thieves and whores everywhere." His bluster was at full tilt now as he ordered, "I've secured a position piloting a ship returning to Boston in six weeks, and I *insist* that you come back with me. As my wife."

The truth was that Greely had immediately squandered most of the money he'd made sailing the Wind Gypsy to San Francisco. Upon his arrival, he'd lost a great deal of his pay by having a run of terrible luck at the gambling tables, and then he drowned his sorrows with too much rum. He remained living aboard the ship in his quarters but had no access to prepared food now that Adeline was no longer cooking for him. This meant he had to scrounge around the city for meals and could barely afford anything decent due to his dwindling funds.

The exorbitant prices of lodging and food in San Francisco were positively criminal. Greely soon realized he could eke out a living by renting space aboard the Wind Gypsy to folks needing lodging. Staying on the ship was infinitely better than sleeping on flea-infested piles of straw on a dirt floor that housed hundreds of bankrupted miners. Many had sought housing in places that were hardly better than a tent with a re-purposed sail for a roof. Those who could not afford any shelter at all merely slept on the beach and prayed it didn't rain. Therefore, Greely let it be known that he had berths he would rent as long as someone's gold held out. When it ran out, he had them dragged away by a hired thug.

He also systematically stripped the ship of usable lumber and any kind of building material he could sell, turning the ship into a floating hull. The Wind Gypsy joined the ranks of abandoned ships littering the bay. Eventually, it would become surrounded by sand, adding to the threat of fire in San Francisco. Often, these ships would catch fire and burn to the water line.

Greely had run out of things to sell. He also became increasingly afraid for his own safety and slept with one eye open, praying he wouldn't be killed by a thief looking for his stash of gold. As prospectors returned from the mining sites nearly broke, he wasn't able to charge as much to let them stay on the ship, and he was smart enough to see this was a one-way trip to destitution for him. He wanted out of this city.

Greely hatched a plan to better his circumstances. It was well known that The Discovery was the highlight of the city and a palace compared to anywhere else. He hoped by marrying Adeline, he could at least move in with her and have a decent roof over his head and a soft bed while he waited for his departure date. He could also save face that way... and it didn't hurt that she was exceptionally beautiful. He was afraid to go to any of the prostitutes in the city for fear of disease, but he was beyond ready for some sexual gratification.

"Adeline," he addressed her in a greasy, placating tone as she glared at him. "Your father put me in charge of seeing that you were safe and well provided for. Surely you want to honor the man's wishes."

"Oh? When did he do that? He certainly never shared that kind of information with me. How would you have known his dying wish? It wasn't as if he believed he was about to expire!" Not waiting for an answer, she persisted, "And how would you make certain of caring for me, Captain? Are you living in a fine, comfortable house with a wonderful chef preparing all of your meals? Are you surrounded by hardworking, talented, and *enjoyable* people? Do you have a means for me to pursue my passion for music?" She shook her head at his sudden awkward expression. "I thought not. You haven't even thought to take a bath, sir, and that is most obvious even here in the fresh air."

It was true. The man had the pungent stink of rum, cheap cigars, and unwashed body odor emanating from him like a nasty cloud.

Jasper and Royal squelched their snickers the best they could, but both of them snorted quietly, nonetheless. Royal tried to make his sound like a cough, but Jasper finally gave up and began to laugh. Finally, he couldn't stand it any longer and spoke up as Greely's eyes sent daggers his way.

"Look, Greely. Adeline isn't just a dance hall girl or an entertainer, and she certainly does nothing that could be considered inappropriate. She is a *full partner* in The Discovery here— one of the proprietors. She is consulted right along with the rest of us when we make business decisions, and we're proud of her accomplishments as well as her good sense." He smiled at Greely. "It's unfortunate that your view of San Francisco is one that focuses on corruption rather than on opportunity, for there are many individuals in the city who are making their lives far better by being clever and by working hard. This city is a haven for the industrious and hell for the indolent. It seems we know which one you are, Captain."

Greely merely glared, so Jasper continued, "It's time for you to run along. Adeline doesn't need your protection. She has *six men* who would lay down their lives for her, and we have armed watchmen around the clock who are well-paid for their vigilance. We know there are dangers in this city and would never take chances with her safety. Can you say that you'd do any better?"

Jasper pointedly directed Greely's attention to a man standing at the far end of the porch. The man had a shotgun and a pistol, and those were just his readily visible weapons. His eyes were shaded by the brim of his hat, but he gave off the impression that he was coiled like a rattlesnake and ready to strike.

Captain Greely glared at Jasper for a moment and then turned and stomped away a few feet. Spinning back around, he nearly shouted at Adeline, "You're making a mistake, girl. You need to be back in Boston with your own kind. You need to honor your father's wishes!"

Smiling benignly, she replied, "Thank you for your opinion, Captain, as misguided as it is. For your information, I am not a *girl*, I'm not from Boston, nor do I ever aspire to make that city my home, and I make my *own* decisions. Good day to you, sir." She rose and gracefully glided through the front door. She didn't go anywhere, though—just waited for him to get the blazes away from her and her friends. She could hear him shouting after her, "Don't forget that *I know what you've done, and I'm willing to forget it and still marry you! I doubt anyone else would be so understanding.*"

After a couple of minutes silently fuming to herself, she peeked around the doorframe to make sure the man was out of sight and returned to her seat between Royal and Jasper. The men were silent and seemed to be studying the path that Greely took, making sure he was really gone.

"I believe that gentleman's roof is minus a shingle," she said dryly, and the men burst out laughing.

Jasper could barely contain himself. "That was the absolute *worst* marriage proposal in the history of mankind."

"Oh?" She looked questioningly at him and batted her eyelashes. "Is there a better way?" She was only kidding and wanted to deflect the conversation away from Greely's threat of exposing her possible guilt in killing that horrible brute aboard the Wind Gypsy.

Jasper sprung up and dropped to his left knee in front of her. He grabbed her hand and looked earnestly into her deep brown eyes. "Adeline, I love and respect you and will for all the days God gives me on this earth and then into the hereafter. You would make me the happiest man alive if you would honor me by accepting my proposal. Will you marry me?"

His expression was so sincere as his eyes bore into hers, Adeline didn't know whether to actually believe him or not, but the spell he had on her was instantly revoked when Royal butted in with, "Jasper! I thought you said Adeline should marry me!"

Her head snapped to face Royal, and she saw the bruised look of sincerity on his face that matched Jasper's. She was completely dumbfounded by this strange conversation, especially when Jasper retorted, "Well, it turns out I may have changed my mind about that now that I've gotten to know Adeline better!"

This got even more confusing when Royal glared briefly at Jasper and then grabbed her other hand and also dropped to his knee, saying, "I don't have a ring picked out yet, Addie, but I would be overcome with joy if you could agree to be *my* wife. Will you marry *me*?" Then he added, "I'll love you forever and ever, amen."

Adeline's eyebrows shot up, and she exclaimed with a nervous laugh, "This must be some kind of a record, gentlemen. Three proposals in less than five minutes!"

"I'm serious," Jasper declared.

"As. Am. I," stated Royal.

Sobering immediately, Adeline hedged, "Uh... are you sure? This isn't some kind of farce? Aren't you both just poking fun at Captain Greely?"

Royal and Jasper gave each other steely looks.

"Jasper, what has come over you? A long time ago, you said you wouldn't marry again because you were somehow unworthy." Royal rolled his eyes a little. "Then you said you wanted a family, and now you want Miss Addie's hand even though you said I'd be the better candidate. Make up your mind, man!"

"You're a fine one to talk, Roy. You said *I'd* be the better man for Adeline. Now you've changed your story!"

"Wait, what? Stop bickering for a moment, you two. What do you mean you've both decided whom I ought to marry? You barely sound any better than Greely!"

Crestfallen, Jasper's whole countenance looked sad as he rose from his knee. "I'm sorry, Adeline. Just the thought of you falling into the arms of someone heinous makes my blood boil."

"And now I'm heinous?!" cried Royal as he too jumped to his feet. His hands were clenched, and he seemed primed for fisticuffs.

Jasper appeared horror-struck as he reached for Royal's arm. "No! I wasn't referring to *you*. I don't know what I'm saying. I meant that good-for-nothing Greely." He went very quiet and added, "You know I love you, Roy. You'd make a wonderful husband—to Adeline or any lucky woman you choose. Go ahead and marry her if that's what you want." He looked pleadingly into Royal's stony gaze and whispered, "But I'll miss you."

Royal's hazel gaze softened, and he put a hand up to Jasper's face for a brief moment, whispering, "I understand."

"Well, I certainly do not," huffed Adeline as she abruptly stood to face them. "What is going on with the two of you, and why are you both acting so strangely all of a sudden? Who here gets to decide whom, if anyone, I'll marry? I do, period! And why do you act as if Royal is leaving?"

Royal turned to her and seemed for a millisecond to be reminding himself of her presence. "I'm not going anywhere, Addie. I'm sorry if we've come on too strong for you. We want the best for you in all things." He squinted at her slightly. "What was Greely carrying on about? He said he knew something about 'what you'd done.' Care to explain that?"

Adeline's face lost all of its color, and she plunked herself into the chair she'd just vacated. She choked out the words, "If I tell you, you'll probably think even Greely is too good for me."

"I hardly think that could be true," spluttered Jasper at the same time as Royal exclaimed, "No chance in hell! Pardon me, Addie." They sat down in the chairs on either side of her and leaned forward.

"I'll tell you, and if you want me to leave, I'll go back to Philadelphia. Or I'll find another job here in San Francisco. You may not want me to be in business with you any longer, although I promise I'd never do anything to disrupt the harmony of The Discovery. I love it here, and I love what I do, and I lo... uh... never mind." She seemed to lose momentum as her words trickled to a standstill.

Guessing that she was ready to declare her affections, the men caught each other's gaze and locked. They had no idea which of them would be the lucky one. But Adeline was still speaking, so their attention snapped back to her as she let out a long, sad sigh.

"I... ki... I think... I killed a man."

"Well, is he dead or not?" asked Royal.

"Oh, he's definitely dead. I just don't know for sure whether I merely precipitated the event or if he actually died by my hand." She hung her head and covered her face. "I'm so ashamed, and I think that I will no doubt burn in hell for such a horrible sin."

"Adeline, maybe you ought to tell us more than that. What exactly happened?" asked Jasper. "First of all, how does Greely know about it?"

"He was there. Well, not when I actually struck the man with a frying pan full of hot grease and pieces of pork."

"Why did you strike a man with a hot pan?" Royal asked.

"He attacked me roughly from behind, even after I told him to leave the galley. He thrust his hands onto me in an offensive and most terrifying manner, and I just lashed out with the pan without thinking."

Jasper looked almost amused when he asked, "And you think that one blow from your pan might have killed a man? Seriously, Adeline, I had no idea you were that strong."

"No, that was not all. The sea was terribly rough that day, and a particularly hard swell caused the ship to roll crazily just as I swung at him. He fell and slammed his head, and then he just lay there looking... dead. I ran to get Father and Greely then, but when we got back, he hadn't moved a muscle. He was an extremely large person and a most frightening one." She shuddered.

Royal asked, "What did Greely do? Was he angry with you?"

"Not at all. In fact, he looked somewhat relieved, now that I think about it. They had been in a ferocious argument a few days prior to this... event, and the man seemed to be nothing but trouble. Greely went quickly and found two more large sailors to come and throw the man overboard."

Jasper looked suspicious and asked, "Did Greely check for a heartbeat or breathing?"

Adeline narrowed her eyes, looking thoughtful. "No. I believe all he did was lean over and look at him for a moment, and then he left to find the other men. They never questioned his authority; they simply carried out his order. That was that."

Breathing a sigh of relief, Jasper locked eyes again with Royal, then turned to her and said, "It sounds to me that you were merely defending yourself from a violent attack, but Greely was the one to send the sailor to his watery grave. I wouldn't think anything about it again if I were you. And if he ever mentions it again, he's nothing but a lunkhead. You were there and saw him order a man to be executed who wanted to rape you aboard his ship. He has some nerve acting as though you're somehow to blame in any of this. The man's logic is flawed, and he's merely trying to bully you."

Royal took Adeline's hand and remarked in a soft voice, "We know you could never kill someone, Addie. It's just not in your nature. I'm proud of the way you defended yourself, however. That man sounds like a terrible person, and I'm sorry he was ever allowed access to you. Greely and your father ought to have been more careful out at sea with a monster like that aboard his ship."

"Father did tell him several times to leave me alone."

"Too little, I'm afraid," Jasper said on a sigh. "Men like that aren't so easily dissuaded. And all the more reason that you should not have been left alone where he could get to you. I think everyone let you down, and you are still, fortunately, all in one piece after that harrowing experience. It makes me admire you even more, frankly."

"Me too." Royal noticed that Adeline's color had returned to her cheeks, and he asked, "So... back to the issue at hand. What are we going to do here? Are you interested in either Jasper or me? Do you wish to marry? One of us or someone else? Do you want a family?"

"Slow down, Royal, and let the woman answer," Jasper laughed. The two men looked at her expectantly.

"I... um... I... think you are both wonderful men."

"Uh-oh. Sounds like she's trying to let us down easily," Royal deadpanned. "But...?" he prompted.

"I'm not. Not at all. I actually have rather strong feelings, I must admit, for both of you." That admission made her cheeks flame. "Since I can only marry one, this rather puts me in a dilemma. But before we go into this any further, I have bared my soul to the both of you, and you know my darkest, most fearsome secret—a secret that has robbed me of sleep on many nights. I thank you both for attempting to make me feel better about it, but I still have questions regarding your earlier conversation."

Jasper chewed his lip, and Royal looked away toward the view of the bay.

"Are you ready to answer some questions?"

Both men nodded silently.

Addressing Jasper first, she asked softly, "Were you married before? Is that why you look so sad sometimes?"

Looking down, he let out a protracted sigh. "Yes. I had a wife. She died."

"I'm so sorry, Jasper. What was her name?"

"Isabella."

"That's a beautiful name. Did you leave the east to get away from losing her?"

His head rose, and he saw the compassion in her eyes. "No. I was enough of a fool as to think I could drag the poor woman across the country in a Prairie Schooner with a team of oxen." His voice cracked. "She was far too good for me, and it's my fault she didn't make it. And our baby died inside her. And now, with the lack of reliable mail service here, I have yet to even tell her family of her fate." The anguished look on his face would have made a stone weep.

Royal spoke up in a soothing voice, "Jasper, we've been over this. It was a tragic accident that could have happened to any-one at any time. It wasn't your fault at all. You need to stop beating yourself up about it." He looked at Adeline and told her, "She took a nasty fall out of the wagon and died instantly. She was a lovely person, and everyone was enormously fond of her."

"Oh, so you knew her as well?" A tear of sympathy trickled down Adeline's cheek, and Royal softly wiped it away.

"I did have the pleasure of knowing Isabella, yes. It was a sad time for everyone on the wagon train when we lost her. She was something special, alright."

Both Royal and Adeline reached out and gently stroked Jasper's arms. He was looking down into his lap, and a fat tear plopped off the end of his nose onto his trousers. "I know I need to get over it and move on, and I desperately want to. Thank you both for being here."

After a polite moment of silence while they all recovered their wits, Adeline asked them, "Is this why Royal always seems so solicitous and affectionate with you, Jasper? He seems like the best of friends to you. I've often noticed your kinship and how it seems to keep you centered."

Jasper's vivid blue eyes first looked at Royal, and then he locked them onto Adeline's gaze. "Royal is the best man I've ever known. He's loyal... hah! 'Loyal Royal'... I never thought of that. He's smart and kind. He's brave and hard-working. I do not mind admitting that I love Royal with my whole heart." He paused for a moment before adding, "And... my body. That is not to say that I don't want a wife and a family. I know Izzy is gone forever." He hung his head and then spoke with resolve, "I loved being married to her, and I would love being married to you as well, Adeline. You would never be second best compared to Izzy. I promise you that because I admire you tremendously. I just don't know... how *hard* it will be to give up Royal after having Izzy ripped from my life. So... there you have it."

"So, you're saying..."

Royal spoke up and explained, "He's saying that for the past couple of years, we have had what they call a bachelor marriage, and as we told you a while back, that is an accepted way of life in the West. I also love Jasper, and I think that we may be one of the special couples who have genuine affection in our arrangement. Many of the partners we've seen just use each other for... to be blunt... sexual release. We're different. I also know how difficult it will be to give up a life with Jasper, but I want a wife and children, and as pretty as he is," Royal chuckled, "Jasper isn't going to be giving me any of those."

Adeline blushed again and let out a thoughtful breath. She chewed the inside of her cheek for a moment before she spoke up again. "I think you're both wonderful men, and I thank you for telling me this and making me feel better about Greely. I have a lot to think about now, and we all need to go have supper and get ready for tonight. We'll talk again later; is that acceptable?"

As Jasper nodded, Royal agreed, "It's fine with me. Have we scared you off, Addie? That may have been a lot to take in."

"No. You have not." She stood to go indoors and then stopped abruptly. Turning around, she seemed to have a sudden thought. "How about this? What if you both allowed me some time with each of you privately? I never see one of you without the other, so you seem almost like a team. Perhaps I could ascertain my feelings better if I could concentrate on one at a time."

The men looked at each other, and a message passed back and forth through their eyes. Simultaneously they looked at her and said, "Yes," and "Good idea." Then Jasper added, "We'll work out a schedule."

Royal tried not to snicker. *Jasper's always so organized and proper*, he thought to himself. *He'll make one helluva husband.*

Royal had another plan altogether, but for now, he was keeping it to himself. He had a bit of work to do.

Chapter Seventeen

As San Francisco grew in leaps and bounds, entertainment opportunities sprung up everywhere. Not only was the city replete with saloons and gambling establishments, there was also a flourishing array of brothels. But as men continued to flow into the city—more and more of them bringing along their wives and children—a higher level of entertainment also began to take root.

Theaters became popular, and everything from locally written plays to Shakespeare routinely sold out. Famous actors, musicians, and singers arrived from Europe and the east coast seeking new audiences to enchant. And the San Franciscans couldn't get enough of them.

Jasper heard that a famous pianist named Henri Herz had arrived in San Francisco from Paris and would be playing at the National Theatre, which had recently opened to great fanfare on Washington Street. He rushed off to buy two tickets, knowing that Adeline would not be able to resist seeing the performance. He couldn't wait to treat her to the show.

And the very next afternoon, they did just that. Jasper delighted in watching Adeline's rapt expression as she soaked in every note the man played. However, after the concert ended, he thought she looked more thoughtful than transported. He decided they needed to take a walk and look at some of the city up close rather than from The Discovery's high perch on the bluff.

The streets were filled with people—almost all men—rushing here and there at a frantic pace. Laughter and music spilled out from many doorways, and not a few drunks staggered out on wobbly legs. When they saw no less than three fights break out, Jasper hurried Adeline away from the scene so she would not be harmed.

"I understand a bit of what Greely was speaking about now," Adeline ventured. "We're in such an ivory tower in The Discovery, we forget... or at least I forget, that there are lesser saloons and seedier establishments scattered all over the city."

Jasper chuckled, "This isn't even the bad part of town." He guided her across the street, dodging mud puddles left and right, and said, "Let's take a look in here and have some refreshment. It's not a bad place, and it's actually where we were able to find your piano."

"Oh!"

"I think the owner was strapped for cash, and it was a quick way for him to make some."

Inside, they found a table where they could have a drink and watch people dance. A flute and a banjo provided the music, but it was nothing like the lively melodies she and Isaac produced. This was just passingly decent.

"Is something on your mind, Adeline? You seem subdued."

She looked thoughtfully into his concerned gaze and didn't answer for a moment. Finally, she frowned slightly and said, "You're probably going to think I'm a crackbrain." She took a moment when he raised his eyebrows at her. "I said I thought you and I ought to spend time together, and then I could spend time with Royal without you. But the truth is, all afternoon I've been wondering what Royal is doing by himself—even though I know he's probably busy working. And I kept thinking how much he would have enjoyed the music at the wonderful concert you took me to."

With a crestfallen expression, Jasper sighed. "Well... I suppose that tells me something. You obviously prefer Royal's company to mine. I can't blame you. He's so affable and..."

"Oh no! That isn't what I mean at all," she cut in as she grasped his arm. "Please don't take this the wrong way. I'm delighted to be out with you, but it just feels so odd to not have Royal with us. It's like we're missing a main ingredient in the soup or something. Does that make any sense?"

"I guess it does because honestly, I feel the same way." His brow furrowed as he said, "I ought to be thrilled to have you all to myself, and I truly do have the deepest affection for you, Adeline. But you're right. I miss Royal as well."

"So, now what do we do?"

"Finish our drinks and go find the man."

"That sounds like an excellent plan," she laughed. Sobering, she added, "Royal kissed me once."

Jasper's eyes widened, and he smiled. "He didn't tell me that, the scoundrel. Why are you telling me?"

"I don't really know exactly, but I can tell you that I was very pleased by it. And it made me wonder..." There came her blush again... "if you'd ever do the same thing."

Laughing and regarding her hand that still clasped his arm, Jasper admitted, "I've certainly thought about it plenty, and I guess I just never thought the time was right. I could certainly do it right now, but a bit more privacy would be nice." Then he looked around the room and saw several people hanging onto each other with obvious carnal intent and realized no one would care one way or the other if he kissed her. With this revelation, he added softly, "Or maybe right now would be the best time."

The timbre of his voice sent a thrill through Adeline.

Jasper gently put his hand under Adeline's chin and drew her close. Her eyes widened and then closed as she realized his intent. His lips grazed her gently at first, but when he felt the softness of that mouth, his hunger for her suddenly took over. He increased the pressure of his lips and pulled ever so gently on her chin, allowing him access for his tongue.

Feeling his gentle invasion, Adeline gasped—-for this was nothing like the quick buss on the lips that she'd received from Royal. It shocked her. Jasper took advantage of that, thrusting his tongue inside her mouth as he slid his hand around to cup her neck. She tasted like heaven, and her softness was so welcome to his senses. He probed her mouth until he felt her tentatively slide her tongue against his in an enticing dance.

They stayed like that for what felt like a lifetime to Adeline. She'd never experienced anything like it. Her insides felt all hot and jumbly, and she craved more and more of Jasper's touch. She didn't know exactly what she wanted or needed, but it was... more.

Eventually, Jasper pulled back and took Adeline's hand in his. His large, warm hand dwarfed hers, and she immediately felt protected by it. At the same time, his skin against hers aroused more of the beautiful sensations she felt roiling through her body. It was all so foreign and so exciting to her.

"Jasper?" she asked. "That was..."

She realized then that she had no words for what that was, but it made her deliciously happy. So, instead, she gave him the most beautiful smile he'd seen in his life. Her eyes shone with glittering reflection of the candlelight around them. Then she took a deep breath and admitted, "I also share a very deep respect and admiration for you as you have professed to feel for me. You make me feel safe, and I love that." He kissed her again, quickly this time, and then she added, "I feel such a strong kinship and affection for you. I do believe I love you."

Jasper beamed then, and his whole face lit up with joy. "That's the best thing I've heard in a long, long time, Adeline."

Sobering for a moment, he asked, "What about Roy? Do you still want him to join us?"

Adeline's brow furrowed for an instant as she thought, and she answered, "Strangely, yes, I do. What that says about me, I have no idea. I hope it doesn't hurt your feelings in any way."

"Not in the least. As strange as it sounds, I actually feel the same way." Then he got a cocky look in his eye. "Did he kiss you like that?"

Laughing, she answered, "Heavens no. It was quick and friendly, but since it was the first I'd ever received, it was still pretty exciting to me."

Thinking about what a lovely and obviously untouched creature Adeline was, he said, "Let's go find our man. Maybe we can figure out what to do." He rose and gave her his hand, once again giving her the sensation that she was cared for and safe with Jasper.

Chapter Eighteen

When they returned to the hotel, however, it was to find that Royal had left on some unidentified business and had yet to return. It was nearly suppertime, so they took their places at the large table in the dining room with Walter, Isaac, Timothy, and Séamus.

Noticing how Jasper had ushered Adeline in with his arm around her waist and then held firmly onto her hand after they say down, Walter gave him a knowing look. Then he winked at Adeline, who ducked her eyes and turned pink.

They were all just about to tuck into their meal when Royal came bursting through the door, all smiles and apologies. "Sorry, I'm late! I had some interesting business to attend to, and I had to run all over town to accomplish everything." He sat down in the empty chair next to Adeline and leaned over to tell Jasper, "Wait until I tell you what I found out!" Turning back to her, he continued without hardly taking a breath, asking, "Are you ready for our engagement tomorrow?"

"We have an engagement?" she asked with a chuckle. Royal's sunny demeanor always made her happy.

"Of course, we do! I have some special plans for us." Seeing her apparent joy at the prospect of spending time with him, he grinned. "How was the concert?"

Blinking at him, she realized he'd asked her a question about the day, and she shook herself a tiny bit before answering, "Absolutely marvelous. I hope to hear more of that kind of music in the National Theatre in the future. It was most inspiring."

Smiling broadly with a tiny nod—and apropos of nothing that was apparent—Royal turned to everyone at the table and asked, "Remember those men we met at John Sutter's mill? The Mormons?"

Everyone answered affirmatively because they'd also toiled alongside them for months and months as they all panned for gold. They'd all become friends.

"Remember how some of them kept saying how anxious they were to get home to their *wives?*" Once again, everyone either nodded or mumbled something like "Yeah" or "Of course."

Royal continued, "Wouldn't that be something? To be married to more than one person at a time?"

Jasper caught onto what Royal was suggesting then and interjected, "It's part of the *Mormons'* customs, though, Roy, and it only works for the men of their religion to take multiple partners."

"Yeah. I know. Just saying... It's just something I've been thinking about."

Timothy snorted. "You'd have a hard enough time in this city finding one woman to marry you, let alone a number of them."

As the laughter petered out, the conversation went back to Jasper and Adeline's account of the day's concert and how much they'd enjoyed it. Finally, it was time to open the saloon for business and get busy keeping the San Franciscans entertained.

Chapter Nineteen

Adeline Hart's Journal

May 24, 1850

I shall not soon forget this day! Jasper took me to the most wonderful piano performance, and it rivaled any I'd ever been to back in Philadelphia. Maestro Herz was born in Austria but raised in France and clearly had access to the finest instructors in Europe. He transported me to a place I've never been while listening to that music. He displayed such raw passion, the sound that emanated from his instrument felt like a living, breathing entity all on its own. I shall strive to practice more of the classics I've learned and see if I can incorporate some of that feeling into my music. The dance tunes we play are nothing compared to the concert, but I love making our guests happy with that kind of music as well. I feel so blessed to have arrived at this place and to have such incredible opportunities at my disposal.

I startled myself by enjoying Maestro's music as much as I did, for it was a far cry from my normal favorites. Perhaps it was the conviction he played with, or perhaps

I am merely starved for hearing someone play other than myself. Whatever it was, I was terribly grateful to attend the concert. I could not help but remember how Louis Moreau Gottschalk was enamored with Herz's compositions. Now I understand, even though I still do not particularly wish to play them.

My surprising reaction to the recital is not the only reason I feel so unlike myself tonight, however. I embarrassed myself tremendously by flirting with Jasper today, and it resulted in an exquisite kiss from him. If I thought Royal's kiss inflamed my senses, I surely might have burned up from Jasper's attentions. This is such a strange city, for no one seemed to be conscious of our activity—right under their noses! I shocked myself kissing him in public that way, but I'd do it again in a heartbeat; it was so divine.

It's terribly late, and I must rest because tomorrow I have plans with Royal to see if my affections are swayed more in his direction. He's going to have to do a lot to top that kiss from Jasper, however. The thought makes me giddy. He told me, as we all three said our goodnights, to wear something especially beautiful tomorrow. I cannot imagine what he has in mind.

I thought Jasper might kiss me again when he walked me to my door this evening. Sadly, he did not. I wonder if he was embarrassed or considered it inappropriate to do so in front of Royal. His eyes seemed on fire as he took his leave.

Chapter Twenty

The next afternoon, Royal arrived at Adeline's room dressed in a dapper, tailored suit and looking as handsome as a man could in her eyes. He was all long limbs and broad shoulders, and his unruly mop of blond hair was combed carefully for once. His glittering hazel eyes looked her up and down with obvious appreciation.

"Addie, you're so lovely; you take my breath away," he told her as he offered his arm.

Before they left, Addie turned to someone in her room and said, "Thank you, Olivia, for helping me get ready."

"It was my pleasure, Adeline. Have a wonderful time today," the young woman answered as she scooted out the door ahead of them. She took a quick peek at Royal, who hadn't even noticed she was there—he was so entranced by Adeline. Olivia chuckled to herself and headed down the hall quickly.

And off they went, though Royal would not tell her where, no matter how she pressed the issue. "You'll see. It's something special," was all that he would say.

She was a little dismayed when they arrived once again at the National Theatre, assuming Royal had procured more tickets to Herz's concert for the afternoon. But she was also confused. "Why are we here so early, Royal? No one is even here yet to take our tickets."

Smiling enigmatically, he answered, "We don't need tickets today. He opened the door and led her inside. Taking her by the hand, he ushered her deep into the building to the rooms in the back of the stage.

"Are we going to meet Maestro Herz himself?" she asked with hushed excitement. Maybe this was going to be something different after all.

"We are," Royal answered but didn't elaborate. His eyes seemed to sparkle as he looked at Adeline.

A few moments later, he knocked on a dressing room door, and they heard a man call out to them to enter. The voice, as it turned out, was not that of Herz but of his interpreter, for the pianist did not speak English. It was through this interpreter that Adeline was to get the shock of her life.

"Monsieur Herz wishes you to know that he has heard you play while he was gambling at The Discovery."

Adeline smiled shyly as she looked at Herz. His eyes were fixed on her.

"Monsieur would like to request that you play at the beginning of his recital this afternoon."

Adeline gaped at him. "What? Play? Play what? Why?"

Everyone chuckled at her response, and the interpreter explained, "He is very taken with your command of the keyboard and thinks it would be most enjoyable to hear you play something other than dancehall music, although he was charmed by your rendition of the little Mozart piece you used to quiet everyone down after so successfully causing a frenzy on the dancefloor. We understand from your gentleman here that you are well-versed in the classics. Monsieur would like you to choose a piece and play it for everyone before he takes the stage."

Her eyes snapped to Royal, who had a decidedly smug look on his face. He explained, "I wanted to see if they might let you play, Addie, but Mr. Herz already knew all about you when I got here yesterday. He was thrilled with the idea."

"I couldn't possibly!"

"And why not? You play every night at The Discovery, and people adore you."

"That's different, Royal. It's easy music, and I have Isaac with me."

"Addie, I hear you practicing by yourself in the morning before the saloon opens, and I know you have an extensive repertoire even though I've never seen you use sheet music. Of course, you can do it. Just play that wonderful piece that Walter calls the 'passion song' or something."

"Beethoven's Appassionata?" She still looked like a scared rabbit, but a bit of eagerness was taking over. It was her favorite thing to play in the whole world. "I'd be terrified, Royal. I'm afraid I'll forget the notes and make a fool of myself."

Gently, Royal took her into an embrace and whispered in her ear. "I know they'll love it if you let them hear you, but forget the audience. Play for yourself and for me. I'm so proud of you, Addie."

"But the Appassionata takes over twenty minutes. Surely Maestro won't want me to monopolize his stage for so long."

There was a pause while the interpreter had a conversation with Herz. Quickly he turned back to Adeline and announced, "Monsieur would be honored if you would play the third movement."

Adeline's attention shifted to Herz, who stood beaming at her like a proud uncle. He nodded at her encouragingly and said, "*Oui! Allons!*" Apparently not taking no for an answer, he indicated to her to follow him out to the stage and gestured to the piano that stood in the middle of it. The house was still devoid of an audience, so Adeline gave Royal a flustered look and sat down at the piano, adjusting her distance and feeling the keys for a moment. As she was accustomed, she played a few scales and then a Bach prelude to warm up. After she was half the way through the prelude, her entire countenance relaxed, and she seemed to be listening to the music as it filled the hall rather than worrying about anyone. This time, rather than stopping after the prelude, she continued on and played the fugue that was written with it.

Henri Herz smiled through the performance. He seemed both captivated and enchanted by her. "*Eh, bien!*" he exclaimed as she finished. He gave her a courtly bow and left the stage.

A worker appeared and announced, "We're opening the doors now for the audience, so you'll want to vacate the stage. There is a dressing room for Miss Hart to the left of Mr. Herz's where she can relax."

"Don't you want to practice your Beethoven piece now, too?" asked Royal, looking less sure of himself than he had just moments ago.

It was Adeline's turn to be calm as she announced, "As long as I can see you off stage, Royal, I think I'll be fine. But... here goes." She played the opening bars to get a feel for the sound and abruptly quit. She laughed and continued, "I can scarcely believe you talked me into this, but now that you have, I can't wait to begin!"

Relaxing, Royal gave her his best smile. "I knew you'd come around."

Adeline tried not to fidget as they waited for the seats to fill. Time seemed to slow down to a crawl and then suddenly speed up when someone knocked on her door and announced, "Five minutes!" Adeline found she needed to practice some deep breathing exercises so she wouldn't pass out from fear.

"Just remember, Addie, these are the same people who hear you play all the time at The Discovery. This will just be something new for them to hear from you. They already love you, but not as much as I do. Play it for us. And play it for yourself the way you love to hear it."

But Royal was incorrect. There was one person seated in the front row who had not yet had the pleasure of experiencing her talent and who was shocked to hear Adeline's name announced from the stage. It was with great skepticism that this seasoned music critic watched the ethereally beautiful young woman glide across the stage, bow politely, and take her place where he'd expected to see Henri Herz. He narrowed his beady eyes as she adjusted her position and got ready to play.

Adeline shook out her hands and placed them above the keys. Then, as if Beethoven himself invaded her spirit, she played the first crashing chords of the movement. She immediately had her audience riveted. Then the piece made a descent from high to low in a charming cadence that ended in a playful low rumble, and she was off. Her fingers flew up and down the keyboard, and she gave off the impression that she was truly one with the music. She sped up and slowed down, never once faltering, and had everyone on the edge of their seat. It was passionate and transcending. She played with power and with obvious joy.

When she finished, she bowed her head, appearing to almost be praying, and the audience was silent for a couple of heartbeats as they let the last reverberation of sound die away, then collectively they jumped to their feet, shouting, whistling, and applauding. Soon a chorus of, "Adeline! Adeline! Adeline!" broke out.

Adeline stood to take her bow and smiled almost confusedly at the riotous reception she was receiving. She bowed again and took her leave off the stage. The crowd didn't stop, however, and Royal gave her a tiny shove to propel her back out to take a second bow. This time happy tears flowed down her face as she heard feet stamping along with the clapping and cheering. She exited the stage one more time, although many people shouted, "Encore!"

Henri Herz himself took her firmly by the arm out to face her fans for her final bow. He grinned at the audience, let go of her arm, and raised his hands to flamboyantly applaud her himself. This little show made the crowd grow even louder. Herz bowed to Adeline and raised his chin slightly, looking off-stage. She got the message immediately that he was done with her and wanted the audience all to himself. She curtsied to him and waved to the crowd. A few men shouted, "Marry me, Adeline!" as she left the stage for the final time.

Royal grabbed her by the hand and rushed her back to her dressing room. Breathlessly they burst through the door, and Royal engulfed her in his embrace. His lips smashed into hers, and he kissed her with the heat of twenty suns. Adeline's eyes had closed as his lips descended on her, but feeling his un-bridled passion, they flew open again, and she met his fervor head-on. They became completely lost in each other and did not hear the thunder of footsteps approaching in the hallway outside. The door flew open, and in poured Jasper, Walter, Isaac, Timothy, and Séamus. Some had bouquets of flowers they pressed upon her with hugs, while Timothy and Séamus brandished bottles of champagne that they opened immedi-ately and messily.

Royal kept his arm firmly around her waist as their friends laughed and wiggled their eyebrows at him while they congrat-ulated Adeline on her tremendous performance.

She kept laughing and exclaimed, "I can't believe I just did that, and I can't believe you're all here!"

"We wouldn't have missed this, Adeline. Are you ever going to want to bother to play with me again?" worried Isaac. "Now you're famous!"

"I'm still me, and yes, of course, I still want to play with you," she laughed.

Jasper snuck up behind her and whispered suggestively into her ear, "I'd love to play *with* you, too." She could have sworn she felt him lightly pinch her bottom through her volumi-nous skirts. Royal still held onto her and was at that moment nibbling her ear. She was so beside herself; she didn't know how to react to anyone. She kept wondering to herself, *Is this really my life now?*

After they finished their champagne, Jasper asked, "Does anyone want to hear the rest of Herz's recital, or should we head back to The Discovery?"

Unanimously, they agreed that leaving suited them. Who needed Herz when they had Adeline?

Back at The Discovery, Chef Guillaume had a special dinner planned for them, explaining that in honor of her performance with Monsieur Herz, he had done his best to recreate his own favorite French dishes. Adeline laughed and asked Royal, "Did everyone in San Francisco know about today except for me?"

"No, there were a few cutthroats and thieves I neglected to bring into my confidence, but I thought your friends certainly would have shot me if I hadn't let them in on it. We all knew you'd be wonderful." He took her hand and kissed it, looking into her eyes with obvious deep affection. "I'd do anything for you, you know that, don't you?"

On Adeline's other side, Jasper gently lay his hand on her thigh and began to lightly stroke up and down. She shuddered at the brazen attention and then felt herself growing terribly warm. This was something new and odd to be basking in the attention of two suitors simultaneously. And the strangest thing of all was that neither man seemed to want to hide their actions from the other. She looked across at Walter at one point because he seemed to be assessing the devotion they were paying her. When she caught his eye, all he did was wink at her and smile happily. Then he turned his attention to Isaac, and she was suddenly aware of a fondness in Walter's gaze at Isaac that she'd overlooked before. *Well, well,* she thought.

After their supper, they opened the saloon for business and enjoyed a raucous, successful night like they'd never had before. Word had spread, and people either wanted more from Adeline after already hearing her play at the National Theatre, or they just wanted to bask in her beauty and talent. Flowers and gifts piled up on the stage around her, and Isaac and guests shouted encouragement and compliments to her all night long.

Finally, completely exhausted, Adeline had to call it a night. Jasper and Royal were embroiled in settling a scuffle that had broken out between a couple of inebriated gamblers, so for once, she was escorted upstairs by Isaac and Walter.

Chapter Twenty-One

Adeline Hart's Journal

May 25, 1850

I am completely exhausted after my long, exciting day, but I find I am far too keyed up to sleep. Writing does relax me.

So many times, I have written in this journal that this was a day I shall never forget, but this one surpasses them all in the best of ways. And yet, I am so confused.

Dearest Royal arranged to get me a place on the recital program at the National Theatre along with Henri Herz, and I played! I played Beethoven's Appassionata— the third movement. The reception was incredible! I felt such support from my friends from The Discovery who showered me with flowers and celebrated with champagne after I played.

It seems that now my name must be on the lips of all San Franciscans, and I wonder what became of the sad young woman who spent the past two years sequestered in her mother's sickroom or on a ship—frightened and surrounded by ruffians. I certainly have no care for fame, but I loved bringing such happiness to my audience by doing what I love.

And speaking of love... I am so confused by Jasper and Royal. I thought perhaps Jasper felt more strongly about me, judging by his passionate kiss, but then Royal flabbergasted me with his. Neither man seems the least bit bothered that the other sees what we are doing, and they also do not seem to mind that their friends are aware of this. Never in my life would I imagine being in the middle of two men.

And such men they are! Jasper is the dark, broody one who is full of profound thoughts and a deep well of emotion. Royal spreads joy around like autumn leaves in the wind. One might discount his intention as frivolous because of his sunny nature, but I know in my heart that he is serious. When I was afraid to take up the challenge to play at the National Theatre, it was only because Royal was there to encourage me that I was able to do it. I think he has had the same effect on Jasper—he's brought him out of the darkness and back into the light. I can see why Jasper loves him so.

Is there possibly something wrong with my nature that I cannot make up my mind between these two men? They are so delightful, am I greedy to want them both, or have I suddenly become unable to make a sound decision? I fear it is not fair to either of them to carry on as if we should all be a unit. We cannot pursue that course of action, so I need to purge it from my thinking.

The hour grows terribly late, and I must get some sleep. There is no telling what will be expected of me tomorrow. I accept the challenge!

Chapter Twenty-Two

"*A*deline! *Addie!* Wake up! Are you up? You need to see something!"

Someone who sounded a lot like Jasper was outside pounding on her door the next morning as Adeline was securing her hair into a proper style. She chuckled at how Jasper finally seemed ready to use the familiar form of her name the way Royal usually did. "Just a moment," she called out.

"Hurry, woman!" he bellowed, but he seemed to be laughing, so she was not alarmed. Quickly, she rose from her dressing table and opened her door. Jasper's hair was a mess as though he'd run his hands through it a few times, and his face was pink—no doubt from running up the stairs.

"What is it?"

"Read this!" Jasper thrust a copy of the *Alta California* newspaper into her hands. His eyes were on fire as he grinned at her.

Local Talent Outshines Celebrated French Pianist
By Albert Newland, Music Critic
For several days now, we San Franciscans have been treated to the virtuosic piano talent of M. Henri Herz, who has given several barnstorming recitals at the National Theatre. Herz entertained us with

his flamboyant style and his lively compositions that many critics around the world see as merely his means of showcasing his own talent. There are few other pianists who are ready to take up the gauntlet and try to play anything the man has written, but Herz seems content with keeping the repertoire all to himself.

Although he may have thrilled his audience to a degree, there was a lovely local lady who stole the show right from under Herz's nose.

Yesterday, I had the tremendous pleasure of hearing Miss Adeline Hart, formerly of Philadelphia, who now resides and entertains at The Discovery, a popular local hotel. She normally plays piano with violin accompaniment so the saloon patrons and hotel guests may dance. Yesterday, however, she enthralled the National Theatre's audience with her transcendent performance of Beethoven's Sonata #23, Opus 57, known as The Appassionata. I've heard many a piano aficionado try to stumble and bumble through this piece in recital, but Miss Hart was surely channeling Ludwig van Beethoven himself. She played with strength and passion that belied her small stature and feminine comportment and interpreted the music with grace and with an ear to every nuance of the piece. Brava, Miss Hart!

My single regret about Miss Hart's performance was that she only played the

third movement rather than the entire sonata. The reason why became clear, however, when M. Herz rushed her offstage,
ignoring the raucous pleas for an encore
by her ardent devotees. The showman evi-
dently had not expected to be upstaged so
dramatically.

The audience's reaction to Herz's performance was merely polite in comparison to
how they responded to Miss Hart. Several
even left at intermission when it became
apparent that we would hear no more from
her. There is no doubt that Herz can play
the dickens out of a piano, but after too
much of his music, one's ears tire with the
sameness of it all.

We hope that Miss Adeline Hart will
allow us to enjoy more of her classical per-
formances in the future. Are you listening,
National Theatre?

"Jasper!" she gasped with a hand to her chest. "If I'd known
I was playing for the music critic of the newspaper, I probably
would have fainted on the spot."

"No, you wouldn't have. You'd have done just what you
did—make everyone fall in love with you. Not like *I* love you,
mind." He leaned in and sealed his statement with a searing
kiss. "Good morning, my love," he added softly. Then his eyes
sparkled again as he announced, "I also heard through the
grapevine that Herz left town this morning. He plans to head
to Mexico!"

Adeline was speechless for a moment and merely stared dreamily at Jasper. Shaking herself, she finally said, "Well, that was the loveliest way to be greeted in the morning that I've ever experienced."

"Ah, good to know." Jasper wrapped his arms around her then and continued kissing her like there was no tomorrow.

In fact, they may have gone on kissing that way except that they became aware of some thundering footsteps coming up the stairs and another voice—this time Royal's—calling out, "Addie! Addie! We need you downstairs!" Then he came to a screeching halt and grinned at the two lovebirds who were just then pulling apart. "There you are, Jasper. I was looking for you too. You both have to come downstairs. But it can wait a moment or two." He then wrapped his arms around both Adeline and Jasper and kissed first her and then him. Then he went back to Adeline's lips once more. Pulling away with a satisfied sigh, he lightly tugged on them. "By God, I love both of you so much. Come on," he said softly and urged them to follow.

Adeline's insides did a funny flip and felt terribly warm. She hoped she wasn't going to need to make a lot of sense if someone asked her a question downstairs.

But that was not to be, though her full attention was definitely required. When they reached the lobby of the hotel, she was greeted by Isaac, who was in conversation with three nicely dressed women surrounded by a flock of children.

"Good morning, Adeline. May I introduce Mrs. Hawkins, Mrs. Lawrence, and Mrs. Simmons? And these are their children. The ladies would like a word with you." He smiled broadly at everyone as he gestured to the parlor off the lobby. Then to Adeline, he added, "I'll see you at breakfast in a bit." Looking a little relieved, he muttered something to himself about coffee and took off for the dining room.

About twenty minutes later, Adeline waltzed into the dining room and gracefully took her place between Royal and Jasper.

"What did they want?" asked Jasper.

"Piano lessons for some of the older children," Adeline answered with a chuckle. "Apparently, there is not a lot for the youngsters to do, and the mothers are thrilled with the idea of bringing a bit of culture to their education. One of the mothers was at the recital yesterday and told her friends."

Royal grinned at Adeline happily and asked, "Are you going to do it?"

Adeline looked at Royal and then across the table and answered, "I'd be happy to as long as Isaac adds violin lessons too. We could start a small music school for the children! Will you do it too, Isaac?"

"Sure, Adeline! I'll have to find some instruments for the children to play. Maybe I can make a few small-sized ones. I know there are new families disembarking from ships every day now. The population is beginning to normalize a little with wives and children showing up rather than just men for a change." He looked around the table and exclaimed, "Did you all know that we have gone from only one thousand residents here in 1848 to over *twenty thousand* now? Incredible." He looked pensive for a moment and then mused, "I think I'll head down to the docks and look around for some suitable pieces of wood..." He trailed off deep in thought. Besides making music, Isaac loved nothing more than creating beautiful things out of wood, and the idea that he could fashion some violins—wonderful!

"I'll go with you," announced Walter. "This city is dangerous enough without venturing out alone in it with your head in the clouds. I'm afraid you'll be studying pieces of wood and ignoring possible hazards in your surroundings." He winked at Adeline. "You two will make The Discovery even more famous with this project."

For the next few weeks, Isaac worked feverishly creating a collection of child and adult-sized violins while Adeline set up a schedule of lessons for her prospective piano students. At first, she only had a few, but as the weeks progressed and more and more families disembarked in San Francisco, she became terribly sought after. Because she still wanted to play piano with Isaac at night for people to dance, she had to limit her students to three a day. Even that was a heavy load, and she already had to keep a waiting list.

The Steinway's piano bench compartment yielded a treasure trove of sheet music that Adeline found extremely helpful. She painstakingly copied the pieces she thought would work well for her beginners, and she was delighted when she discovered that some of her new students had studied before they made the voyage to San Francisco. She had music for them as well. Some of the families were so dedicated to musical education they'd even brought along their beloved pianos and, happily, more sheet music.

It was inevitable that the saloon stayed busy well into the night, and she tended to be too keyed up to sleep right away after they closed, so Adeline's routine was to write in her journal at night to relax. She then had to sleep late in the morning, so she wouldn't be too exhausted to teach her students. Teaching became almost as important to her as performing. She loved them both, and she loved her students.

There was also another aspect of her life that needed attention—her promise to Royal and Jasper to spend time with them.

She intended to set apart an hour or two—or at least about twenty minutes if that was all they could spare—to do something with Jasper and Royal individually each day. As a unit, they spent all of their mealtimes and much of what they had left of free time together already. These trysts, though important, ended up being few and far between, however.

It was during these private moments that she learned all about Royal's broken heart and why he'd felt so compelled to leave his family farm in the east and make the perilous journey across the continent.

"I never felt as if I fit in," he explained. "My brothers and my father were so dedicated to their work, and I just put in the time knowing it was my duty. No one in my family could ever understand why I wanted to read so much or ask so many questions. They thought a book-learning education was a waste of time. So, when I lost the woman I loved because her father saw me as nothing but a dairy farm worker, I had to go make something of myself finally. I wasn't going to prove anything to that man, but I sure needed to prove to myself that I had merit. We need dairy farmers, obviously, and there is no shame in that profession, but I was not cut out for that life."

"And look at you now," Adeline said with a smile. "A successful businessman with a wonderful career and a group of partners who are unparalleled. Things definitely worked out for you, and you're still young. You are undoubtedly lucky you weren't saddled with that closed-minded, overbearing man for a father-in-law."

"I was lucky. I took up with a wagon train and managed to find Jasper and the other men, and we got here to California before the crush of hopeful prospectors. If we'd have even been a few months later, I doubt we could have had the success we achieved." He smiled at her fondly. "And then we met the *most* wonderful woman in the world. She's talented, kind, and generous and is the most beautiful lady I've ever laid eyes on. My feelings for you far surpass anything I felt for that other woman. She didn't even try to stand up to her father on my behalf, so I doubt we could have been all that happy over the long haul." He kissed her softly, and Adeline's toes curled in her shoes.

A couple of days after this encounter with Royal, Adeline went to Jasper's office to meet him for an afternoon they'd planned to spend together—doing what, she was unsure. She burst through the door all smiles and sunshine, only to find the poor man with tears pouring down his face as he sat at his desk. He had a pen in his hand and a kerchief in the other. He seemed to be staring into space.

"Jasper? Whatever is the matter? Are you ill? What's going on?"

Shaking himself slightly, Jasper set his pen down and made eye contact with Adeline. He let out a long sigh and answered, "I'm sorry, Adeline. Now that we have some semblance of mail service here, I hoped I might be able to get some letters to the east finally. I haven't been in contact with my parents since I left, and I would like them to know what has transpired with me. But..." he looked down and chewed his lip. Finally, he roused himself enough to say, "I also need to write to Isabella's parents. They are such a fine family, and it will kill them to know what became of their beloved daughter. It seems as if it happened so long ago now..."

"Oh, Jasper," she said in a soft voice. "I'm so sorry. Is there anything I can do to help? Do you want to be left alone today so you can concentrate on writing?" He had to be feeling atrocious, she knew.

"No. I very much want to spend the afternoon with you. I thought I could write these letters and be done with them. I did, in fact, get the one written to my parents." He gestured to a sealed envelope sitting nearby on his desk. "But then I tried to begin writing the other one, and I felt my heart break for Izzy and for her parents all over again." He watched as Adeline lowered herself into a chair across from his desk and wiped away a tear that was leaking down her cheek. "Please, Adeline, don't ever think mourning Isabella lessens how I feel about you. I cherish you. You must know that."

"I do, Jasper. I just feel so horrible for you, knowing what you've been through, and I see how hard it is for you to write the letter. I'm just so terribly sorry."

"You've known loss as well, Addie. I know you understand the pain." He roused himself then and looked deeply into her lovely brown eyes. "I think maybe one letter today is enough for me. We need to go have some fun. Would you like to go to see a play this afternoon? Or would you rather take a buggy ride? It's a beautiful day."

"A play sounds nice, but frankly, I'd rather just spend the time we have together so we can talk, if that's alright with you."

"That sounds perfect. Are you wearing comfortable shoes?" When she nodded, he added, "Then let's go take a walk and have a light picnic. We can sit on the bluff and watch the city below us. And we can talk as much as you like."

And so, on that day, Jasper and Adeline poured their hearts out to each other. They both desperately wanted children, and they both harbored guilt for their previous deeds that no amount of reassurance from others would erase. Adeline still feared that eternity in hell might be part of her future, and Jasper believed he'd been a terrible, worthless husband who'd neglected his wife. But each time they voiced their concerns and realized they were still worthy of love in this lifetime, the great anxieties they had fell away in minute portions.

The next day, Jasper resolved to write the letter. There was something about unburdening himself to Adeline that bolstered him enough to get through it. He knew it could still be months before Isabella's parents read it, and he hoped and prayed that the missive actually reached them. He could only imagine their horror and grief at reading his words, so he made sure to write about how much Isabella had been loved by all who had the great fortune of knowing her. More than one of his tears stained the paper.

Day after day, Adeline grew to love Royal and Jasper more than she ever could have imagined. Her ability to choose one over the other, however, became a hopeless impossibility.

At one point, she decided that perhaps the kind thing to do would be to distract one of the men. Perhaps she could encourage Jasper or Royal to fall in love with someone else. So, she asked them with false hope in her voice, "How would you like it if I included my lovely friend Olivia in our outing to-day?" Her insides clenched for a positive response from either of them, for it would break her.

Royal's answer was a blank, "Who is Olivia, and what do we want with her?" Apparently, he'd forgotten even hiring the woman.

Jasper's simultaneous reply was, "Why on earth would you do that? We want to spend as much time with *you* as we can."

"Yes, well, never mind then. I shan't bother her." *What a relief, though we still face the same dilemma.*

During the personal time they spent with Adeline, the men had to refrain from being overly physical with her. They desperately wanted to do more than kiss, but since neither felt they had a claim to her, they resolved to be perfect gentlemen.

Adeline, however, privately wished something would happen. When the men kissed her, that unmistakable thrill scorched through her body, leaving her longing for more. Much, much more.

At night, the men continued to love each other, and after their lovemaking, they often discussed Adeline. They began to wonder if they could realize her love at the same time, although that seemed an almost inconceivable possibility. A life with her—sharing her—became a beautiful fantasy, however. The more they spoke of it, the idea sprouted roots and began to blossom.

Jasper might whisper to Royal, "Imagine if she were here with us right now. We could have each other and her at the same time. I'm positive she's untouched, so we could teach her all about how to make love. Pretend I'm Adeline right now, Roy, and see how you like it." He bent down and engulfed Royal into his mouth and began to suck on him voraciously.

Royal started to chuckle, and that grew into a belly laugh when Jasper added some high-pitched moans that he supposed were meant to sound feminine.

Leaning back, Jasper pulled off with an audible pop and asked with a comical expression as he batted his eyes, "What?"

Royal wiped his eyes and chortled, "It's hard to imagine Addie with a tickly beard. But don't stop. You know how much I crave that from you." He gently stroked his fingers through Jasper's hair.

When Jasper returned to business and Royal's laughter subsided, his voice took a much more serious turn. "Jas?"

"Mmmff?"

"Have you ever heard of two men having a woman at the same time? One in front and one in the rear?"

Jasper's jaw dropped, and he suddenly popped his head up to stare at Royal. Clearing his throat, he finally answered, "That sounds... almost too good to be true."

And a whole new bunch of fantasy scenarios were born—each featuring their possible threesome. When they talked about it, their own lovemaking took on a deeper significance and the excitement level they felt went through the roof. It had always been good for them, but this was beyond belief now.

Royal felt compelled one night to say, "Jasper, I have to tell you that no matter what happens with Addie, I'll love you until the day I drop. I adore her and want a family so badly, but you're in my heart forever."

With his head on Royal's chest, Jasper idly stroked him, saying, "I understand. Completely. It's the same for me. I don't want to belittle the affection I feel for either of you when all of it is so utterly profound." Then he nuzzled Royal's belly with his nose and his lips, leaving a trail of kisses.

When they were with Adeline, they made sure to show affection to each other as well as kissing her whenever the opportunity presented itself. She almost purred like a kitten when they loved on her, and they observed how her eyes would dilate when they kissed each other in front of her.

Noticing this, Royal asked her with a bit of a smirk, "How does it make you feel when Jasper and I kiss, Addie?"

Blinking as if to clear her vision after the sight of the two men swallowing each other's tongues took her somewhere in her head, she finally answered, "I want to see more of that. It makes me as excited as when one of you kisses me."

The men looked at each other with matching grins then, and both leaned in to kiss her simultaneously. "And how does this make you feel?" asked Jasper as he nibbled her ear. Royal busied himself with her neck.

Adeline gave a visible shudder and grinned like a Cheshire cat. She reached for both men's thighs and squeezed.

That night, the two men discussed Adeline for hours. They had to get her to make up her mind. They vowed to each other that they would work harder at it.

Chapter Twenty-Three

Adeline Hart's Journal

July 1, 1850

Life is delightfully exciting. And life is so confusing. I have never known myself to be so conflicted.

Two wonderful men are courting me, and I fear I am taking advantage of their good natures by not selecting one of them. Both wish to marry, and yet they also love one another. I am confused by my reaction to their mutual affection, and I wish I could make up my mind. The turmoil in my brain robs me of sleep at night.

What should I do? I cannot deny that being with both men together makes me happier than I have a right to feel. At some point, I must break a heart that is as dear to me as my own. I cannot face that decision.

Chapter Twenty-Four

Royal and Jasper had a meeting with Chef Guillaume to discuss the restaurant and how things were going with purchasing supplies. When the two men entered the kitchen, however, they discovered Guillaume deep in a lively conversation in French with another man roughly the same age. They seemed to have been laughing about something, and they both looked so joyful; their mirth was infectious. It was hard not to laugh along with them, even though the Americans couldn't understand a word of what they said.

Immediately, Guillaume smiled at his employers and switched to English, "Good afternoon, sirs. I would like to introduce you to a friend of mine. We sailed here from France together. This is Louis Montrachet—an esteemed physician. Louis, these are my employers, Mr. Langley and Mr. Dawson."

The man was dressed like a typical prospector and not the least bit like a doctor—though an awful lot of men looked like that these days. While chatting with the man, Jasper and Royal discovered that Louis had come to California to find gold. It was a typical story. He was rapidly becoming flat broke because he hadn't found any.

"Now that I see how difficult it is to make a living that way, I would prefer to set up a medical practice here instead. Unfortunately, I have dwindling resources."

Chef Guillaume interjected at that point, "Louis was working with a famous physician in France. Perhaps you have heard of Pierre Briquet?"

"That sounds vaguely familiar," answered Jasper.

"He is better-known in France, but as soon as his study is published, he will be world-famous," Louis said, beaming at them. "I should have stayed in France and completed the study with him for all of the success I've had finding gold. But I was in a rush. The ship was leaving, and I was anxious to come to California... at least I have had a big adventure coming here."

Always the curious one, Royal asked, "What was this important study about?"

Louis winked at him—which Royal found a bit odd. Then Louis answered, "It was a treatment for female hysteria called *'la titillation du clitoris.'*"

Jasper stared at the man blankly, but Royal's jaw dropped. "Interesting," he said after collecting himself.

"Useful!" laughed Chef Guillaume. "Something we all need to know!"

"Why is a medical procedure important for anyone but a physician?" asked Jasper. "Female hysteria? What does '*la tit...* whatever that was mean?"

Smiling broadly, Louis explained, "It is a technique that is guaranteed to make any woman relaxed and content. It cures her 'hysteria' or bad mood instantly. Do you have a woman who needs pleasing, sir?" He looked at Jasper.

"I... uh... well... perhaps."

"If I teach you this technique, you will never be so unsure again," Louis boasted. "She will be happy and devoted to you for life."

"But you say this is a medical procedure. I'm not a physician."

Louis burst out laughing. "The medical community would love for the world to believe it is purely science, but I call this technique essential for *all* lovers. It is all about creating the most beautiful sexual experience for a woman, no matter what these stuffy physicians would like the public to believe. It's crucial! Do you want to be trained?"

Jasper looked at Royal, and they both grinned at each other. Royal looked at Louis and asked, "What is your price for training? We're in."

Grinning, Louis requested a peach from Chef Guillaume—who'd handed it to him with a wink before getting back to his cooking. Regarding his new pupils, Louis answered, "I will let you two gentlemen decide on the value of the lesson. Just remember, it will be life-altering."

Jasper and Royal wondered why, if the man was so hungry, he didn't eat the fruit.

A few moments later, the three of them were seated in Jasper and Royal's office. Louis produced a very detailed drawing of the female genitalia and proceeded to give the men a crash course in how to properly stimulate a woman's clitoris. He demonstrated how to do it both manually and orally.

"The oral technique is my own addition. It is not what Pierre Briquet uses on the women in his study," he assured them.

Eventually, Louis sliced the peach in half and pulled out the pit. He had the men practice on the peach as though it were a woman. After much laughter, while watching them slurp up dribbling juice, he pronounced them adept at a skill they would use the rest of their happy lives.

Before he left, they handed him a generous sack of gold.

"You've earned it, Louis. Thank you. Now go out to the staff dormitory and find yourself a bed," Jasper offered. "There should be room, but if nothing is available, let me know. No charge."

"*Merci, messieurs,*" Louis said with a huge grin. "It has been a pleasure doing business with you both. Tomorrow I will set to work on my new medical practice, now that I finally have some gold." Then he winked at them and added, "Do not worry. I can also stitch people up and set broken bones. *Amusez-vous!*" Laughing, he left to stake out the most comfortable sleeping arrangement he'd had in weeks and weeks.

"I think it might be a good idea," Royal suggested dryly after the office door closed, "to send Adeline to a different doctor, should she ever need one."

"Agreed," said Jasper.

They both had a good laugh and headed back to the kitchen to meet with Chef Guillaume so they could finally speak to him about work.

Delighted with their newly acquired information and anxious to try it out as soon as possible, Jasper and Royal decided that they were going to make certain Adeline caved to their wishes, no matter what.

It was time.

Chapter Twenty-Five

At the end of breakfast the next morning, Jasper asked, "What do you have planned for today, Adeline?" He reached up and toyed with a loose tendril of her hair that had escaped its confines. "Would you care to spend some time with Royal and me? We have a few things we'd like to discuss with you."

Adeline felt a thrill go through her as his fingertips slid gently along her jaw. She studied his piercing blue-eyed stare for a bit before gathering her wits enough to answer him.

"I have a fitting with Madame Beaufort soon, and after that, I'm all yours."

"Oh, I like the sound of that. Did you hear, Roy?" he chuckled. "She's ours."

Adeline ducked her chin in embarrassment. "I didn't mean...."

"Of course you did, Addie. Jasper and I can't wait to spend the day... discussing things with you." He leaned in and pecked her on the cheek, enjoying her blush. Whispering in her ear, he said, "I'll be thinking about you dressing and undressing while we're waiting for you."

Adeline gasped wide-eyed at him, and there were those tingles again, running through her and turning her to mush.

As soon as Adeline finished her seemingly endless fitting appointment, she exited Madame Beaufort's quarters and nearly collided with Royal and Jasper. "Oh!" she cried and then laughed. "Have you been waiting long?"

"Yes," Jasper grumbled. "I thought that confounded woman would never finish."

Royal chuckled at Jasper's exasperation and asked, "Would you like to come have a private conversation with us, Addie? We can use our office."

Adeline raised her eyebrows, answering, "I'm intrigued, gentlemen."

Pressed in on either side of Adeline on a lovely rosewood and brocade sofa, they both took one of her hands. Jasper cleared his throat and then opened his mouth. Nothing came out, but his eyes looked a little wild. He finally closed his mouth and looked to Royal to start the conversation. Royal smiled crookedly and winked.

"Addie, I did a little research around town the day you and Jasper were at Henri Herz's recital. Have you ever heard of a man named Sam Brannan?"

"Oh, yes. His name has come up a few times. Isn't he the gentleman who used to publish rather sensational stories in his paper *The California Star*?"

Royal nodded and explained, "He's become an extremely rich man by spreading inflated stories about the availability of gold in this area, and he's duped people into spending lots of money on mining equipment that they could only get from him."

"What does he have to do with us? Does he want to buy into The Discovery?"

"No, nothing like that," Jasper assured her. "He's also a Mormon and has some very strong personal opinions."

Adeline frowned slightly. This wasn't explaining much to her. She looked back and forth between the men with confusion.

Royal stood and dragged a chair over in front of Adeline and Jasper. Sitting down with their knees touching, he took their hands. "There, that's better. Your neck was going to get stiff, swiveling back and forth between us, Addie. And this way, we can all see each other easily." Smiling at his two favorite people, he continued, "Brannan has been a Mormon for years and years, but he's had a falling out with the church recently. He does, however, perform non-Catholic marriages—one of the few who will in this area, in fact."

Jasper's hand tightened on Adeline's.

"Marry? Does he mean to convert people to the Mormon church this way?" she asked, clearly confused.

"Not at all," Jasper interjected. "He is far more interested in making lots of money for himself, and that is how he's gotten into the marrying business. He charges a hefty sum for his services. But before Royal goes on, perhaps we ought to ask you if you've decided on a preference for one of us over the other. Your opinion is terribly important to us."

Adeline ducked her head for a few seconds. "I haven't, actually." Then she laughed softly. "I love being with you together as well as apart, though you've scarcely offered me much opportunity for the latter." She saw their sheepish smiles and laughed again. Obviously, they were aware of that. "We spoke about this, Jasper. You remember." He nodded, and she continued, "I have found on the *rare* occasion that I was alone with one of you, I was constantly wondering what the other was up to and privately lamenting that we weren't all together. I don't know what that says about me. I have never considered myself to be particularly fickle or indecisive." She smiled with sincerity in her eyes, "This is not to in any way diminish the enjoyment I took from being alone with either of you. It just somehow always feels... I don't know... incomplete? It's very strange."

"No, Addie," soothed Royal. "It's perfect."

She blinked at him in confusion.

Royal looked solemnly at Jasper, and in unison, they turned their eyes on Adeline, saying, "Marry us."

Adeline gave a tiny gasp as her head jolted back. "How? I can't marry two men."

"Why not?" laughed Royal. "Brannan told me he performs marriages for men who want to marry multiple wives, so why not the other way around? It makes more sense in the long run anyway. If something were to happen to one of us, you'd still have the other to take care of you—not that you're not self-sufficient now that you're such a wealthy, successful businesswoman as well as a talented pianist and teacher. But your *personal* needs would be still be fulfilled."

"How is that legal?"

Jasper spoke up. "We don't have many ordinances here in San Francisco, but that may change soon once California becomes a state. I've heard rumors that it will happen before the end of the year. There isn't anything at this point to prevent us from all three marrying. Oh, and speaking of Henri Herz? Did you know that he's married to a woman who has another husband?"

Adeline's eyebrows shot up, and she blinked at the news.

Royal continued explaining, "What I discovered is that all we have is an ordinance that says an unmarried woman over the age of fifteen and an unmarried man over the age of eighteen may marry, and the definition of a marriage is 'a civil contract to which the consent of the parties is required.' Brannan has agreed to perform the wedding, and when I asked him where he would file the documents, he just laughed and answered, 'No one cares about documents, but you can file them with the local judge if you feel some desperate need.' I also discovered that the ordinance doesn't specify gender—so theoretically, Jasper and I can marry each other the same way we marry you. Granted, it's a technicality and one that will someday, no doubt, be clarified, but in the meantime, we can take advantage of it."

"Also," added Jasper, "the most important point is that no one will care one way or the other, even if eventually our union were to become illegal. It'll be too late then. You've seen how just about any behavior is tolerated in this city. As long as we're not stealing anything or killing anyone, no one cares about our morals. When we were back at Sutter's Mill working with the Mormons and the Indians, most of the Mormon men had multiple wives, and some of the Indian men were married to other men—sometimes more than one. No one thought a thing of it." He looked deeply into her eyes. "Marry us, Adeline. We may be unusual compared to people in the east, but here we'll be perfect. Royal and I feel the same way that you've described. We're happy together, but it's so much better when you're here with us—all three of us."

"I... ah..."

"Say yes, Addie. Jasper and I love you so much. Be ours. You love us too, don't you?"

"I do."

"Just the words we want to hear!" laughed Royal as Jasper grinned.

Adeline shook herself and closed her eyes for a brief moment, then asked, "When would the two of you want to do this... wedding?"

"Today is fine with me. Jasper?" Royal asked with a beaming smile.

"Today sounds wonderful. Adeline?"

"I... ah..." She looked into Jasper's eyes and then into Royal's. The depth of love she saw mirrored in them nearly robbed her of breath. Finally, she asked, "Where shall we meet this Mr. Brannan?" She hazarded a shy smile. "I accept."

"That's positively splendid, Addie! Jasper and I will love you until our dying days and then some. You won't be sorry, dearest."

"I must be mad," Adeline murmured as if to herself and then burst into a fit of giggles. "It's so ridiculous; it's perfect. You're both correct."

Jasper jumped up, grabbed Adeline around the waist, and kissed her soundly. Then he kissed Royal before Royal had his chance to kiss Adeline. Once that was accomplished, Jasper ordered, "We have a wagon standing ready for us. Let's go see Brannan!"

"You were that sure of yourselves?" she asked.

"Not really. We hoped, but if you'd said no, Royal and I would have just gone somewhere to drown our sorrows, I suppose."

"He's teasing," Royal said firmly. "We never doubted your affections for a moment. Who could resist us?" He gave them both a saucy look, and they were off.

But when they arrived at Brannan's office in the Plaza, Adeline appeared panicked. Standing in front of the closed door, she looked at Jasper and then at Royal. Both men seemed to be beside themselves with excitement, and all Adeline could feel suddenly was a sense of dread. *What on earth am I doing?* She asked herself. *I was never raised this way. My parents would die if they knew I'm considering marriage to two men.*

Sobering, Royal asked gently, "Addie, what's wrong? You look like you're about to faint. Are you unwell?" He took a firm hold of her arm as Jasper grasped her other one.

Her brown eyes seemed to increase in size by at least half as she again looked from one of them to the other. "I feel like I ought to be able to choose one of you. Am I doing something that is completely immoral?"

Jasper softly cupped her cheek and asked, "Does it feel immoral to love me?"

"Of course not, Jasper! You are the most caring, wonderful man I've ever known. It pleases me immeasurably to love you."

Royal kissed her on the other cheek and demanded, "Does it feel immoral to love me then? You know how deeply I'm in love with you." His eyes flicked to his friend, "And with Jasper as well," he added.

"Not in the least, Royal. You are infinitely dear to me and make me happier than I have the right to feel sometimes."

Her face looked troubled still, so Jasper made one last effort to right her mood. "Dearest Adeline, if you still think that you're bound for hell, then what is one more sin? You cannot be more damned than you already are!" Then he burst out laughing.

His laughter was contagious and spread immediately to Royal and finally to Adeline. They laughed until their sides ached, and Royal put his hand on Brannan's doorknob. He sobered finally and told them, "When I was passing through New York on my way to Missouri, I traveled a while with a Jew. He and I got into many fascinating debates about philosophy and religion, but he told me one thing that will stay with me always." He saw that he had their rapt attention and continued. "He said that no one, no matter what they tell you, has any idea about the existence of either heaven or hell. So, what he believes is that the important thing is how you conduct your life while you still have control over it. The rest will sort itself out after you die. Unless you see some truly horrible reason that you cannot love two people equally who love you back the same way, then don't worry about hellfire. You don't even know if it's real. It could just be a constraint the church imposed on its members to control their behavior and collect their money." He opened the door then and immediately demanded, "Mr. Brannan, could you please tell us whether the

Mormons believe that having multiple spouses is a guaranteed ticket to hell?"

Brannan's eyebrows shot up and then relaxed as he answered, "Exactly the opposite, Mr. Dawson. God instructed us to participate in plural marriages, and it became law."

Turning to Adeline, he said, "Jews *and* Mormons can't all be wrong, can they?" He looked deeply into her eyes and continued in a whisper, "Addie, you have to do what you think is right, but I can guarantee that if you go through with this, we will strive to make it work by assuring you our devotion. So?"

Adeline was very quiet for a moment and then finally extended her hand toward Brannan, saying, "How do you do, Mr. Brannan. My name is Adeline Hart, and I am here today to marry these two wonderful men. Shall we begin?" She smiled as he took her hand, but her smile faltered as the man stepped back, clearly having second thoughts.

"Now see here, folks," he said seriously. Addressing Royal, he said, "When you told me you wanted to marry two people, naturally I assumed two ladies. I'm not at all sure this arrangement is suitable in the eyes of the church."

"We're not members of the Mormon church," explained Jasper. "We're trying to do what is right for *us*." As he said this, he produced a large buckskin sack of gold from his pocket. "But if you don't want to marry us, perhaps we can locate one of the wagon masters who are still in town. They have the right to perform weddings, I understand, under maritime law. Or...we are also well-acquainted with a man who is a ship's captain, and he's always looking for some extra income."

Adeline fought to not roll her eyes as Royal covered his snort with a cough at the idea of Greely agreeing to marry them. He'd be the last man on earth who would do so.

"You'd have to be aboard his ship for him to perform the wedding," Brannan said with a scowl.

"That can be arranged. The ship under his command is in the harbor right now." That was stretching the truth a bit, he knew. The remains of the Wind Gypsy were only a flophouse for Greely, and Greely was barely in command of himself on a good day. Besides, hopefully, by now, the man had finally left for Boston. Just in case Brannan was persuadable, he went on, "I'd certainly rather pay you, Mr. Brannan, than give it to a sea captain who'll probably just squander it on rum and gambling. You'd surely find a better use for it."

Brannan's jaw twitched as Jasper jiggled the sack of gold as though weighing its heft with both hands.

"I thought you had broken ties with the Mormons anyway," Royal said with a perplexed look. "Did something change?" It had, after all, been weeks since they had spoken. That morning he'd only sent a messenger to tell Brannan that they would be coming in today for the ceremony.

"Well, yes, I have realigned myself with them, and since I paid my tithe, I am back in their good graces once again," explained Brannan—whose eyes had not left the sack of gold for a moment. He licked his lips greedily, and no doubt considered all of the money he was suddenly out now that he'd paid his exorbitant tithe. Finally, he seemed to shake himself out of the magnetic draw of the gold and announced to them, "I'm sorry, but I can't do it. It's not right. Men take care of their wives, not the other way around. Go try your captain or maybe the judge. He's just up the street."

Brannan ushered them toward the door. He seemed to be in a bit of a hurry to be done with them. "That way," he said, indicating to turn left.

It took the disgruntled fiancés less than five minutes to locate the judge's chambers, during which time Royal apologized over and over for dragging them to Brannan's office on a fool's errand. They assured him just as many times that they weren't angry with him about it and understood how he could have misinterpreted Brannan's opinion.

As soon as Jasper brandished the sack of gold in front of the judge, it took no persuasion at all to get the man to agree to marry them. He was an extremely unscrupulous man who'd do just about anything for the right price.

The actual marriage ceremony was about as anticlimactic as shopping for a sack of flour. The judge had them sign a piece of paper, and he asked them, "Do you take each other to be wedded?" When they each answered, "I do," he continued in a monotone. "I now pronounce you lawfully... er... *married*." It wasn't even clear whom he was addressing, but they were all three so giddy, they barely noticed.

"Thank you for your time," Jasper told him sincerely and handed him the sack of gold.

The judge's eyes lit up as he hefted its ample weight, and as he cheerfully stuffed it into his pocket, he showed them the door. "I'll keep the file in my records," he assured them. All of a sudden, the judge seemed to be in a big hurry to do something with his payment.

"Jasper, we made a blunder!" cried Royal as they exited the judge's office. "We forgot to give our bride her rings."

"Well, it's not as if anyone wanted to bless them or anything. You have yours, don't you?"

"Right here." Royal fished around in his pocket and took Adeline's hand. She trembled as he slipped a gold band on her ring finger. Then Jasper took the same hand and slipped a similar one on as well. Then together, they slipped on a third band.

Adeline oohed with pleasure as she realized the rings fit together as one, but in the center, there were three beautifully cut rubies. "Each of the bands has a stone, and the rubies each represent one of us—our hearts," Jasper explained. "It's our version of a gimmel ring for you. And, of course, we had them made from our personal stash of gold."

Royal continued, "As we see it, the rings can stand on their own, but all three together are far more beautiful and stronger." He kissed Adeline, who kissed Jasper, and Jasper kissed Royal. Bringing their foreheads together, Royal exclaimed softly, "We did it. We're *married*. There were times I thought this would never happen for me. Thank you, both. I feel blessed."

Chapter Twenty-Six

They headed back to The Discovery, where all of their friends and business partners were waiting for them in the dining room. It was decorated with a banner that said, "Congratulations!" and everyone was holding glasses of champagne to toast the newlyweds.

"You certainly were self-assured about today's outcome, you two!" Adeline laughed. The men merely beamed at her; they both ignored the fact that it could have gone so very wrong.

One by one, their friends shook hands, hugged, kissed, and showered them all with the best of wishes. When that was accomplished, they all sat down to an incredible wedding feast specially prepared for them by Chef Guillaume. It was so magnificent; they cheered for him until he came out to take a modest bow. The man looked extremely smug about it as he winked at Adeline. He knew he was the finest chef in the city.

As they were about to commence with dessert and more champagne, Walter stood, clinked his glass, and launched into a long-winded speech about how he'd known Royal and Jasper were headed for greatness way back when he'd first met them in Missouri and how he felt so fortunate to have become such a close friend. Walter was just starting in on his feelings about Adeline when Jasper jumped to his feet and asked, "Does anyone else smell smoke?" Running for the window, he peered out and cried, *Fire! The city is on fire!* The sun had set long before this, but the brightness of the flames created an eerie glow.

He turned to Adeline and ordered her, "Stay here and do not go upstairs to bed. The fire shouldn't reach us up here, but if it somehow does, you'll need to evacuate immediately. We're going to help. Come on, men!" Then he rushed out the door with his partners hot on his heels.

Adeline sat in bewildered panic for a moment until one of the hired guards came back into the dining room and announced, "Your husbands ordered me to not let you out of my sight until they return." The man was on the short side, had a spare, wiry build, an honest face, and looked to be as tough as nails. She immediately trusted him.

"Oh! Yes, of course, Mr....?"

"Cooley, ma'am. Caleb Cooley, at your service."

"May I offer you some supper, Mr. Cooley?"

"Caleb will do, ma'am. And yes, thank you. I haven't had much to eat yet today, and I'm as hungry as a bear."

Adeline rang for service, and shortly Caleb was treated to a dinner like none he'd ever tasted before. He dug in like a starving man and laughed, "These are some fine vittles, ma'am. Thank you."

Adeline's hand shook as she sipped her champagne and stared out the window—scarcely paying him any attention. Now that she'd seen to his nourishment, she turned her focus on worrying herself sick about her brand-new husbands and the city below. The black smoke and engulfing flames were terrifying from their lookout on the bluff above the city. The fire seemed to be growing exponentially.

I feel useless, she thought. *I know nothing about how to fight a fire, but I certainly hate just sitting here and watching the city burn down. Unfortunately, if I tried to help. I would just get in the way.*

The smell was atrocious.

As Jasper, Royal, and the others reached the Plaza, they could see that in just a few moments, an entire city block had gone up in flames, and the fire was spreading quickly. The dry wind whipped up the heat to a terrible degree as people ran up and down the crowded street looking for their friends and loved ones and trying to escape the inferno.

Sobbing, terrified people hollered everywhere as the smoke choked their lungs and soot filled their eyes. Men used whatever they could to beat back the flames, but the fire spread in what had become a gale-force wind. Another block and then another exploded into a rapidly increasing inferno.

Adeline's frustration ended abruptly as soon as she heard Royal's voice bellowing from the front door of the hotel. "Addie! Take care of them! We'll be back with more!" and he was gone just as quickly as he'd arrived.

About a dozen bedraggled people piled into the foyer, bloodied and filthy from mud and soot. Some were crying, and others appeared to be in shock.

Quickly, she ushered them into the saloon and sat them all down where she could bring them water to drink and wash with. With their hands and faces clean, at least, she could assess who needed medical attention. Unfortunately, she'd seen the physician Louis Montrachet rush out with the other men to fight the fire. She got the kitchen staff to come out to help her dole out salves for their burns, and she patiently listened to each of their stories and worries. Their fears and grief were palpable, and she heard the word "arson" muttered angrily over and over in connection with "Sydney Ducks."

The Sydney Ducks, a ruthless gang of expatriated Australian convicts, had a terrible reputation for setting fires. They would request payment from a merchant for fire "protection," and when the man did not pay, his business burned to the ground, taking lives and many other businesses with it. They also roamed the streets during a fire, offering help to citizens who worried that the fire would spread to their homes. Valuables needed to be systematically removed from the structures before going up in flames. However, the Sydney Ducks "helpers" merely helped themselves to the valuables and ran off with them to Sydney-Town—the worst crime-filled area of San Francisco.

The idea that the frightening ex-convict gang from Australia could be behind such a crime made Adeline's blood run cold. She wished fervently that the fire could be brought under control quickly so she could see that Jasper and Royal were unharmed.

She was just about to pour some of the men harder things to drink than water when the next group of fire refugees arrived. So, Adeline assigned one of the kitchen staff to man the bar while she tended to more arrivals.

This cycle went on for hours, with more and more homeless, sad, and terrified people showing up. Adeline had a kind word for each of them and had Chef Guillaume lay out a large spread of food for them to eat.

To his immense credit and Adeline's appreciation, Caleb Cooley worked tirelessly alongside her, helping in any way he could. It turned out he had a caring nature for all of his gruff exterior.

When the influx of people seemed to slow down, at last, she could finally relax a little and decided to do what came naturally to her. She played the piano for them. By then, there were people sitting or lying all over the saloon, either in chairs or on the floor. Their lives were a mess, they smelled to high heaven of smoke after the tragic loss of their homes and businesses, but for the moment, they could relax and listen to something beautiful that soothed their troubled hearts.

Hours after that first cry of "fire," Royal and Jasper trudged through the door. Adeline hardly recognized them. Their faces and hands were blackened with soot, their clothes were torn and filthy, and their boots were covered with ashy mud. They were physically indistinguishable from the homeless fire victims. The big difference, however, was that they both made a beeline for Adeline and engulfed her in their arms.

"Sorry, Addie, we're getting you all grimy," Royal croaked into her ear with a voice hoarse from smoke inhalation.

"I don't care! As long as you're both safe. I've been sick with worry for you. How bad was it?"

"Several blocks of buildings were completely obliterated, and quite a few people died," choked out Jasper. His voice was as bad as Royal's. "Thank you for taking care of these people. You're a saint."

"I didn't do much—not like the two of you. Feeding people and cleaning them up is nothing like fighting a fire with your bare hands!" She looked around wildly then and demanded, "Where are the others?"

"Séamus and Timothy are seeing to the livestock and the wagons. I think Walter and Isaac went straight upstairs to bed. Don't worry," Jasper assured her. "Everyone is safe." With tears in his eyes, he added, "I just wish we could have said the same thing for some of the poor bastards down there whose houses exploded into flames with them inside. What a disaster. This city has to do something soon about all of these fires. Our volunteer efforts help, but we need far more equipment and better organization."

Royal added, "The fire spread so quickly, people didn't even get out of their houses fast enough, and they... you can figure out what happened."

"Oh, my lord," breathed Adeline with tears in her eyes. "I cannot imagine." Looking from man to man, she suggested gently, "Why don't the two of you go upstairs and get yourselves cleaned up, and I'll bring you some drinks. Your throats must feel awful."

"Thank you," choked Royal as Jasper nodded. "We could both use a bath." Snorting, he added, "All of the city's records, including our marriage document, burned up tonight." He turned to Jasper with a resigned shrug and said, "Let's get cleaned up. Addie, we'll meet you in your new room in a little while."

"New room?" She looked confused. She was still reeling from hearing their marriage document had just gone up in smoke, even though the men looked unconcerned with this development.

"While we were out today," Jasper rasped out, "and during our wedding dinner, we had some of the staff move you into the suite we had reappointed for all three of us. Don't worry." He gave her a saucy wink. "You'll love it."

Chapter Twenty-Seven

Adeline followed shortly after the men had gone up, carrying a tray with some hot tea and a bottle of brandy. Royal had provided her with a key and directed her to head down the hall in the opposite direction of her old room. "Last door at the very end. You can get cleaned up in there. Sorry we messed up your pretty gown with our grime."

When she entered the room, she was taken aback. Her previous room had been, in her opinion, quite pleasant, but the men had obviously gone to great lengths to make this suite something special. Her breath caught, and she couldn't pull her eyes away from the enormous bed that occupied much of the space on one side of the room. The other side had a lovely fireplace and sitting area where she placed her tray. There was a private alcove off the back where she could see a washbasin sitting on a beautiful marble-topped rosewood dressing table. The soothing smell of lavender filled her senses. It was the best thing she'd smelled in hours. She headed for the washbasin and moved a privacy screen across the alcove so she would not be seen if the door should open. The alcove was also equipped with a small closet that held a commode that was designed similarly to the medieval Scottish castles and their garderobes.

Walter's hopeful plan to have indoor plumbing in the hotel was still a work in progress. He had seen to it that The Discovery had a deep well so that the kitchen had plenty of water, but a municipal water system and a decent septic field were still a few years in the future due to lack of public interest or funds. The guests had shared bath and toilet facilities, but apparently, Royal and Jasper had insisted that they would all three have a modicum of privacy.

Someone had kindly left a new, silken dressing gown for Adeline to put on, so she quickly removed her soiled clothing and washed up. She undid her hair and let it cascade down her back in mahogany waves.

Looking in the mirror, she asked herself, *Nervous?* Her mirror image smiled enigmatically and decided for her that she was actually too tired to feel any particular nerves. She was excited and curious but not the least bit scared. She was, unfortunately, bone tired. She could just imagine how the men felt. After passing her brush through her hair, she padded on bare feet over to where she saw a lovely little writing desk. Sitting on the top, clearly waiting for her, was her journal and a fancy new ink pen. Her men had thought of everything.

Adeline got herself situated at the desk and was just considering what to write when the door swung open, and her two delectable husbands burst in laughing hoarsely. They both had nothing on besides towels wrapped around their waists, and their hair dripped water down their shoulders.

"We forgot to get any clothes before bathing! We were so anxious to get that smoke and filth off," laughed Royal in a raspy voice. Grabbing Jasper's arm, he asked, "Look at her. Doesn't she look like an angel sitting there?"

Adeline had never seen so much bare male flesh in her life. Their hard bodies reminded her of the drawings she'd seen of Greek statues—only these were in full, glorious color and radiated heat and energy. Royal seemed to be all sparkling and golden, while Jasper's pattern of black chest hair stood out in stark contrast with his skin. The flickering lamp cast shadows across their sculpted torsos. She stared at them wide-eyed, but when Royal struck a pose and flexed for her, she couldn't help but giggle.

Jasper seemed spellbound as he regarded Adeline. He cleared his throat, but that seemed to hurt, so he just nodded and smiled. "Lovely," he finally whispered. Then he seemed to sway a bit where he stood.

"Are you feeling alright?" Adeline asked. Without waiting for a reply, she jumped up and led Jasper to the sitting area where she asked, "Tea or brandy, or both?" Seeing him slump onto the sofa, she looked at Royal with worried eyes. But it was then she realized that Royal didn't look much better. Both men were utterly exhausted, and no doubt emotionally spent after seeing the horrors of the inferno. She poured them both cups of hot tea and laced them liberally with brandy. "Here, maybe your throats will feel better after this, you poor dears. You must be dead on your feet after what you've been through tonight."

Jasper gulped his hot drink and stared into the empty fireplace. The weather was far too warm to suggest lighting it, and Adeline instinctively knew that neither man would be charmed by more flames. It was past four o'clock in the morning, and they would have been tired anyway at such an hour even without the hair-raising experience they'd just had.

Grabbing a couple more towels, she dried Royal's and then Jasper's hair while the men sat quietly downing their drinks. Then Jasper raised his bloodshot eyes to Adeline and announced with a few coughs, "This is certainly not the wedding night you may have imagined. I think more than anything, however, we all need to sleep for a while and then revisit... getting... acquainted."

Royal stood then and let his towel unravel and fall to the floor. He took Adeline by the hand and led her to the huge bed. Jasper followed, also leaving his towel behind in a damp heap. He approached Adeline and kissed her lovingly while

Royal untied her dressing gown. She shivered as Royal drew the robe slowly off her shoulders and encouraged it to flow down her body like a silken river. Her skin suddenly felt more alive than it ever had. Both men smiled at her with shining—though bloodshot—eyes, and Royal kissed her as deeply as Jasper had. Then the men kissed each other with the same hunger and affection. Jasper finally reached over and extinguished the lamp.

As they all piled into the huge bed with its crisp, cool sheets, Adeline was made aware of naked, velvety flesh surrounding her on both sides. The men were hard of muscle and bone and downy with body hair on their chests and legs. It felt wonderful to her to be cocooned between the two people who were the most precious to her. Jasper's warm breath tickled her neck where he nuzzled in, and Royal's arm was draped over her protectively. This was surely heaven. It took less than a minute for each of them to fall asleep. Adeline's last waking thought had been, *Why don't I feel embarrassed? I've never been naked in front of anyone, and yet, this seems completely perfect.*

Only a few hours later, the fierce sunlight forced its way in around the edges of the window shades, and Adeline awoke to the feeling of hands on her body. And, oh, how they felt! Jasper was busily toying with her breast, and Royal was making large circles on her belly, getting closer and closer to an area of her body she'd never paid a lot of attention to. If the sensations had not felt so delicious, she might have been embarrassed, but she found she wanted to purr like a cat and rub against the men instead. When Royal's hand slid down her thigh, she moaned.

"Our queen awakens, Royal," Jasper chuckled with a hoarse rasp. He snuggled closer and began to kiss her neck tenderly.

Adeline wasn't sure of what to do with herself. Her hands were at her sides, and both of them seemed to be touching some very intimate parts of her men's anatomies. Her curiosity got the better of her, and she began to explore. When Royal gave a hiss and Jasper moaned into her ear, she pulled away immediately. "Sorry!"

The men laughed, and Jasper explained, "Never apologize for that, dearest one. Keep doing it. We promise you, we love it."

"And we love *you*," added Royal, sounding as gravelly as if he'd swallowed glass shards. Coughing, he pulled away and climbed out of bed. Then he strode over to the sitting area where he quickly downed a gulp of the now cold tea. "Ah, that's better."

Adeline stared unabashedly at him as he returned to the bed. His body was a sculpted work of art, and she couldn't fill her eyes with him enough. Unlike the Greek statues, Adeline noticed something quite different about his male appendage. Rather than looking like a sweet little twig nestled among the berries, his stood straight out, looking proud and a bit intimidating. It seemed to be at least three times larger than the Greek statues. Adeline blinked. *Oh my. I wonder if he is normal!* she thought to herself.

"He's beautiful, isn't he?" asked Jasper with a twinkle in his eye. "Come here for a second, Roy."

Royal stood beside the bed next to Jasper, who reached out with the hand that was not still stroking Adeline's breast and grabbed Royal by the hip. He caressed the man's thigh and buttock before he wrapped his hand around Royal's immense erection. "He's happy to see us this morning," he chuckled to no one in particular and then proceeded to surprise the dickens out of Adeline. Jasper scooted to the edge of the bed and engulfed the end of Royal's cock with his mouth. Immediately, Royal's head fell back, and he groaned.

Adeline's chin dropped, and her eyes grew wide as she took in the pleasure both men were obviously enjoying with this act of... what exactly, she wasn't certain. She only knew that seeing it made her insides feel funny in a very pleasant way.

Jasper pulled the covers off Adeline and himself and immediately took her hand and carefully wrapped hers around his cock, encouraging her to get the feel of him. *It's as large as Royal's!* she exclaimed to herself. *Maybe those artists didn't know how to draw very well, or Greek men are...* Her thoughts trailed off to nothing as she became aware of both men groaning in ecstasy.

"Enough, Jasper. Addie needs attention now."

"She certainly does, now that we're all awake."

Royal knelt on the bed beside Adeline and bent down to kiss her. "Good morning, my love," he whispered. Then his mouth began exploring her neck, as Jasper became his mirror image on Adeline's other side. Both men's mouths nibbled and licked their way to her breasts where her nipples stood out rosy and hard. The tingles going through her body so far surpassed those she'd felt from the men's kisses up to now; she could hardly believe she was the same person.

Jasper's tongue circled around one nipple, and he suckled the hard bud in and out of his mouth, while Royal nibbled gently at her other breast a few times and then gave her a small bite. She sucked in a deep breath as unexpected desire shot through her like a spear. She squeezed her legs together, for the pleasure in her breasts seemed to be traveling down her body and settling between her legs in a most unusual—and pleasurable—fashion.

Before she knew it, both men had scooted down in the bed, and each gently took hold of one of her legs.

"We want to look at all of you, Adeline," Jasper croaked. "You're so lovely."

Adeline finally succumbed to embarrassment and smashed her eyes closed, turning a bright pink in the process.

Chuckling, Royal crooned at her, "Addie, you're the most beautiful woman I've ever encountered. Don't be shy. Open your eyes and see how much in love with you we are."

She slowly blinked them open, feeling her cheeks burn nevertheless. Both men smiled at her as if they were proud of her. "Incredibly beautiful," Jasper whispered. Then he bent and kissed her hip and then her thigh. By now, Adeline could barely hold still. His soft lips and raspy whiskers were driving her insane with want. She didn't know what to do exactly, but doing nothing was difficult, so she squirmed a little, and her breathing sped up.

"What is it, Addie?" Royal asked with a humorous leer.

"I... need..."

He chuckled at her. "I know the feeling." Slipping a hand between her legs, he slid up into her warmth and grinned, and she moaned. "You're so wonderfully female and wet," he nearly purred with a groan. "Look at her, Jas. She's so ready for some love. Join your hand with mine on her."

Jasper stopped his explorations with his mouth and put his hand to Adeline alongside Royal's hand. Together they stroked her where no one had ever touched her aside from herself in the bath. Shamelessly she raised her knees to allow them better access because this was truly the most incredible feeling she'd had in her life. Adeline knew she was extra sensitive there, but she had no idea what she'd been missing. She felt their fingers stroking up and down on her most intimate parts and thought she might faint dead away from the pleasure, but then... *oh my!*

"Look at how responsive she is, Roy! She must love this, and isn't she as pretty as a peach?" He grabbed Royal's hand —who was nodding and grinning in agreement—and together, they probed and circled a cluster of nerves that made Adeline nearly jump out of her skin.

"What was that?" she asked, panting suddenly.

"It's your clitoris," Jasper explained with a wink. "Just you wait; it's your pleasure center."

"Oh, my stars..." Adeline thought she could barely breathe with the sensations now rolling through her body. "What's happening to me?"

"Relax and enjoy it, Addie. Jasper is going to use his mouth on you, and I'm going to put my finger inside you, and it will feel incredible."

"You're...?" Adeline suddenly felt her insides turn to mush as Jasper's lips and tongue touched her clit. "Jasper!" But then, *oh my glorious stars*, Royal pushed his large index finger against her opening and cautioned her to relax. *Relax?* She could barely remember how. Her breathing sped up, and then suddenly, she felt something hard and warm slide into her body. Royal's finger was *inside her!* And even better, he began pumping in and out while Jasper began to probe her pleasure mound with his firm tongue.

"Damned if she isn't as tight as a vise, Jas! Wait until you feel this. Am I hurting you, Addie?"

"Hurting me?" she laughed. "I should say not! This is the absolute opposite of hurt!"

"Well, some of it's going to hurt a bit, sorry to say. But I don't think it lasts very long. Just relax for now, and enjoy the sensations."

But Adeline wasn't even listening. She was concentrating on a strange building and building inside of her. It wasn't pressure exactly, though her breathing was certainly changing with whatever was taking over her senses. Just as she thought something inside of her was about to detonate into something unknown, Royal gently pushed on Jasper's shoulder and ordered, "Let me have a taste."

Reluctantly, Jasper gave a little suck to Adeline's clit, nearly sending her through the roof, and he was gone. But immediately, Royal's hungry mouth latched on, and she was back on the road to heaven once again as what felt like liquid fire lit her up from the inside. He kept up a completely different rhythm than Jasper had—not better or worse by any means—just his own brand of manipulation. Then he upped his suction to such a degree that Adeline let out a long keening wail and felt her body tipping over some invisible cliff into a place beyond reason. Pleasure that challenged belief washed over her like a tsunami.

With her eyes squeezed shut, Adeline missed the self-satisfied look that passed between the men. She felt her muscles spasm as Royal's finger exited her, only to return immediately locked together with Jasper's equally large index finger. She felt them push inside of her together, eased in by her slickness, but halfway in, they seemed to hit a snag. Jasper crooned to her to stay relaxed as Royal continued his pulsating attention to her clit.

"Stay loose, Adeline. We don't *want* to hurt you, but we're going to. Like Royal said, it won't last long. Here we go." For good measure, Jasper added a second finger along with Royal's, and they gave a big push just as Royal sucked her clit into his mouth one more time.

Adeline bucked and writhed so hard she couldn't tell what was pleasure, what was pain, and what had actually happened. There was a searing, sort of burning sensation that made her cry out, but it was blurred by an intense wash of pleasure that poured through her body at the same time. She knew something profound had just occurred, and her two wonderful husbands had done it for her with love. Her great spasms went on and on still, gradually abating after a minute or so, and Royal finally removed his mouth after kissing her gently. Their joined fingers were still inside her, however, and she could feel herself rhythmically squeezing them with interior muscles she had never known she possessed. The burning feeling began to quell as they gently stroked her from the inside.

Breathing hard, she opened her eyes again and looked at the sweet, caring faces of the men she adored. Jasper looked concerned, and Royal looked a bit smug as they faced each other and wordlessly leaned in for a blistering man-to-man kiss. "Mmm, you taste like Addie," Royal whispered with a small laugh to Jasper.

"That was... transcendent," she breathed finally as they pulled apart. She would never tire of watching her men love each other.

"It was just the beginning," Jasper assured her. He and Royal slowly removed their fingers and examined them. "Not too bad," he announced. "Barely any blood."

"Ohh," said Adeline. "So that's what that was? Taking my virginity together?"

"In a manner of speaking, yes," agreed Jasper. "We've breached your maidenhead, and I'm terribly sorry about the pain, but in truth, you're still a virgin until one of us actually makes love to you. From here on out, the pain ought to be over. Who do you want it to be? Lady's choice, dearest."

Blinking at them, Adeline pondered a moment and then answered, "I don't know. If it could be both of you, that would be ideal, but that wouldn't work. Can you just... surprise me?" They all three burst out laughing at the thought.

Royal sobered first, however, and said, "I have the perfect solution for that if you're serious, Addie. Are you?"

"Of course."

Royal first went to fetch a clean towel and gently cleaned the slightly bloody reminder of her breach. "Am I hurting you?" he asked with concern.

"Not at all," she replied, trying not to feel embarrassed by his scrutiny. Jasper also looked on with rapt attention, smiling fondly at her.

The two men washed their hands, and Royal went to the wardrobe to grab something. Returning, he coaxed Adeline into a standing position next to the bed and tied a cravat snugly over her eyes. "Are you comfortable?" he asked as Jasper chuckled.

"I'm fine. I feel a little silly, though."

Royal patted her bottom and assured her, "You've never looked more beautiful." He kissed her shoulder, making her shiver.

The men stepped away for a moment for a whispered conversation that she could not decipher, and then Adeline could hear their footsteps return to her. She felt the heat of their bodies against her back, and then four hands began to caress her body. They stroked her back, her shoulders, her bottom, and her breasts. They kissed her neck and nibbled her ears, and all the time, that warm feeling within her grew and grew. She now understood it to be some kind of sexual excitement for which she had no name, and she loved it. Silently, the men continued their ministrations on her body as she moaned and hummed her pleasure. Holding still became impossible as she responded to their caresses and rubbed against them like a cat.

One man's hand gently pushed her upper body down so that she was leaning over the bed, where she turned her face to one side and braced her arms on either side of her. The other man wordlessly encouraged her to spread her legs as he stroked her bottom and tapped at her feet with one of his. The only sounds she heard were some heavy breathing and happy-sounding moans coming from her men. She had no idea who was on the right or the left. Even their moans sounded raspy and unlike their normal voices.

Two hands cupped her sex and stroked around and around until she was tingling once again with that incredible, building sensation. Adeline could not help but demand, "More, please!" She heard chuckles behind her but still could not differentiate them. She felt herself becoming moist again, and the men seemed to approve, judging by their satisfied hums.

The hands disappeared, and two warm, blunt male members took their places. One stroked up and down for a moment, and then the other took over as the first retreated. Then the first was back again, and Adeline's breathing sped up. *This is surely the moment!* she thought to herself. But the cocks played this parry and retreat game until she thought she would lose her mind with want. "Please!" she cried finally, and one of them— she had no idea whom—penetrated her entrance at last.

Adeline gave a huge intake of breath as she felt this large, silky-but-hard cock push into her a couple of inches. "Yes!" she breathed. "Finally." But she was to be teased again, for the man retreated, and a different one entered her. She thought, anyway, that it was a different one. *Maybe not? Maybe it was the same man? It doesn't really matter anyway.* But then the game went on and on, each time she was entered a little more deeply until finally one of the men stayed inside her and began thrusting in and out without pulling out all the way. A hand reached around and found her clit, causing her to cry out, "Oh yes!" as he stroked it over and over in time with the organ that was pumping in and out.

The pleasure she felt was like nothing she could have ever imagined. Emotionally, it was even better than the feeling she got when she played her music—but it was like that in some ways. Her heart pounded with so much love and emotion, tears began to gather in her blindfolded eyes.

But then something odd and astounding happened. The hand on her clit retreated, and a different one took over from the other side. She heard the sound of some fumbling around behind her for a moment as the cock inside her stilled, and then both men simultaneously cried out, "Yes!" The pumping in and out of her body immediately took on a new rhythm, and the strength of the motion became more like a pounding— as if it were made by the force of both men at once. *Glorious* pounding that sometimes felt as though a particular thrust reverberated through her like a pump-pump. She felt alive and wanton and nearly insane with the pleasure coursing through her mind and body. Her legs shook, and her heart sped up as she gripped the sheet on the bed. She wanted so badly to touch someone with her hands; this was pleasure that was positively ridiculous and unimaginable to her. *How can a body withstand such an overload of bliss?* Her sensations grew and grew as she felt herself reaching that incredible precipice once again, and then an enormous thrust combined with the nearly pained-sounding cries of her two men—first one and then the other—carried her over the ledge. Her body became suffused with light and pleasure as she shook involuntarily. She joined her men in exclaiming her relief and joy, feeling her muscles contract and release over and over again as if some strange force had taken control of her body.

When her spasms finally stilled, whomever it was who'd entered her slipped out and pulled away. This left her momentarily bereft of warmth and sensation, but that was only fleeting. She could feel a strange warmth dripping down her inner thigh until one of the men carefully cleaned it away. *Was that more blood?* she wondered. Surely there would have been plenty of pain accompanying so much liquid, but there was none. *All I feel is an afterglow of that incredible pleasure.* The other man, who turned out to be Jasper, removed her blindfold and kissed her closed eyes. He stood her up and encouraged her to climb back into the bed.

Her men disappeared for a bit, and Adeline could hear water splashing for a few moments behind the privacy curtain, and then Jasper and Royal sandwiched her in on either side once again.

"I love you so dearly, Adeline," Jasper whispered to her. His voice was still rough and sore sounding from all of the smoke. "Thank you." His eyes fluttered closed as she wondered about all of the things he might mean to thank her for.

On her other side, Royal played with a lock of her hair and nuzzled her behind her ear. Then he cupped her breast and re-iterated, "I love you both more than I ever imagined possible."

Dreamily, Adeline asked, "What was that wonderful rush I felt? It was like nothing in this world."

Jasper kissed her as Royal explained, "It's called a climax, dearest, but if you like, we can call it your golden rush." Both men chuckled softly as she purred with satisfaction. Royal thought of the sack of gold they'd spent on learning how to please her and how it was well worth any price to see her this content.

"I like that," she murmured sleepily. "A golden rush. It *is* beautiful, and it sparkles like gold. Can we do it again?"

Before they knew it, she'd fallen asleep. A couple of more hours went by until they all awoke to a polite knock on the door. It had to be afternoon by now, she mused.

"Someone clearly wants to make sure we're still alive," Royal rasped. He grabbed a discarded towel, wrapped it around his lower body, and made sure his bedmates were modestly covered.

It turned out to be two workers from the kitchen with large trays of food and drinks that they deposited on the sitting-room table. One of them—a woman with steel-gray hair and very few teeth—explained, "Mr. Walter sent this with the mes-sage to stay in bed as long as you like since this's yer honey-moon. But he was sure you all need some grub by now." She dropped into an odd curtsy—or maybe just tripped over her own feet—and sped out the door, blushing a florid crimson shade. The other server—an enormous bear of a man—stood mutely staring first at Royal, then flicking his eyes to the people in bed, and then back to Royal with such a look of longing in his eyes, it was palpable.

After a few seconds, the beldame shot back in and grabbed him by the arm. "Git outta here, you puddin'-head turnip!" she ordered as she yanked him out the door.

"Thank you!" Royal called down the hall to their rapidly retreating forms.

Chapter Twenty-Eight

Jasper's stomach gave a growl as the smell of a delicious meal wafted through the room. He handed Adeline her dressing gown and padded to the wardrobe to find himself and Royal some trousers. Adeline was thrilled they didn't bother with shirts. It was a fine, warm day, after all, and she appreciated the view.

As they sat down to their meal, Royal asked Adeline, "Are you feeling alright, and do you have any questions?'

Giving him a sweet smile, she answered, "I feel alive and wonderful actually, and I do have a question."

"Thought you might," rasped Jasper.

Adeline looked thoughtful as a blush tinted her cheeks a lovely pink. She nibbled at a piece of toast for a moment and finally blurted out, "I felt one person inside me, but it seemed there was a kind of an echo as if both of you were controlling the... movement."

"Very insightful," Jasper answered with a smile. "Our wife is as clever as she is beautiful, but we knew that, didn't we, Royal?" Royal nodded with a wink as he shoveled food into his mouth. He was famished.

Jasper took a swallow of his hot coffee and explained, "One of us had the honor of being inside of you, but the actual process of making love to you—the speed and the rhythm— was dictated by the other of us who was inside the man who was inside you. Does that make sense?"

Adeline pondered that for a moment and then surprised them by saying, "I would very much like to see that the next time." As she did, she squirmed almost imperceptibly in her seat. The idea was heating her up all over again.

"We can certainly accommodate you, Addie," laughed Royal, who'd paused eating long enough to pile more food onto his plate.

Beaming at her, Jasper said, "Nothing would make us happier. Now eat up before Royal gulps down every last bit of this meal they sent us."

"No more blindfold, please. I enjoy the sight of you both far too much to be deprived of that." Adeline sipped some coffee and then continued, "I know I said to surprise me, and you did a perfect job of it. But I... um... have so much to learn."

"We all do, Adeline. None of us has ever done this with two lovers before."

Royal gave a funny cough, and they both stared at him. He swallowed and laughed, eventually able to explain, "Well, there was this one time in Pennsylvania I was offered a place to sleep by two sisters... I've never had a night like that again!" He closed his eyes and gave a comical shake of his head as if remembering the good times.

"Royal!" Adeline huffed at him with a giggle.

"I'm just joking, Addie. Relax. I never did that."

"I have no say over your past, Royal. If it had happened, that would be fine. It is just difficult to comprehend, I suppose. And it's even stranger to call that odd, given my situation with the both of you."

"It sounds like fun to me," laughed Jasper and then coughed. "Anyway, my point is—before Royal sidetracked us with his fantasies—that we all have to learn how to make our physical relationship work for each of us."

"Well, I'm up for some experimentation if you think we need to explore some more." Royal winked at them. "Addie?"

"Yes, please."

Unfortunately, before they could have any more fun—or finish their breakfast—there was another knock at the door. This time it was Walter, looking terribly apologetic. "I'm so sorry, everyone. I would never have thought to disturb you today of all days, but we have a... situation."

All three of them stared in alarm at Walter, who cleared his throat. "There is a gentlema... er... a *man* downstairs who insists he needs to see Adeline and is telling everyone within earshot that she is betrothed to him according to her father's wishes. He is even carrying some kind of letter that he's been waving around under our noses. He says it's proof."

"Ridiculous," huffed Adeline at the same time that Royal scoffed, and Jasper spluttered, "Balderdash!"

Then Jasper conceded, "I suppose we all better get dressed and go see what this man is about. It's the only way we'll get rid of him, I'm afraid. We don't want him continually bothering everyone here."

Fifteen minutes later and respectably attired, the three of them descended the stairs and found the rest of their partners in the parlor glaring—unsurprisingly—at none other than Captain Greely.

Adeline groaned and whispered, "I thought he'd left by now! Wasn't he supposed to sail back to Boston?" Then she raised her voice and addressed the man in question. "Good day to you, Captain. Still here, I see."

Jasper's face took on an angry expression as he asked, "What do you want this time, Greely? Do we need to have you tossed out again?"

Adeline's eyes went swiftly to Jasper's, and she looked at him questioningly. "You've tossed him out?" she asked.

Royal stepped up and announced, "He was caught cheating, and he's lucky he wasn't stabbed or shot. We probably saved his miserable hide. Serious gamblers who know what they're doing don't take kindly to cheaters."

"Untrue!" shouted Greely and then seemed to gather his wits. "Anyway, it's beside the point. I have come to fetch my betrothed because I have decided to stay in San Francisco after all since she loves it so much. See? I can compromise! And I have proof this time of her father's wishes in the form of this document that he left with me on the Wind Gypsy. I apologize for not having it with me the last time I called."

Adeline gave a decidedly unladylike snort and asked, "You term coming here and making ridiculous demands, insulting me and smelling up the hotel like a pigsty 'calling?' You are sorely mistaken, *Greely*!"

"*Captain* Greely to you, miss. Your father would be appalled at your behavior," he huffed. Then he muttered something under his breath about her needing a "firm hand."

Laughing, Royal asked, "There you go again, sweet-talking the lady. Have you no sense whatsoever, Cap'n?" He shook his head as if sad for the man. "What is this about proof?" He looked at Jasper, who rolled his eyes.

Greely had a soiled piece of folded paper in his hand that he waved in Royal's face. "Here it is," he said in an oily, smug tone. "Her father and I wrote this up together when we were off the coast of Chile. I had it locked in my trunk for safekeeping all this time."

Royal calmly took the piece of paper, glanced at it, and handed it to Adeline.

She frowned at it and asked Greely, "Who signed this paper?"

Rocking up and down on his toes and puffing out his chest, Greely answered, "Well, clearly I signed it and your dear, departed father signed it. That is, he signed it before he departed, obviously. And I must add, the sea was terribly rough that day —not the best conditions for writing neatly."

Adeline pursed her lips and nodded. "I see." She handed the paper to Jasper, who burst out laughing, much to Greely's astonishment and anger.

"*Captain* Greely," she said patiently as if to a child. "The next time you try to make a false claim, perhaps you ought to try a bit harder. My father may have been in compromised health, and I can personally attest to the challenges a rocking ship causes to one who writes, but he surely would have remembered how to *spell his own name*. Hart is not spelled with an E in the middle like the organ in your chest. Believe it or not, Father was aware of that, and this is a common misspelling he no doubt had to contend with his whole life. So, I don't know whom you persuaded to forge his signature, but they did a poor job of it. And you failed to take note of it, so more's the pity."

Greely's face turned purple, and he opened his mouth undoubtedly to say something vile when Adeline stopped him in his tracks by announcing, "Furthermore, you are too late, for I am already married. And, I might add, blissfully happy. So, it's time for you to run along. Again."

Jasper called some of his hired guards into the room and ordered loudly and clearly, "Escort this man off the premises immediately."

Greely struggled and writhed as two strong men grabbed him unceremoniously by the arms and dragged him out the door. He shouted vile threats that made Adeline's cheeks burn, calling her names and hurling insults at her. When he was finally out of earshot, she looked at her husbands and deadpanned, "Such a pleasant, charming man. Perhaps I should have considered his offer months ago." Then she lifted her skirts delicately and trotted up the stairs laughing over her shoulder, "Coming, husbands?"

Jasper followed immediately, but Royal said, "Just a moment." He ducked into the kitchen and reappeared with a strange little bottle in his hand that he carried up the stairs.

After entering the room, they watched as Jasper produced the fake document from Greely that he'd stuffed into his pocket. Jasper momentarily turned up the flame on one of the kerosene table lamps and held the edge of the paper over the lamp chimney until it ignited. Then he carried the burning paper over to the fireplace and deposited it in the grate where it quickly flared up, burned out, and became nothing but a small bit of ash.

"Now we can forget about that man completely," he told them with a smile. "I just wish he were going back to Boston and leaving us alone, but it appears he must have lost the position as captain that he was counting on."

"My thought exactly," said Royal. "He is now forgotten."

The three of them finally polished off the rest of their meal, and Adeline announced, "I think it would be lovely to *lie down* for a while. I find myself quite in need of repose." She winked at them and headed toward the bed as she began to unbutton her blouse.

Jasper and Royal stacked their dishes onto the trays and set them outside the door in the hallway. They reentered the room and locked the door firmly as Jasper muttered, "No more interruptions!" Turning to Adeline, he smiled and said, "Take off your clothes, beloved."

"I am. But will the two of you do something for me?" she asked softly.

"Anything," Jasper replied. "What do you need?"

"I want to see how the two of you love each other."

"Well! Are you feeling a bit adventurous, dearest?" asked Jasper with a soft chuckle.

Royal began to untuck his shirt.

Adeline merely stared at Jasper. She smiled angelically and raised her eyebrows.

After they stripped down to nothing, the men reached for each other. They kissed deeply with their bodies smashed together.

Adeline sighed, thinking, *They are so beautiful like that.* She proceeded to discard more of her clothing and made herself comfortable on the bed with pillows propping herself up for a good view. With her knees raised, she offered the men a tantalizing view, but for now, they concentrated on each other.

The men kissed and reached for each other's erections, stroking and pumping them with increasing force.

Royal sneaked a glance at Adeline and smiled. He pulled away long enough to tell her, "Use your fingers on yourself, the same way we did. It will feel wonderful while you watch us." Then he stepped away from Jasper completely and walked to the bedside table, where he grabbed the bottle he'd carried upstairs. With a pleased smile, he said to Jasper, "This is olive oil. According to Walter, it was a favorite of the ancient Greeks. And you know how much the man likes to learn *important* facts. Anyway, it's supposed to be far better than spit."

Adeline looked confused, but Jasper leered at him, saying, "That sounds promising. Now turn sideways so Adeline can watch." He took the bottle from Royal and unstoppered it, pouring a small amount into his palm. He dipped his index finger into the puddle of oil and told Royal, "Spread 'em."

Royal sighed happily and grabbed his buttocks, stepping his feet apart at the same time.

Jasper began to paint Royal's puckered entrance with oil, dipping his finger into his other hand to reload every so often. His finger went round and round for a while, then began to dip inside, causing Royal to moan happily. His finger entered deeper and deeper each time, and then he added a second finger. Royal stiffened a little, so Jasper poured a bit more oil out and liberally greased up both fingers this time.

"Yes," whispered Royal. "That's it. Feels so good." He didn't seem to be able to keep his eyes open for a moment, but then he commanded in a voice that broke with emotion, "I'm ready."

Jasper pulled away long enough to generously lubricate his erection and suddenly burst out laughing.

Adeline stopped what she was doing, and Royal turned around to look at him.

"Sorry, sorry," Jasper explained. "It just occurred to me that I am 'anointing my head with oil.'" He continued to laugh at his joke.

"Sacrilege." laughed Adeline.

"Get on with it. I need *comfort from your rod*—or is it your staff?" Royal demanded with a chortle.

That just made Jasper laugh harder, but then his throat seemed to give out, and he coughed for a moment. "Sorry, I'll be good now," he promised.

"You're always good," Royal assured him. "Now do it before Addie falls asleep."

"Not a chance," Adeline said with a quiet laugh. She had taken Royal's suggestion and was curiously fingering herself. It was a new experience, so it took some experimentation and investigation. She discovered she liked to put two fingers onto what Jasper had called her "pleasure center." She sighed with delight as her body seemed to heat up from the inside out. It was interesting to her to feel her intimate parts become slick the more she watched the men and touched herself.

"Ready?" asked Jasper.

With an impatient moan, Royal insisted, "Do it!"

Ever so carefully, Jasper began probing Royal's backside with his shiny, oily erection. Adeline was so spellbound she momentarily forgot to diddle herself. She loved the sight of

Royal and Jasper's faces as they seemed to be transported with pleasure. "Oh, my stars," she whispered.

Once Jasper entered Royal all the way, Royal opened his eyes. He appeared almost pleasure drunk as Jasper slowly began to thrust in and out of him. Jasper had a firm grasp on Royal's hip with one hand, and his other reached around and grasped Royal's cock. "Yessss," hissed Royal. Then he said, "Addie, move over toward the end of the bed here. I need to be inside you. Let me fuck you."

Adeline gave a gasp at the crude word, but at the same time, she felt liberated and excited by it. She immediately complied and scooted to the edge of the bed.

The men turned to face her, and together they made their way to her—looking like some four-legged creature the way they were joined.

Royal bent over and kissed right where Adeline's fingers had been playing. She grasped his head with a shout of, "Yes!" and used her other hand to pinch her own nipple.

Royal's tongue went stiff as he vibrated it against her sensitive clit. Over and over, he alternated sucking it into his mouth and probing it. He slipped one of his hands beneath his chin and slid two fingers roughly into her.

Adeline's sharp intake of breath whooshed out of her in a moan.

Royal pulled his face away and told Jasper, "She's positively soaked. Apparently, she loves the show." Then he groaned with his own pleasure as Jasper thrust into him extra hard.

"Please," Adeline moaned. "More!"

Within moments, she was shaking from head to toe with pleasure so bone-crackingly sharp and delightful, she thought she might die from it. Never could she have imagined this. But then Royal pulled his face away from her and raised his upper body. Jasper was still entering and retreating from Royal's ass, and he was still busily pumping Royal's willy in front.

Adeline thought she could hear Jasper's balls smacking Royal with each thrust. *This view is spectacular, but what I wouldn't give for some strategically positioned mirrors right now. I wonder if one ever faints from sheer pleasure!*

"I'm sure we won't need any of that oil for this," Royal announced as he gently removed Jasper's hand and lined himself up with Adeline's opening. As Jasper gave a mighty thrust from behind, Royal impaled her in one long shove.

"Ohhh," breathed Adeline. "Yes. This is so much better now that I can see you both!" She then gulped as Royal slung an arm under her leg and hoisted it up in the air. She looked at him questioningly.

"Better access," Royal explained with a satisfied smile. He put a finger from his other hand into his mouth. She watched as his slick finger disappeared from her view and shuddered when she felt it probing her bottom. She'd certainly never imagined this!

"That's um...!" She had no words for it.

"Are you alright?" asked Jasper.

"Yesssss!" She shuddered as a long digit penetrated her. "I see why you like this," she exclaimed. It's so... more!" It seemed to Adeline that a whole world of pleasure had invaded her body.

"You're both so perfect," growled Jasper as beads of sweat broke out on his forehead. He had a firm grip on Royal's hips and began kissing his shoulders. Kisses morphed into nibbles, and as his thrust grew in intensity, he finally bit the back of Royal's neck. A low, growling moan poured out of Jasper as he filled Royal with liquid heat.

Royal shuddered through Jasper's release, fighting to keep his own from happening too quickly. "I. Love. You. Both. So. Much!" he bit out with each mighty shove he made into Adeline.

Adeline fought to keep her eyes open and became aware that Jasper had removed himself from Royal and was now leaning over her to kiss her breast and play with her nipples. *More pleasure! Is the rush like this for everyone?* she wondered.

As Adeline stiffened and began to shake with her incredible release, Royal upped his rhythm to an even greater degree and shouted "Yes!" as his seed poured into her.

Jasper turned to look at him, and they both grinned like drunken babies at each other.

This was definitely more than they had ever expected.

Life was perfect at last.

Chapter Twenty-Nine

Greely still planned to get back to the east coast and wanted Adeline to go with him, no matter what. She would cook for him and warm his bed, and life on the sea would be perfect. He'd wanted her so badly on the trip to San Francisco, but her confounded father had thwarted his attempt to get closer to the woman. So, he'd played along and befriended the man instead. That hadn't been too bad. The old guy was entertaining enough. But when that horrible sailor had actually touched what he thought of as *his* Adeline, Greely made sure the man was disposed of immediately. Good thing the sailor had been knocked out, or it may have been harder to manage.

Greely had the same problem many ship's captains had in San Francisco—their men abandoned them, and they had no one to work for them. He had what was left of his ship, but he desperately needed a crew. There was no one paying his way either—that had been a lie. All of the potential sailors had taken off to prospect for gold, not even collecting their wages—they were so anxious to get to mining. No one wanted to go through another dangerous voyage. The ships in the harbor, including the Wind Gypsy, were so stripped down they were barely seaworthy anyway. They looked like death traps.

Greely spent so much of his time drunk that when he plotted and planned, his ideas made complete sense to him but were not always well thought out. His frustration grew and festered in his mind and his gut, and he was becoming desperate to accomplish something. That was why he'd concocted the false paper he'd shoved in Adeline's face. It had seemed brilliant at the time. His face burned with embarrassment as he remembered her laughter when his fakery was revealed.

Since he spent so much time wandering around San Francisco's many saloons and gambling halls, Greely heard things. There were rumors about the Sydney Ducks that ought to have been frightening, but he saw the Ducks as men of influence and power rather than wretched criminals. He finally decided he needed to learn from them without getting himself into any trouble, so he quietly began asking around. The name he heard over and over was Boolie Bollinger.

Boolie Bollinger—a sly, odd-looking man—saw himself as something special and dressed in fashionable clothing, unlike many of the Sydney Ducks. He had a lucrative life of crime in the city, organizing the looting of houses and setting fires to his enemies' homes and businesses. So, he could afford incredible niceties that he'd never had as a convict and would take his pick from the stolen goods before letting his underlings have the rest. If anyone argued with him, he shot them.

He liked to hobnob with the elite of San Francisco whenever possible and could often be found gambling in The Discovery. He always bought the most expensive whiskey and smoked the finest cigars. He loved the atmosphere of the hotel and its casino. Being there made him feel like everyone knew of his importance. The fact was, the vast majority of those around him didn't give a damn. They were all there for the gambling and the entertainment.

The only exceptions to that were the city officials, who might have protested his presence if it weren't for the large sums of money he paid them regularly. His criminal escapades were ignored, thanks to his generosity and goodwill.

Chapter Thirty

Throughout 1850, San Francisco went through many changes. The influx of hopeful prospectors continued, but little by little, more women and whole families began showing up by sea. Although it was becoming more common to see petticoats on the streets, the ratio of men to women was still lopsided.

Men still craved the companionship of women to such a degree that just seeing a woman or some feminine object was an exciting event. Lonely miners paid in gold for such mundane items as a woman's shoe or a piece of clothing just so they could handle it and look at it. One enterprising "landlord" who rented out boarding space on a ship placed lacy, feminine laundry where it was visible to make prospective tenants believe women lived there. It was just false advertising, but it worked.

The autumn rainy season hit, turning the streets into a dangerous quagmire once again, and no matter what they poured into the muck, nothing helped. The streets turned into mud so deep it threatened to engulf anyone foolish enough to try to navigate them by foot. Several attempts to create impromptu sidewalks did very little to alleviate the problem. All manner of refuse was cast out into the streets—tree branches, boards, sails, broken furniture, and in one famous case, a grand piano. Residents told tales of the time when horses and wagons were swallowed up in the mire. None of their stopgap measures did a thing to permanently fix the mud situation.

One afternoon, Walter returned from attempting to run an errand and told everyone, "I watched workers try to erect pilings in the ground so they could build a street over the mud. The pilings were twenty feet long, and one just sank straight down out of sight! Then they tried to bore another one into the ground right on top of the first, and it sunk too. Forty feet of mud, at least! Unbelievable. We need to do something. People are throwing anything they can find out into the streets just so they can return to their houses. Nothing works, and these streets are so steep, it's horribly dangerous."

San Francisco suffered from two distinct problems that perpetuated this situation: its population increased enormously in a short time, with no budget for city planning or repairs, and there were almost no workers who were willing to do the manual labor required to improve things. Most of the able-bodied men who arrived in San Francisco left immediately for the gold fields, not caring to earn laborer wages when the promise of gold was so tempting.

So, it was considered a great improvement when the town finally managed to build a series of raised wooden sidewalks along the business district's streets. It was wonderful for a while—until once again, the city burned, and the raised wooden sidewalks went up like rows of matches, helped along most horribly by the air beneath them.

Jasper, Royal, and Adeline grew closer as the weeks passed. The men were delighted with their situation now that they had each other as well as the woman they both adored.

However, Adeline—blissfully happy though she was—began to suffer from exhaustion. Teaching, entertaining late into the night, and keeping up with her husbands even *later* into the night was taking a toll.

She and Isaac had a wonderful time with their little music school and planned for their students to give a recital. This gave Jasper a great idea for how he could lighten Adeline's responsibilities.

"Let's use our stage for plays and other entertainers," he suggested one day. The idea took hold and became an instant success. Now Adeline and Isaac were finally able to relax some evenings and turn over the stage to others. The patrons were still fabulously entertained by visiting singers, actors and other musicians who appreciated the attention and the pay.

Adeline had never complained of being too tired, but her men privately knew she must need more sleep. They'd caught her yawning and rubbing her eyes too many times. Now that she was more refreshed, they worried less about how their nights were filled with excitement and enthusiastic experimentation. Adeline surprised her men now and then when she came up with a new idea for them to try, and they all embraced her suggestions with zeal.

One such night was so memorable they recreated it on a minimum of a weekly basis.

Adeline lay in bed between the two men and had just performed a thorough examination of both of their penises—all in the spirit of education—though she'd also tried out different kinds of oral exploration on them as well. "These are quite fascinating the way they wax and wane, you know," she said with a giggle. "Soft, then hard. Wrinkled, then smooth. It's rather a miracle. And these..." she cupped Jasper's testicles in her hand as he sucked in a breath.

"Careful, sweetheart. You need to treat those with care."

"Really? Why is that?" She found them somewhat humorous, not that she'd ever say so. They were just so... dangly and hairy.

Royal peered over her shoulder and explained, "They're very sensitive to pain."

Adeline let go of Jasper's balls and turned her attention to telling them what was on her mind. "I'm curious to know what it feels like," she ventured, "to have two men at the same time. I've heard it's possible and quite... stimulating." She shivered, thinking about what it was like to have Royal inside her with his cock and his finger in her bottom and how much she'd loved it. This surely had to be even better.

"Where on earth did you hear about that, sweetheart?" asked Jasper with a quizzical look. He couldn't imagine.

"Oh..." she answered vaguely. "From... a friend. It's not important."

Shrugging it off because they were more interested in getting to the deed itself than ferreting out the source of information, the men smiled at each other knowingly. They remembered their earlier fantasy about just this particular act. Quickly, the delighted men produced the bottle of olive oil and pulled the covers off Adeline. They flipped her over and started kissing and stroking her shapely bottom to the sound of her soft laughter. She calmed down and grew serious, however, when they put a pillow beneath her hips and spread her legs.

"Look at our beautiful wife, Jas. She's so perfect. Don't you just love her dimples?" He kissed one. "And her little pucker here?" He stroked her gently with a well-oiled finger. Adeline could then feel Jasper's hand join Royal's. With soft words of adoration, they took their time circling and probing her with their fingers. "We'll make sure this is good for you, Addie," he assured her. "We need to take it slowly." He snorted then and shoulder-bumped Jasper, saying, "Sometimes our husband gets a little *eager*."

Jasper rolled his eyes and shook his head good-naturedly.

Adeline waffled between total embarrassment and tingling excitement as the men explored and played with her bottom.

They made sure one of them simultaneously kept contact with her clit, exactly as they'd been instructed so ably by Louis Montrachet—whom they'd privately come to think of as the Patron Saint of Adeline's Golden Rush. Adeline's tingles won out over her embarrassment. Her breath hitched, and she couldn't hold back her whimpers.

Finally deciding she was ready after many kisses and lots of gentle play, Jasper lay back on the bed and encouraged Adeline to lower herself onto his lap, facing away from him. Ever so slowly, he breached her backside, and they shivered as Adeline moaned in surprise and pleasure, "Jasper! Oh, yes." Jasper was so excited he had to force himself not to explode. He and Royal were spellbound as they watched him disappear inside of her.

Kneeling beside them, Royal stroked himself absently as he watched—and then had to squeeze hard so that he didn't lose it before getting inside of her too.

As Royal maneuvered around and carefully entered Adeline from the front, she clung to him with a surprised expression. Relaxing, she stared deeply into Royal's eyes, seeing the love there and projecting her own trust and devotion.

"This is amazing, Roy. I can feel you rubbing against me inside of Adeline," Jasper groaned. "I thought this would be good, but I had no idea just how incredible. Are you doing alright, Adeline?"

She merely moaned and nodded—she was so overcome with these new sensations. This fullness was almost too much—but not. More like perfection, she decided.

All three of them were bowled over with the feeling of the two cocks sliding together, separated only by a thin barrier. Jasper also kept up a firm pressure on her clit with his hand as they alternated kissing Adeline and kissing each other.

The room filled with gasps and groans of rapturous pleasure as the tempo of their thrusts increased. Faster and faster,

Royal pumped into her, stroking along Jasper's hard shaft, and Jasper prodded and pulsated Adeline's clitoris harder and harder as he stayed buried deep within her. Finally, Adeline trembled and shook with her release, keening in bliss as she clung to Royal, and one after the other, the men spilled inside her. When it was complete, they remained tightly locked together in each other's arms. No one wanted to break what felt like a dream. And they didn't—until gravity finally took over, causing them to slide out.

After they'd all cleaned up and retired to the sitting room for a drink by the fire—without a stitch on because doing so felt reckless and decadent—Adeline came up with another suggestion.

"I think each of us enjoys being in the middle of our triangular lovemaking, wouldn't you both agree?" Royal winked and nodded, and Jasper smiled and gave an affirmative groan. "In that case, I think we should make a game of it," she finished.

With raised eyebrows, the men blinked at her, loving her mischievous nature. "Game?" asked Jasper.

Adeline rose and went to a drawer in the bedside table. They watched her hips sway and admired her adorably dimpled bottom as she sashayed away from them. Equally entranced by her shapely breasts as she returned, they scarcely breathed. She sat between them on the settee, and they both immediately began stroking her soft skin up and down her body.

Adeline produced a deck of cards that she'd swiped from their casino. "I propose a game called 'Middleman,'" she laughed. "We shuffle the deck, and each of us draws a card. Whoever is holding the middle card gets to be in the middle."

"Genius," Royal answered with a laugh.

"I love it," chuckled Jasper.

And so, it began that the three of them played "Middleman" whenever someone felt especially lucky.

No one ever considered themselves a loser... no matter what happened.

Chapter Thirty-One

Adeline Hart Dawson-Langley's Journal

October 31, 1850

Months have passed since I last put pen to paper, and I have missed it. My life is full in many ways I never dreamed possible, and each day is an education. Our young music students are a challenge and a joy, and I am so proud of their progress. My husbands are an even larger source of joy, of course.

The men were right. No one has so much as batted an eyelash at our marriage. Such is the life in this city.

Last month, California joined the United States as its thirty-first state, and we San Franciscans celebrated two days ago with incredible fanfare. We had parades and dignitary speeches—one of them was by the U.S. Supreme Court Chief Justice Nathaniel Bennett. A military regiment gave a thirty-one-gun salute in the Plaza, and later there was a magnificent fireworks display. The city was lit up all around by large bonfires, which was a stunning sight to behold. Best of all, we attended a fantastic ball that night. Madame Beaufort designed a gown for me that I simply adored. I've never felt so fashionable and elegant in my life. I even danced... and enjoyed it. But who would not have with two such handsome and attentive partners?

Speaking of Madame, she has been an interesting confidante and source of advice. Sometimes it feels good to unburden my doubts and worries on a sympathetic female ear, and my friend Olivia is still an inexperienced young woman who has not wed and therefore would not be the best one for advice. I love my husbands so dearly, but they are as new to this arrangement as I, even though they were more experienced—Jasper having been married previously, and Royal probably had lovely young women flocking around him since he was a boy. He is just so charismatic and beautiful, both inside and out. If I were to have met either of them and married one, I would have felt blessed, but to have both of them, knowing they also love each other... I can barely describe the joy and satisfaction this brings to me. It's not as if we never quarrel. To say that would be unrealistic as well as untrue. However, we each try to be fair to one another at all times. And the love I feel is immeasurable.

But back to Madame. She is a beautiful, worldly woman whose English is impeccable, though charmingly accented, and was tragically widowed at a young age. I feel certain she is somewhere in her early to mid-thirties. She determined that coming to California would be good for both her dress design business and her broken heart. Frankly, I wonder if she has her eye on our Walter. She could have her pick of anyone in this city with her beauty and intelligence, and he might be an excellent match for her. I understand that the men here find the

French ladies in town exotic. Sadly for the women, many are prostitutes, but they make a seriously good living at it. That's at least some compensation for what must be a difficult existence.

Madame explained to me rather dispassionately that she and her beloved husband used to take lovers into their bed now and then for extra excitement. As if it were a normal, everyday occurrence! (I should not be shocked, for look at my own marriage, but sometimes Puritanical thoughts still pop into my brain.) Lovers of either sex, apparently, and by mutual agreement. She has explained several, shall we say... "techniques" in most graphic terminology that she says the French are accustomed to. When I brought these ideas into our marital bed, my husbands were elated. We have tried things I would never have imagined, and we have invented a few ideas of our own after trying her suggestions. Some of the activities make me blush to think about, but the ecstasy! I have one more suggestion that I will bring up at the next convenient opportunity. Madame said she was waiting to tell me about this one because she feared at first she might shock me too much, so this is something that is... oh my... I don't know how to word my curiosity and excitement. I hope the men are willing to try it. Since it supposedly benefits them greatly, I cannot imagine that they would balk at it. It would be another version of the game we play that includes a deck of cards and chance. I shall need to come up with a new name for this, although it will not require the cards.

Chapter Thirty-Two

One night soon after Adeline's journal entry, they had a visiting troupe of actors perform an original comedy on the stage of The Discovery. The house was packed, and people laughed throughout the production from beginning to end. The evening was a joyous respite for miners, who were exhausted from trying to eke out a living from the dwindling supply of gold left in the ground, and the locals, who were reeling from yet another fire that had demolished a small part of the city once again.

Adeline, Royal, and Jasper were relaxed and in high spirits once the play ended, leaving the saloon as soon as they were able to get away. They retired upstairs with eager looks at each other.

Adeline had an especially mischievous look on her face that caused Royal to ask, "Does our beloved wife have something she wishes to tell us?"

"I might. That is if you both want to try something new and exciting." She chuckled softly at their raised eyebrows and avid expressions. "I may have a suggestion for an activity that was recently brought to my attention."

"I knew asking Madame Beaufort to move in was a great idea," Jasper said with a laugh.

With a mock gasp, Adeline asked, "How do you know this came from her?"

"Really, Adeline? Who else do you spend time with privately who could possibly be filling your head with such tantalizing notions? Isaac? Hardly. He might confer with you on your music, but nothing as delightful as the ideas she's given you."

"I see your point. Just please don't make her feel uncomfortable for confiding in me."

Royal snorted then, laughing. "We'd *never* do that. The woman is a godsend. She dresses you like royalty and makes the most delicious ideas come out of your head." He moved in to kiss her and added, "Out with it, woman. What's on your mind?"

Taking a fortifying breath, Adeline sat down in front of the fire, surrounded by her husbands. She looked at Royal and then Jasper and said, "Madame says the most exciting thing she and her dear, departed husband ever did was to share her with another man."

"We do that every night," Royal pointed out. "So?"

"That's not all, Royal. She meant that the two men... penetrated her at the same time."

This time it was Jasper who asked, "Again, we do that often, and it's wonderful for all of us, but it's not new. Is there something else?"

"She did not mean one man in front and one man behind, although that is the physical position it would have to take to accomplish this act, I understand." She took another deep breath and squirmed a little. "She says it is possible for both men to penetrate the woman in the *same place* at the same time." Now her words came tumbling out. "She said the men especially loved it because their members rubbed deliciously against each other while being held in place with the woman's tight muscles. It takes a bit of effort and care, but it sounds exciting to me." Blushing, she looked down.

"Well!" exclaimed Jasper as Royal blew out a surprised breath. "I've never heard of that, but if you don't think it would be painful for you, Adeline, it certainly sounds... titillating."

"I think you'll want to use plenty of that olive oil and proceed carefully, but I... um... want to try it!"

Royal kissed her, kissed Jasper, and exclaimed, "Let's do it!"

"Now?" Adeline batted her eyelashes at them and then shivered. She could already feel desire coursing through her, along with a tiny bit of anxiety. The nervousness caused her excitement to increase with a sharp edge to it. When the men indicated their agreement by ripping off their clothes like their pants were on fire, she added, "Madame said to be sure that I have at least one climax before attempting this kind of penetration." Adeline slowly began to disrobe. "I need to be utterly relaxed. So, I will leave that part up to you, gentlemen." Then as an afterthought, she added, "I used to think that Madame was sweet on Walter, but yesterday I saw that man you call Doc Louis exiting her room at an odd time. Did you know about that?"

Jasper laughed and answered, "No, but they make an interesting pair, for sure. Good for them. Then again, maybe they just wanted to speak French for a while."

Royal snorted and exclaimed, "Of course! That's it. Maybe they were discussing French politics. Or more likely... she needed some *medical attention.*"

For some reason that Adeline couldn't fathom, that comment made both men burst out laughing. "Well, I certainly hope that Madame is well," she said in a worried tone. "The alternative would be terrible. And it's not funny! Is Louis really a doctor?"

Jasper stopped his guffaws long enough to look contrite. "Yes, he was a physician in France and is starting up his practice here in San Francisco. Please don't worry about Madame Beaufort, Adeline. I'm sure she's fine, and it was a *social* call."

Royal moved next to Adeline in all of his naked glory and began kissing her neck, murmuring, "Here, let us help you with all of those buttons, dearest. You're too slow."

"It's not my fault," she pouted. "Take it up with Madame and her fashion sense. Ooh, careful!" By now, both men were attempting to get her out of her layers of garments as quickly as possible. It seemed as though there were buttons and ties everywhere.

"Women wear entirely too many clothes," Jasper grumbled. He pulled her dress off and beheld her in her layers of undergarments, shaking his head. Letting the petticoats fall to the floor, they regarded her in her bloomers and chemise. Not wishing to wait a moment longer, he slid his hand between her legs and discovered how wet she was already, just thinking about what they were planning to do.

"At least your bloomers are practical and offer access to your body nicely." Jasper's hand fit nicely through the slit in her garment, so he took full advantage and stroked her damp flesh. He immediately located her clit and began to play with it.

Royal continued getting rid of her light undergarments as Jasper growled with pleasure, and Adeline sighed and writhed against him.

When she was at last divested of every stitch, they settled her onto the bed, and Royal placed the bottle of oil on the nearby table. "I have an idea of how to do this," he said softly. They looked at him expectantly, so he continued, "Lie back, Jasper, but prop yourself up with pillows so you can see. Addie, you sit on his lap facing me with your legs spread." They crawled into position. "There you go, yes, that's right. Now get comfortable and lean back onto Jasper's chest." Adeline's juices sparkled in the lamplight, and Royal licked his lips. Straddling Jasper's legs, he knelt down and gave her a kiss between her legs.

Adeline immediately groaned with pleasure, and Royal began to probe her pleasure center with a firm tongue. Round and round her nub he licked and sucked, making her take in a deep breath and stiffen her body. Just as it seemed as though she might be heading over the edge with delight, he pulled his mouth away. "Be sure to watch, Addie," he ordered. Jasper's cock was already as rigid as a post, and Royal sucked it into his mouth.

Jasper and Adeline's moans of pleasure joined in a chorus of heavy breathing and humming with ecstasy. "Oh, my stars," Adeline whispered. "That's a beautiful sight, Royal. I love seeing how much you love Jasper."

Jasper couldn't hold still, and even with Adeline sitting on him, he writhed and pumped into Royal's eager mouth. Royal's cheeks hollowed out as he sucked, all the time using one hand to pump the base of Jasper's rod. "You need to stop, Roy!" Jasper finally croaked out. "I don't want this to be over too soon."

Royal's mouth popped off Jasper, and with a pleased look on his face, he went back to playing with Adeline using his mouth and fingers. This time it took just seconds before she cried out, "Yes! Ohh, yess..." and shook with a mighty release. "So beautiful." She was still shaking when Royal grabbed the bottle of oil and generously greased up Jasper's cock.

Jasper couldn't hold back his groans as Royal carefully fed him into Adeline. It was already a tight fit once Jasper was all the way in, so Royal worried that he'd hurt Adeline if he got in there too. His body tensed with concern.

As if she sensed his reluctance, Adeline pointed out, "You know a woman's body expands tremendously when she's giving birth, Royal. This works. I've been assured. You'll fit if we're patient."

Royal had a most unwelcome vision of all the calves he'd seen born on his family's farm and knew she was correct. He had to shake himself mentally to get back into the mood. He watched Adeline rise up and down on Jasper's shaft and then sat up and kissed both of them, then kissed his way down to Adeline's beautiful breasts, sucking on first one and then the other. He was rewarded by a long, happy purr from her.

Deciding all was well, Royal took his oily finger and stroked around Adeline's opening. Slowly he invaded the space and was gratified to think that he was stimulating her tender flesh as well as Jasper's shaft simultaneously. The idea excited him, causing his cock to ooze. He was so hard, it nearly hurt.

Jasper whispered, "That feels so good. I can't wait, Roy. Make love to both of us at the same time. Please."

Feeling Adeline's body relax a fraction, Royal introduced a second finger. Her muscles were still slightly spasming from her recent rush, and this made him even more excited. He began to pump his fingers in and out until he felt her relax more, and he shoved in a third digit. Adeline gasped.

Stopping immediately, Royal asked, "Did I hurt you? If this is too much, we can try again another time."

"Not on your life," she chuckled. "Proceed. It feels incredible."

So, Royal grabbed the bottle with his other hand and drizzled oil onto his rock-hard cock. Just the feel of the oil dribbling onto him caused so much excitement he wondered how long he'd last. He set aside the bottle and squeezed himself, spreading the liquid around carefully. Taking a deep breath, he slowly pulled his hand from Adeline's body and lined himself up alongside Jasper. Ever so slowly and carefully, he forced his way inside.

Adeline moaned and cried out, "It hurts!" then, "Don't you *dare* think of stopping!" She grabbed one of her own nipples and gave it a hard pinch as she threw her other arm around Royal's neck, pulling him closer. She invaded his mouth with her tongue and clung to him, shaking all over. It was as if she'd become possessed with rapture with this astonishing act of lovemaking, and Royal wasn't sure what to think.

As she kissed him, he calmed down and began to realize he could feel every inch of Jasper as if they were squeezed together with an iron fist. But this iron fist was warm and wet and pulsated around them.

"Roy..." Jasper breathed. "Do you feel it? I've never imagined anything like this. I love you and Adeline so much; this is perfection. I want to stay like this for days and weeks on end."

"I feel it, and I agree. Addie? Are you alright?""

Adeline laughed and answered, "It's the most incredible sensation! I feel another rush building now. It's... ohh...."

When her climax hit, it was all over for the men. All three of them shouted and groaned with abandon. It was messy and outlandish and entirely extraordinary.

Later that night, Adeline announced dreamily, "I think I'll call that one Two Peas in a Pod. It's definitely my favorite." She snuggled closer and fell asleep.

Chapter Thirty-Three

The amount of alcohol consumption and the general out-of-control behavior of miners who either needed to blow off steam or drown their sorrows—partnered with a city filled with kerosene lamps and candles—resulted in fires being a constant threat. The resiliency of the San Franciscans was legendary, however. Each time a fire happened, within a week, the town was rebuilt and back to as much normal as could be expected. Sometimes it was a faulty chimney or an accident that caused the fire, but more often than not, it was arson. And in a city with no protective system of justice, this was disastrous.

When the raised sidewalks were discovered to be a contributor to the spread of fire, some enterprising person went around selling great sheets of corrugated metal to residents who needed to rebuild. The thinking behind this was that, unlike wooden structures that went up like tinderboxes, the metal buildings would be fireproof. Thus began a time when construction was done with metal and, when it was affordable to the builder, bricks. People developed a smug sense of safety with these new, improved materials.

Disastrously, the corrugated metal did not help. Gullible, frightened people ran into their houses to be protected from the fire, only to have their house turn into an oven—with them inside. Likewise, shoddy brick houses, rather than protecting their residents, exploded in the massive heat. During 1850 and 1851, a series of devastating fires burned the city to the ground, and still, its citizens rebuilt and rebuilt and rebuilt again.

At last, the city formed a designated volunteer fire department and took some serious measures to combat the problem. All businesses and homes were required to keep buckets of water handy at all times in case a flame should break out, and construction became a lot better. They began building houses with thick walls and small, deeply inset windows, and the effect was that many people's lives were subsequently spared.

San Francisco continued to have a huge influx of treasure seekers, causing the population to change, but nearly as many men were now leaving on the ships that arrived. Ships bringing supplies flooded the harbor, however, and much of what they brought was downright overkill. Prices dropped for everything due to the overabundance of goods and underabundance of consumers. Whole ships loaded with cargo were auctioned off, and the unused material was dumped into the streets, where it was covered with dirt. They were going to pave those terribly hilly streets come hell or high water, and they didn't seem to care with what. Street material may have included barrels of spoiled goods, bags of coffee, tree limbs, anything someone wanted to discard. The rubbish only provided a temporary means for people to cross the streets to get into their houses.

Sometimes, the use of questionable materials caused the streets to melt during a fire.

Prices for goods had been exorbitant while they were scarce and gold dust was everywhere, but now, there was a surplus of just about anything, and merchants were feeling the pinch. They couldn't make nearly the money they had been making previously. The gold had dried up finally, and no one had mountains of it to spend anymore. Supply and demand had swung the opposite direction at last, and sadly for them, many merchants became just as bankrupt as the unsuccessful miners.

Despite the change in fortunes, the pleasure-seeking immigrants continued to make The Discovery a success. San Francisco had developed a reputation for being sophisticated and cutting-edge with some of the best entertainment in the world. In its relatively safe location away from the Plaza, people had a sense of calm when they visited the gambling house or the saloon. And the entertainment continued to be spectacular.

The Discovery's proprietors were making names for themselves as leaders of the community. They were active in the attempts to improve conditions for residents and businesses alike, and they often made generous contributions to the city's ongoing progress programs. All of the men of The Discovery joined the volunteer fire department, setting a good example among their young, able-bodied peers.

San Francisco finally had sewers installed to direct water out of the streets, and mud, at last, became much less of a problem.

The Discovery became such a sought-after place for entertainment even the higher-ranking Sydney Ducks found their way to the saloon and the gambling hall. Their ringleader Boolie Bollinger owned a few of the seedy bars in Sydney-Town where he employed unscrupulous men who earned him plenty of money. He also ran a brothel that made him a fortune. No one who knew Boolie ever thought to cross him because his temper was monstrous, and his revenge tactics were horribly cunning.

Boolie, dressed like a gentleman, always managed to get a good seat at a gambling table by an unsuspecting dealer. For the most part, he kept his mouth shut and his nose clean and didn't try to cheat, but The Discovery was something he studied. He scrutinized how the proprietors acted, and he couldn't keep his eyes off Adeline. Often, he'd quit gambling early just so he could sit in the dance hall and feast on her beauty. He had plenty of women who were ready and willing to satisfy his needs, and after a night of watching Adeline play her piano, he'd seek out three of the best prostitutes in the city for the rest of the night.

Boolie wanted Adeline, but he wasn't in a hurry. An undertaking such as this took planning.

But sometimes, fate has a way of interfering in the best way possible.

One night, as Boolie swirled his whiskey absentmindedly in his glass while staring at Adeline from across the room, a tipsy clod sat down in the chair beside him. Boolie could smell the man's stench mixed with a powerful bouquet of rum and knew this man had to be drunk. Boolie ignored the lout until the man stuck out his hand and slurred, "I'm Captain Greely of Boston, sir. Perhaps you've heard of me. I see you're entranced with my Adeline over there."

"Yer Adeline?" *In what part of the swamp of his brain can this buffoon think she's his?*

"Uh... yeah! Her father, God rest his soul, betrothed her to me, and I aim to get her away from these two bootlickers who think they can both have her!"

Boolie narrowed his eyes at Greely. Not only did he smell to high heaven, he was wearing threadbare clothing that may have been a captain's uniform once upon a time. His clothing must have been dragged through the dirt and slept in for a long, long time. San Francisco was full of down-and-out miners who were similarly attired, so it wasn't exactly rare to see this. Some men were stupid enough to set out for the gold fields in their best Sunday clothes, believing they'd just bend over and collect large chunks of gold that they'd fill their pockets with. Greely appeared to be as unlucky as those fools. But if he knew something about Adeline, Boolie was willing to listen.

"That so?" Boolie asked.

"Absolutely! I plan on getting a crew together right away and taking her back to Boston with me. My ship, the Wind Gypsy, is all ready to go. I just need some men, and we can be on our way. She'll come with me this time."

Boolie snorted. "If ye say so."

"I know who you are, sir, and I was hoping we could do a little business," Greely added in a low voice, "if you know what I mean."

In a bored tone, Boolie answered, "Not really. Tell me what ye want, Greely."

Greely scooted his chair closer to Boolie, who tried not to gag, and in a stage whisper said, "I hear that you Sydney-Town sorts have ways of finding crew members for sea captains. I have money. I was hoping we could add Adeline to the crew, as well, if you know what I mean."

"Hmm. How much money do ye have? I require one hundred dollars for a regular sailor, and anyone with a specialty—like a carpenter or an experienced pilot—goes for more." He noticed how Greely's swarthy face turned a little green. Still, he could always double-cross the man and sell him to another captain. Let them deal with each other when Greely ended up aboard someone else's ship and tried to act like the captain. This was becoming amusing.

Just then, a ruckus across the dancehall caught Boolie's eye. Someone was trying to get Adeline's attention in the worst way, and she was merely smiling, playing her music, and ignoring the man. When the drunk hopped up onto the stage and tried to kiss Adeline, three more men jumped up there with him and surrounded him with guns pointed at the fool. "She's certainly well-guarded," Boolie pointed out. The trouble was over before it began, and the man was booted out.

"Greely, it's been a pleasure talking with ye. When ye figure out how many men ye need for the journey and have the funds, ye can get word to me at the Boar's Head."

"Oh, I don't need anyone too special," Greely said as he belched. "Adeline can cook, and I can do the rest. I just need men—maybe twenty of 'em, but I can do with ten if they don't die on me. I hate it when that happens—losing an investment that way."

Striding out of The Discovery, Boolie had a lot to think about. Chiefly, what kind of a father would betroth that exquisite creature to a mess like Greely? She clearly deserved a man of power and substance. Like Boolie. And what did Greely mean about those "two bootlickers?" He needed to make some inquiries.

By the end of the next day, Boolie's spies got back to him with the information he needed. The Wind Gypsy was a real ship that was so stripped down it was barely seaworthy. Greely had been making claims for ages about getting back to Boston, and nothing had transpired to help him manage that task. In the meantime, he was eking out a paltry income by letting men live aboard the Wind Gypsy, but the conditions were terribly rough, so he had few takers. Greely was an impossible drunk (no surprise), and Adeline had not one but two extremely wealthy husbands, and she also was a woman of considerable means on her own.

But Boolie hadn't gotten to where he was by dismissing possibilities. The more he learned about Greely, the stronger his plan became. *Maybe I can't keep her for long, but I can certainly borrow her for a time and make some serious money in the process,* Boolie thought to himself.

Chapter Thirty-Four

Good lighting was paramount at The Discovery. The dealers at the gambling tables needed to see clearly to prevent anyone from attempting to cheat, which made the chandeliers, sconces, lamps, and candles critical. When heavy gamblers placed large bets, the room often became stifling due to the number of guests crowded around the tables. Between the light sources and the sweating bodies, there was often a tremendous amount of heat.

It was not all that surprising when late one dark, foggy night, someone smelled smoke in the gambling hall. Quickly the cloud spread through one end of the hall, apparently coming from a storage closet. Shouts of "Fire!" filled the air, and frantic guests grabbed their money and stampeded the doors. The next room to the gaming hall was the saloon where Adeline played the piano and Isaac his fiddle. Right away, the sound of the yells caused a panicked exodus of guests. It was a miracle that no one was trampled. The noise was deafening.

Royal, Jasper, Walter, Isaac, and Timothy ran toward the billowing smoke and escalating heat as the closet door erupted in flame. Séamus hurried to ring the hotel's large bell, alerting any guests upstairs to evacuate their rooms, and then he joined his partners. They quickly doused the fire with the buckets of water they always kept on hand. The door was hacked to bits, and the walls around the closet were badly charred, but the speed at which they got to the flames prevented a terrible disaster. They saw immediately that they would be able to repair things without too much trouble.

If only everything could have been remedied so easily.

Walter made a shrewd observation once the fire was out. "Does it seem odd to anyone else that the fire started in a dark area with no lamp or candles in it? How could the blaze have started from inside the closet unless someone set it on purpose?"

"Maybe someone's cigar dropped on the floor unnoticed and rolled into the closet? Seems rather preposterous, though," Timothy said.

"It's possible, I suppose," answered Jasper. "But it does seem awfully fishy." As he looked around, his entire body tensed. "Has anyone seen Adeline?"

"She must have run outside with everyone," Royal answered in a soothing tone as he squeezed Jasper's shoulder. He didn't like the anxious look on Jasper's face. "I'll go get her and let her know it's safe now."

Royal, closely followed by the others, headed outside where some sleepy-looking hotel guests and straggling gamblers milled around, authoritatively discussing what they knew about the fire and their narrow escape from sure death. The rest of the crowd had already ambled away into the eerie fog— no doubt to find entertainment somewhere else, even at this late hour.

Walter, Isaac, Timothy, and Séamus followed Jasper and Royal through the thinning crowds, assuring everyone that the danger was over. Each of them craned their necks, looking for Adeline. She was nowhere to be found. After a few minutes of searching, they began demanding to know whether anyone had seen her.

Growing more and more anxious, the partners went from man to man seeking information on Adeline's whereabouts.

Their voices grew frantic as the responses were all negative. One man mentioned that a few wagons had left the area, but other than that, there was nothing to report. It was too foggy to see much anyway.

"You don't think she'd have gone upstairs, do you, Roy?" Jasper asked and loped toward the doorway, not waiting for an answer. Royal was right behind him, so Jasper went on, "She wouldn't have been foolish enough to stay indoors during a fire, would she?" He was now in a flat-out run and barged up the stairs, taking them two at a time.

Fumbling his key with shaking hands, Jasper bellowed through the door to their suite, "Adeline? Addie! Are you here?" Finally, the key turned, and the two men nearly fell into the room.

It was empty.

Staring at each other with dread, they heard shouts from below. Séamus was hollering to get their attention. "Come down here!" they could hear the Irishman roar.

Thundering back down the stairs, they were confronted with the terrified face of their friend.

"You need to come outside and see this," Séamus said in a grim voice. "But I'm warning you, it's not a pretty sight."

Royal and Jasper dashed outside, horrorstricken with worry, nearly tumbling down the front steps.

Mist-diffused light spilled from the building. Timothy held a torch aloft that illuminated a grisly scene. Isaac stood shaking, his face and clothing smeared with dirt and blood. His eyes appeared haunted as he explained in a voice that broke with both rage and sorrow, "I found him over by the back entrance near the kitchen. I tripped over him and landed in the dirt. I carried him here because it was so dark back there; I didn't even know who it was. Not until I got him into the light by the front entrance."

Caleb Cooley, who had become Adeline's favorite, trusted bodyguard, was cradled in Isaac's strong arms—looking limp. He was covered in blood.

"Is he dead?" asked Royal in a stricken voice. "What happened to him?"

Walter explained, "It looked like he was clobbered over the head pretty badly—maybe with a rock. He has a weak pulse. We need to get him to a doctor quickly."

Jasper looked like he was about to faint as Royal said with his voice breaking, "He must have led Addie out the back through the kitchen to keep her safe from the crowd while everyone was shoving through the front doors at once. The kitchen staff was all gone for the night, so it would have been a safe route. Caleb is a good man." With wild eyes, he choked out as he swiveled about frantically, "But where is she now?"

All of them craned their necks around as though they expected her to come walking out of the darkness.

All was quiet, unfortunately.

No Adeline.

"We *need* that doctor, men," Walter insisted again.

Royal seemed to snap to attention before Jasper and announced, "I'll go find Doc Louis. He's still around here somewhere." Going on a hunch, he rushed back upstairs rather than heading over to the dormitory. About a minute later, he returned with the doctor, who he had found storming toward Madame Beaufort's room.

Once they got Caleb in a bed and Doc Louis situated, they turned their focus on the mystery of Adeline's disappearance.

"Where should we look? We have to find her!" Royal moaned, by now in tears with worry. "Who would hurt Caleb?" He grabbed Jasper's arm like a lifeline—whether to support Jasper or himself was unclear.

Isaac was enraged—both at himself and the situation. Fuming, he nearly shouted, "I *never* should have let her out of my sight! But I was sure Caleb would watch out for her while I was helping with the fire. One minute we were happily playing our music and the next... she's gone... and Caleb might..." He couldn't complete the thought.

"It's not your fault." Walter tried to assure him while soothingly rubbing Isaac's back. Then he looked at Jasper sharply and asked, "Didn't you say Greely was still hanging around?"

Jasper's eyes flashed angrily. "*Greely.* That rotten son of a bitch! I bet he's behind this. We need to head down to the Wind Gypsy and see if he's still living in that pigsty of a ship." Facing Royal, he cried, "Let's go!"

"Wait!" cried Walter. "We'll go with you, Jasper, but we need to bring weapons. If he's already wounded poor Caleb, there's no telling what else he might do. I never liked that man."

Royal growled, "The last time I saw him, he was acting like a clod-brained fool. He's a drunk and a criminal, and he's desperate for Addie, so he's dangerous for sure."

Séamus spoke up, saying, "As much as we'd like to help find Adeline, I think Timothy and I need to stay here and manage things. If we all leave, we might be leaving The Discovery vulnerable to serious trouble. Taking Adeline could have been a ploy to get us out of here so the place could be robbed and looted."

Nodding, Walter answered for everyone. "You're right, Séamus. You'd best have a talk with the watchmen and make sure they're on their toes."

Chapter Thirty-Five

Armed with pistols and knives and carrying torches, the four men took off for the wharf. The coastal fog smothered them like a blanket in some patches, making visibility spotty. In other places, the way was clear. No doubt they could have been set upon by cutthroats and thieves at this late hour, but anyone who thought they might have spotted a target took one look at the group and disappeared into the shadows like rats. Their ferocious expressions and the purposeful way they marched spoke of men who were seriously on edge and bearing a life-threatening grudge.

When they reached the area where the Wind Gypsy was docked, the men increased their speed. They had to pass by ship after ship, trying in vain to recognize something of the remaining hull. It was useless. There were hundreds of boats in all levels of disrepair, and in the foggy darkness, they couldn't make out a thing. Some ships were still moored to the pier, while others were anchored willy-nilly all over the bay.

Farther and farther, they followed the dock out into the water until they came across something strange. Through the fog, they could hear a male voice making odd noises. Sometimes he seemed to sing the words of a song, and other times he just hummed tunelessly. Unfortunately, it did not sound like Greely's voice.

Stepping around some debris that cluttered the pier, they were met with an odd sight. A ragged man lay on the dock, leaning against a mangled wooden crate. The man held onto something light and lacy, and he seemed to be singing to it, alternately rubbing it on his face and sniffing it. The stench of rum and unwashed human filled the air.

Realizing they weren't likely to be attacked by this drunken mess, Jasper spoke up, "What do you have there, mister?"

The man jumped about a foot and grasped his prize to his chest. "It's mine! She only tore a little off, and I kep' it. She won't need it! Not where she's goin'. And I'm not lettin' you have it!"

"Who is she?" asked Royal quickly. "Is she still here?"

"Nah, they took her off again."

"Who took her?" Jasper demanded. "What did she look like? Did you get her name?"

"Oh, *real* purty. The men took 'em both."

"Both?" Jasper demanded. "Was the woman with Captain Greely?"

"I dunno. He mighta been Greely, I guess. The cheatin' varmint. She din't seem so happy to be with any of 'em."

"What men?" Royal nearly shouted at him.

"Those ones what talks funny and walks like they ain't got their legs to work right yet."

A chill went through both men as they realized he was speaking about the Sydney Ducks. The brutal ex-convicts from the Australian penal colonies had strong accents, and years of confinement in leg irons caused many of them to stagger with an awkward, swinging gait.

Royal reached toward the drunk. Politely and as calmly as possible, he asked, "I promise I won't take it from you, but may I take a look at that material? Just for a moment, and I promise I'll give it back."

He reached toward the man, who got a mulish look on his face and narrowed his eyes on them. "Yer lyin'. You want it fer yerself. It's mine, an' you cain't have it!"

"I'll pay you just to look at it," Jasper announced, reaching into his pocket. He produced a gold coin that glittered temptingly in the flickering light.

The man's eyes shone with greed, but he eyed Jasper suspiciously. "I ain't gonna let go. Jus' a peek. That's all you gets." Jasper reached forward, and the man yanked backward quicker than he seemed capable of managing in his inebriated state. "Pay up first! Then you can see."

"Yes, of course," Jasper breathed out in a huff. "Here's your coin. Now let me see the confounded thing!" He studied it for a second before the wretched man yanked it away again and said to Royal, "That definitely looks like the trim from Adeline's dress." Addressing the man, he asked, "Did she say anything?"

"Nah! She was gagged. Hands tied up too. Those men was plenty mad at the man what they brung her to. Gave 'im a good kick in the nuts too, she did. As soon as she saw him. That woman has spirit!" The cackling drunk seemed to be enjoying having an audience at this point, so he rambled on, "They brung her here to git paid, I 'spect, but when he didn't cough up the loot, they yelled at 'im about it, then beat 'im up good, and then dragged 'em both away. I was jus' comin' back and seen all this on the dock, so I hid 'til they was all gone. I din't wanna get sucked in too, ya know. Found this pretty piece snagged on a piece a wood over there."

"Did any of them say where they were headed?" asked Royal.

"Nah." The man let out a belch as they all turned around to leave. As the men made their way back along the dark pier, they cringed to hear him crooning to his lacy treasure once more.

When they reached the shore, Jasper wondered aloud, "Where could they have taken her? And what would they want with Greely—if it was Greely—after he didn't pay them?"

In a grim voice, Walter answered, "Sydney-Town. It's full of thieves and former convicts and has plenty of shady saloons, opium dens, and terrible brothels where men go in and never come out. I've heard stories about how men get Shanghaied every day. They get beaten or drugged, get shoved down a trap-door—usually unconscious—and when they wake up, they find themselves on a ship already out to sea. It's the only way some of the ship captains can find crewmen, so they pay to have men brought to them. It's a horribly dangerous part of San Francisco. No one should ever go there alone; it's hideously unsafe." He looked like he was about to cry when he added in a broken voice, "They also steal women and imprison them on boats or in their disgusting cat houses where they force them into prostitution."

"Let's go," Jasper growled. "Now!"

Chapter Thirty-Six

In the early predawn light, the city had a strange, sinister look that got worse as they approached Sydney-Town. As they walked the city blocks and scanty sunlight began to emerge, they ditched their torches. It seemed prudent to have the use of both hands. Once they turned onto Pacific Street, they were met with the sight of the meanest sort of establishments. Shady-looking men loitered in the doorways. Leathery men whose faces seemed to have been baked in the sun and bore scars that spoke of hard living and frequent fights. Many wore heavy cotton clothing made of material sometimes called "duck" and woven cabbage-tree hats that seemed too jaunty for their threatening expressions. These men had come from the roughest living conditions in the Australian penal colonies. Whether Australia gave them their release papers because shipping them to California was cheaper than feeding them, or whether they'd actually served their time, was a subject up for debate. In any case, these were men who were hardened by life and had turned into ruthless gangsters. They were cruel, violent, and often deadly.

The curious Sydney-Town locals scrutinized the band of men. Many of them seemed particularly interested in Isaac, who, for all of his gentle nature, was still coated with dirt and blood. He glared menacingly at anyone who looked at him for too long, and they glared right back.

Shoddy buildings and tents lined the streets. Many of them seemed to be brothels and gambling halls. The partners gave a wide berth to one hideous saloon that had a miserable-looking bear chained up in front. "We can come back to this one later if we have to," offered Walter. "I don't want to get near that creature if it's not vitally important." The sign over the door aptly named the place The Fierce Grizzly.

Here and there, they came across someone who seemed approachable, and one of their group would ask, "Did you see a woman brought here late last night against her wishes? She was bound and gagged and was in the company of some rough men."

The answers were generally a nasty laugh, a blank stare, or a quick shake of the head. However, as they approached a seedy-looking—but sturdier than many—two-story wooden establishment called The Boar's Head, the men cringed at the image on the sign above the door. It featured a woman engaged in carnal relations with a boar.

"Lovely place, don't you think?" asked Royal, who was trying to keep his spirits up. Just then, a fresh-faced young man crossed their path, and Royal asked again, "Excuse me. Have you any knowledge of a woman who may have been brought to this part of the city last night? She was tied up, so..."

The young man's eyes lit up, and he smiled graciously. "Yessir! I might jus' know somethin'."

"Well?" asked Royal eagerly.

"Well, yerself, mister," the young man said, extending his hand, palm up. His face suddenly looked a bit more calculating than it had moments before.

Royal fished a gold coin from his pocket and set it in the youth's filthy mitt.

Grinning, the young man snatched the coin and cocked his head in the direction of The Boar's Head doorway. "Heard some men talkin' in there 'bout an hour ago."

Restraining himself from grabbing the guy by his shirt, Royal demanded, "What did they say?"

"Oh, nuthin' much. Jus' that they had somethin' special that'd fetch a good price. That's all I heard."

Just then, a small commotion happened as they were joined by Séamus and Timothy. "We found you!" Timothy cried happily, if a little out of breath. "We thought you might end up here!"

Walter asked, "What are you doing here? I thought you..."

Séamus cut him off, whispering, "We had a chat about it after we set our minds to right. The fire is out, the hotel is safely guarded by the watchmen, and all of the money is locked in the safe. We couldn't just sit around and let you look for Adeline by yourselves. You need our help too!"

Timothy added, "Adeline is more important to us than the hotel anyway."

Jasper was touched by their willingness to put themselves in harm's way for Adeline and said, "Thank you, both."

Timothy and Séamus just scoffed in response.

Royal asked with a concerned look, "How was Caleb doing when you left?"

The smile faded from Séamus' face as he answered, "He was moaning and coming around a little, I think. Too soon to tell, Doc Louis said."

While the group was catching up with their partners, the young man with information had vanished.

The only thing left to do was to enter The Boar's Head and start asking questions.

"I'll go in," offered Isaac. "It's my fault she's lost, and they'll have a harder time doing any damage to me than the rest of you."

Each one of the others spoke up quickly in protest to Isaac's assertion that he was to blame, but he waved them off.

"I'm going with you," stated Walter in a voice that said he meant business. "You'd be a fool to go in there by yourself." He grabbed Isaac's arm and marched through the door without a backward glance.

"Now what?" asked Royal. "We just loiter around here until they come out? This seems ridiculous! But it may not be such a good idea for all of us to go in, either." He paused for a second and shook his head, adding, "What that little scoundrel heard could have meant anything."

Jasper thought for a moment and said, "Let's you and I check out the upstairs and leave Timothy and Séamus here in case Walter and Isaac run into difficulty. They're better shots than we are."

"Aye," agreed Séamus with a grin. "We are."

Discarded empty bottles took up most of the ground surrounding the saloon, so they had to pick their way carefully around the building as they searched for a staircase. A raggedy man lay amongst the bottles in an awkward position that looked so uncomfortable, it made them wonder at first if he'd fallen and died there. However, as they stepped gingerly around him, they realized that he was snoring lustily. The stench of the results of his overindulgence made them cover their noses and mouths.

"Here it is," Royal announced in a low voice. "Shall we just head up there and hope for the best?"

"I suppose so," Jasper answered. "I don't have a better plan."

As quietly as they could, the two of them ascended the wobbling stairs and pulled open a rickety wooden door. They cringed at the screeching sound it made, immediately sorry for disturbing the people inside. For in the room, they found a bunch of straw pallets and nasty, soiled beds that were jammed with sleeping women who were undoubtedly the whores who worked there. The room smelled of sex, cheap perfume, and sweat. Apparently, this was not a busy time of day for business, for there was not a single man in sight. There was also no evidence of Adeline.

"I don't know if I'm relieved or mad that she's not here," muttered Jasper.

A few of the women cracked their eyes open, but most slept on. Of the few who paid attention, one with a bluish bruise on her cheekbone said, "We're closed now, boys. But yer both so purty, I'd look deep into my generous heart and let you mix giblets wi' me." There were a few giggles, and a couple of others added sleepily, "Me too," or "If ya got the cash."

Jasper smiled politely and straightened his spine. "We're just here for information, ladies. Do you have any knowledge of a young woman being brought here last night? We believe she may have been bound and gagged." Then for clarification, he added, "A beautiful lady in a fine gown."

"Nah. No one like that showed up here. But if she had, then prob'ly Boolie Bollinger either woulda kep' her for hisself or auctioned her off. Depends on how greedy he felt—or how horny." She gave a nasty cackle.

"How can we find this Boolie?" Royal asked quickly.

Yawning, the woman answered, "I dunno. Try his house."

Jasper pressed for more details, "Where is that?"

"Do I look like his landlady? How should I know?" she snapped. "If yer not gonna pay to do a bit a business, then get the hell outta here. We need our beauty rest."

"Yes, ma'am," Jasper said as he backed up through the door again with Royal at his side. Once outside with the squeaky door shut, he and Royal carefully made their way down the rickety stairs again. "We have to find her as soon as possible, Roy! Let's get the others."

Once again, they made their way through the bottles, trying to avoid as much broken glass as they could. They were surprised to find that the derelict was missing from the scene; he hadn't seemed capable of moving. They did see a few dead rats, however, and one or two live ones nosing through the debris.

Upon reaching the front of The Boar's Head, they found Timothy and Séamus whispering. Both of their heads turned abruptly as Jasper and Royal approached, and Timothy raised his eyebrows in question. "Anything?" he asked.

"We need to find someone named Boolie Bollinger. Apparently, he's some kind of ringleader who may have Adeline," Royal explained. "Is something else wrong now too?"

Séamus explained, "We thought Isaac and Walter were just going in for a quick chat to ask a question or two, but they haven't come out yet. We're trying to decide whether to go in with guns drawn or make a more peaceful introduction."

"We're worried about them," added Timothy. "They're both too soft-hearted. It should've been us going in."

Jasper and Royal looked at each other and said simultaneously, "Let's go." All four men drew their guns and headed through the door.

The inside of the saloon was barely any tidier than the alleyway had been. Littered with empty bottles, the stench made their eyes burn. A miasma of cheap tobacco smoke and rotgut liquor wafted around them, making their stomachs roil in disgust. In one corner, there was a straw-filled pen, and in it lay a snoring boar that also contributed mightily to the stink.

Suspicious glares from the few patrons met them head-on.

There was no sign of either Walter or Isaac.

Jasper spoke up immediately, "Where are our two men? They just came in here a few minutes ago."

A man behind the bar took the chewed stub of a cigar out of his mouth and smirked, "Sorry, gents. Ya just missed 'em. Signed up for jobs and lit outta here."

"They don't need jobs! What have you done with them?" demanded Royal.

All of the men laughed nastily as the cigar-chomping bar-keep answered, "We'd send you on the same path if it weren't for Boolie wantin' to do a bit a business with ya. We know who ya are."

"What path?" Séamus nearly shouted at them.

"Don't worry. They'll be fed and watered. Might even get a decent ration a rum now 'n then. The big one looked like he'll fetch a good price, that one." He glared more ferociously. "Now take yer stupid guns outta here, go home and wait for Boolie to get in touch with ya. Yer wastin' yer time here. We ain't got yer men no more!"

"If you've harmed our men, I'll personally come back and burn this pigsty to the ground!" Jasper hollered.

"Yeah, right. You do that and see how long you'll live," they heard the barman laugh as Royal dragged Jasper back outside.

Séamus held his gun pointed at the laughing man until Timothy had to drag him away, too, saying, "Come on; you'll be no help if someone kills you."

Jasper shook with fury. "This is getting worse and worse. He must have meant they Shanghaied Isaac and Walter somehow." Looking wildly this way and that, he finally said, "If there's a ship that's heading out today, maybe we can find them before they get aboard it. Let's head back down to the dock."

"What about Adeline?" cried Royal. "We have to find her!"

Timothy pointed out, "That barman said Boolie would get in touch, so I think we need to get Walter and Isaac back first if we can. I don't think we can take any more time. No doubt Boolie has something to do with both crimes. And if he wants to 'do business,' he might be more interested in a ransom than harming her." He did not add all of the other things Boolie might want to do with her first. The thought made his skin crawl.

As they spoke, the men sprinted back toward the dock. It wasn't far from Sydney-Town, but just getting away from the wretched Boar's Head was something of a relief to them.

Now that the sun was fully out, they had a clearer view of the array of ships moored in the bay. As they scanned the docks, their shoulders deflated. There were hundreds and hundreds of ships. It would take a miracle to find anyone in that mess. For a moment, their hearts broke as they collectively realized the futility they faced.

"Oh no. Isaac. Walter," Royal moaned. "Where *are* you?" Then he began to scream their names as loudly as his voice could go. *"ISAAC!! WALTER!! Where are you?!"* And something strange happened. A smallish skiff that was being rowed out to the middle of the bay began to rock in a peculiar way. "Look!" Royal cried. "Maybe that's them! If it's not, it's sure strange, so it's worth looking at." Just then, a large booted foot appeared from inside the boat and kicked around in the air before disappearing again, and the boat began to wobble once more. "That might be Isaac's foot, and I think I heard a shout! Let's go!"

The men took off at a flat-out run down the dock to get closer to the skiff before they lost sight of it behind a ship. The man rowing the boat seemed to be yelling and kicking at something at the same time he desperately tried to navigate the boat in a straight line. It wasn't working out very well for him.

Being the fastest runner of the group, Royal reached the end of the dock first and shucked off his boots and most of his clothes in seconds. He dove into the harbor and swam as fast as he could toward the rowboat. He was such a good swimmer, and the oarsman was having so much trouble, he gained on them quite quickly. Nearer and nearer, he closed the distance steadily. But then...

The man with the oars stopped struggling with them, stood up in the wobbly boat, pulled a gun, and shot Royal.

Jasper, who'd by now also reached the end of the pier, was getting rid of his own boots when he heard the gunshot and saw Royal sink below the surface of the water.

The water was red.

With one boot on and one boot off, he screamed, "ROYAL!" and dove into the water after him. Encumbered as he was by clothes and terror, he was not nearly as good a swimmer. He was winded and weighted down with his clothing, but he used every last ounce of strength he had left in him to reach Royal.

As he splashed his way out into the harbor, Jasper heard another shot ring out. Bracing for the pain, Jasper prepared to die.

Chapter Thirty-Seven

Adeline was less than charmed by her "host," Boolie Bollinger. "You are an arrogant fool if you think you'll get away with this!" she railed at the man.

He smirked at her. "I'm already getting away with it. Yer here, ain't ye?"

"Not for long, I'll bet."

"Oh? My men tell me otherwise. I have eyes everywhere, ye know."

"Arrogant fool," she muttered again. Adeline was tied tightly to a chair, and she knew that struggling against her bonds would do nothing other than hurt her wrists, for the rope was rough and terribly scratchy. The chair, at least, was both beautiful and comfortable—stolen, no doubt, from some establishment Boolie had looted and then torched. She wondered if the unfortunate previous owner still lived.

"Keep grousing, pretty one, and see how quickly ye can be gagged again." He glared at her.

After a few minutes of scowls from Adeline and leers back at her from Boolie, a rough-looking scoundrel came in and mumbled something unintelligible in Boolie's ear. Boolie glowered at the messenger before telling him, "I'll need more information than that! Get yer facts straight, man."

Addressing Adeline, Boolie said in a smug voice, "I just got word that at least one o' yer precious men is floating in the harbor right now. Too bad, really. That wasn't the plan. I guess someone got annoyed with them."

Adeline simply refused to believe such a horrible and certainly false tale that was meant to scare her into submission. What did "floating" mean exactly anyway? So, even as silent, worried tears streamed down her face, she turned her attention to the contents of the room. She needed a plan. She could not give up. Try as she might to be brave and sensible, however, the question burned through her. *Who was in the harbor?*

Adeline pressed her feet hard to the floor, testing to see if she could move herself around at all if she had to. One foot slipped forward, and the other grabbed enough purchase that she nearly toppled herself right over sideways. The chair wobbled and settled back down as Boolie laughed at her nastily.

"I like a little temper," he cackled. "Maybe it's not worth the ransom, and I'll just keep ye. Besides, dead men can't pay me." He reached for the decanter on the table next to him, pouring a draught of something into a greasy-looking glass. He downed it in a gulp, belched, and laughed again. "One way or another, I'll have some fun wi' this."

Chapter Thirty-Eight

Other than an earache from the gun's report, Jasper's pain never materialized. He'd stopped swimming long enough, however, to see the gun-bearing oarsman fall backward out of the skiff and into the water. Turning back to the dock instantly, he saw Séamus and Timothy pointing their guns and scanning the area for more trouble. Relief flooded him for a millisecond and was immediately replaced by terror over Royal's fate once again. Splashing wildly in his nervous haste, he made his way over to where he thought he'd last seen Royal. Ducking beneath the surface, he saw cloudy shapes a few yards ahead. Amidst the general debris, one of the shapes seemed to be sinking, and there was a bloom of red in the water.

Knowing he'd do better swimming if he took off his other boot, Jasper momentarily considered struggling to remove it, but he also feared for Royal's life too desperately, so he rose up and swam closer to where he'd seen what he hoped was his man, took a mammoth gulp of air, and kicked his way down several feet below the surface of the water. *Where is he?* he thought frantically. *And why isn't he floating? He must have a bunch of gold in his pants pockets weighing him down.* Jasper spun round and round, looking up and down until his lungs couldn't take it any longer. He surfaced with a mighty gasp and took in as much air as he could hold. Ducking down again, he dove deeper into the water.

There! Jasper kicked with all his might and struggled to get closer to Royal. Plumes of blood formed a halo around Royal's head in the churning water, but as they descended away from the rocking boat, there was less turbulence. Jasper's vision began to fill with black spots as he neared Royal, his body craving oxygen. Still, he would have sighed with relief—if he could have—when he finally grabbed hold of one of Royal's arms. Up and up, closer and closer to the surface, they rose as Jasper kicked with all of his might, and Royal hung from his grasp like a ball and chain.

With lungs burning like acid, Jasper could only think of one thing. *Get him to the skiff. Get Royal to the boat! The boat is safe... I hope.* The closer he got to the skiff, the more red he saw coloring the water, and the boat itself was still rocking wildly, churning up the water even further. As he breached the surface, Jasper took in a mighty breath at last, wrapped one arm around Royal's chest, and grabbed for the side of the boat. Immediately the thrashing stopped.

"Jasper? Is that your hairy arm? Please say that's you!" a familiar voice hollered from the bottom of the boat.

"It's me. I need help! Royal's been shot! I need to get him out of the water. Help me boost him, Isaac!"

"I'm tied up! We're all bound together and can't move our arms," Isaac explained in a pained voice. "I'd love to help you, but I can barely feel my own hands. We need your help getting loose!"

Jasper racked his brain and finally decided to just use brute strength to shove Royal's dead weight up and into the boat. Having nothing to push against except water severely hindered that idea, but he was like a man possessed. He struggled and heaved and finally decided that would never work. So, he kept a death grip on Royal with one arm and threw his other arm over the gunwale. He held on to the rough wood for dear life and shoved one of his legs beneath Royal. Finally, with screaming muscles and one massive thrust, he got his friend bent over the top of the wooden rail, where it smacked Royal in the stomach.

Sometimes things just work out with sheer luck, divine intervention, or voodoo—but this did the trick. The weight of Royal's own body put so much pressure on his stomach he instantly spewed up about a gallon of seawater (and a few other things) into the boat. Fortunately, the person whose face it landed on was none other than Captain Greely. There was no reaction from Greely, who appeared to be out cold.

"Can someone use a leg to help him in? I can't hold on this way much longer," Jasper shouted.

"The others are unconscious, but I can reach him with my foot now," Isaac answered frantically. "Hang on!"

After a lot of grunting noises, Jasper saw a large boot swing over the gunwale. Jasper tried to direct Royal's body over Isaac's boot. Royal remained limp, and Jasper prayed his man was still alive. There seemed to be blood everywhere. It still poured off the top of Royal's head, and now Royal's poor body was scratched everywhere from the splintered wood of the rickety skiff. Jasper thought, *So much for taking your clothes off to go for a swim. A shirt might have helped. Nothing to be done for it now. Please be alive, Royal, please!*

There was nothing graceful or efficient about the way they maneuvered Royal into the boat, but he finally dropped like a lead weight on top of Isaac and his bound fellow captives. Then it was Jasper's turn to heft himself over the gunwale and into the skiff. He'd never felt so completely drained of all strength in his life. Terror has a way of making one go that extra mile, however, and he was determined to make sure Royal and his other partners were safe. Panting, at last, he too joined the heap of men in the bottom of the boat. The boat looked ready to sink under all their weight.

As he lay there catching his breath, Jasper heard more shots. Peering over the side of the boat, he saw Séamus and Timothy picking off gunmen who'd shot at them from a way up the dock. The Ducks were no match for the Irishmen's sharpshooting skills, and Jasper thanked the stars above that Timothy and Séamus had traded in that old blunderbuss a long time ago for better weapons.

"There's a knife in my boot," Isaac said suddenly, startling Jasper into action.

"Yes, of course." Jasper fished his hand into the boot and pulled out a small knife that he used to cut Isaac and the other men free. Walter seemed to be groaning, but Greely was still unconscious. Once the ropes were cut, Isaac moved into position and began rowing the skiff back to the dock.

Jasper finally grasped Royal and dragged him to his chest. Royal was freezing cold and turning a frightening shade of blue, but he seemed to be breathing. His head was bleeding copiously, so Jasper maneuvered around, trying not to squash Walter in the process, and took a look at the back of Royal's scalp. His stomach roiled as he saw some of Royal's exposed skull, but the bone seemed intact. Jasper sighed with relief when he realized that the bullet had grazed the skull rather than penetrating it. Awkwardly ripping his own shirt from his body, he wrapped it around Royal's head to attempt to stop the flow of blood. After that, he scooted behind Royal, wrapped him firmly in his arms, and tried to warm up the man's body. He fervently wished he had something dry, but everything and everyone was soaked in blood or saltwater in this leaky little boat.

As Isaac rowed toward the pier in long, efficient strokes, Jasper craned around nervously, looking for any other possible gunmen, but there was no sign of trouble. It seemed Séamus and Timothy had taken care of anyone who'd threatened them.

The skiff itself was another matter. It was taking on water rapidly. The cracked hull looked like it needed repair work some time ago. Jasper just hoped Isaac could get to the dock before the boat sank.

Lower and lower, they dropped into the harbor. Jasper considered heaving Greely overboard to remedy the weight problem, but he wouldn't let go of Royal long enough to actually do it. Besides, despite what Greely deserved, Jasper was no murderer.

Finally, feeling disgusted and angry, Jasper grabbed Greely by the shirt and hauled his head up so he didn't drown in the bottom of the boat. The man was still unconscious—whether drunk or knocked out, Jasper couldn't say.

As they approached the dock, Timothy peered inside, finally able to see the water inside the skiff. He said something to Séamus and took off at a run back up the dock.

They got closer to the pier, and deeper and deeper the rowboat sank into the water. Finally, at about ten feet from the edge of the walkway, the boat disappeared slowly out from under them. Jasper treaded water and held onto Royal for dear life while Isaac lunged for Walter, both keeping their friends from sinking to their death. Greely, however, was going down with the boat.

Jasper grabbed onto the end of one of the oars and thrust the other end toward Séamus. The Irishman grabbed the oar and pulled the two of them quickly to the dock. He bent down and hauled first Royal and then Walter out of the water and carefully lay them on the wooden pier. Isaac and Jasper looked at each other and wordlessly made a collective decision. They both dove beneath the water and yanked Greely up to the surface where Séamus dragged the captain out and lay him on his side.

Heavy, hurried footsteps and lots of rattling sounds grabbed their attention as they saw Timothy heading their way. He was pushing some kind of handcart he'd discovered lying about. It was in just about the same shape repair-wise as the rowboat, but everyone immediately saw its value. As Isaac and Jasper struggled to climb out of the bay, scratching themselves in the process on barnacles and rough wood, Timothy and Séamus were carefully loading Walter and Royal into the cart. Then Séamus covered them with the dry clothing Royal had left on the dock. As the Irishmen began to push the cart back toward the city, Isaac and Jasper took a backward glance at Greely.

"I wonder if he'll remember anything if he ever comes to," mused Isaac. "He's been like that the whole time. He was lying on the floor of the basement in The Boar's Head when they dropped us down there through a trapdoor. We landed on top of him. We were damned fools to ever go into that hellhole. I'm sorry we caused you and Royal so much trouble." He hung his head. "They planned to sell us to a captain whose ship is due to leave today."

"I'm aware," Jasper said with a nod. "And I'm relieved as hell you signaled us from that dinghy. We couldn't lose you." He jutted his chin toward Greely. "Look, let's just leave the bastard here. If he wakes up, fine. If not... fine. I can't worry about him anymore. He should be happy we saved him from drowning. I want to hear more about The Boar's Head and what happened, but we need to get these men to Doc Louis right away. And we need to figure out how to find Adeline."

They rushed to catch up to Séamus and Timothy with the cart. Every step felt like an ordeal; Jasper was so exhausted. He was relieved to see, however, that Walter was attempting to sit up. And, of course, Walter was talking.

"I can get out and walk, and it'll make it easier for you to get our young man to the doc sooner."

"It's fine, Walter. Relax," Timothy told him. "You've obviously also had quite a blow to the noggin and need to take it easy. If you want to be helpful, make sure Royal's head doesn't bounce. This road isn't the best, and I don't want him to bleed any more than he already is."

"Yes, right. I can do that." He moved around in the cart until Royal's head was comfortably cradled in Walter's arms. It was an odd sight, but it reassured Jasper to know Royal wouldn't get wounded any worse from bouncing his head.

As they made their way back to The Discovery, Isaac and Jasper tried to keep a sharp eye out for any Sydney Ducks who could be looking for more trouble. What they didn't know was that Boolie Bollinger had called off the remaining gunmen who hadn't been shot by the Irishmen. Boolie was furious that his sale of three talented crewmen had fallen through. He had been hungrily awaiting the juicy payoff for that big, strong carpenter.

At last, they reached The Discovery and located Doc Louis. He'd been attending Caleb, who was now cleaned up and looking a lot more human. Caleb had his head bandaged, but he was sitting up and drinking a cup of coffee when the partners found them.

"Here, I'm fine, and he can have my bed," Caleb announced and tried to leap to his feet when he saw them carry Royal into the room. He immediately swooned and landed back on his ass on the bed with a groan. It turns out that a rock to the head is tougher to come back from than he'd have liked.

Doc Louis gave Caleb a deprecating look and cleared some medical equipment off the other bed in the room. He lay a heavy blanket down and said, "Put him here, and we'll have to get him out of those wet pants. He needs to warm up, and I'll take a look at that wound."

Isaac spoke up, "When you're done with Royal, I'd appreciate you looking at Walter. He got clobbered with a liquor bottle to the head, and he might need stitches as well."

Doc Louis muttered, "I've never seen so many busted-up skulls in one day as you men have."

"I'm fine," groused Walter. "Just took a little nap for a while, you know?"

Ignoring Walter's comment, Isaac continued, "It probably didn't help you any when I lunged for you as you were falling, and they shoved me down that trapdoor where I landed on you. I could have broken your bones."

"Isaac, it's just fine! I'm fine!"

Despite his worry about Royal, Jasper smiled at their ribbing. Apparently, Walter *was* actually just fine despite being unconscious for a while. "Why don't the two of you go get into some dry clothes and come back when you're cleaned up? Doc Louis can take a look at you then, Walter. And we have a lot to discuss." Still wearing one soggy boot and dripping all over the floor in his saturated clothes, Jasper was hardly one to talk. He dragged up a chair opposite Doc Louis and grasped Royal's hand while the doctor examined Royal's gunshot wound.

"Your man here is going to need some stitches, Jasper. That will stop the bleeding, but I don't think there was a lot of damage to his head. You say he was shot while he was swimming?"

Jasper nodded.

"If he'd been in more of a vertical position instead of keeping his head down in the water, he'd likely have gotten his head blown off. I guess good swimming skills saved his life."

"So, he'll recover?" Jasper looked at Louis with pleading eyes.

"Yes, son. He'll have a mighty headache for a few days, but he'll be fine."

Tears of relief stung Jasper's eyes. Now they just had to get Adeline back to safety. *How?* Suddenly the lack of sleep, lack of food, severe nervousness for his loved ones, and general fury all swamped Jasper at once, and he began to shake.

"Jasper, go get some dry clothes and come back here. You're going to be no good to anyone if you can't function properly, and you look to me like you're going into shock. Actually, here

—have some of this before you go." Doc Louis poured Jasper a cup of coffee to warm him up.

Jasper swallowed the warm liquid and kissed Royal's forehead before taking the doc's advice. It would be nice to get clean and dry. He was covered in salty water and blood with bits of kelp and sand in uncomfortable places. Making a lot of squishy noises with his soggy clothes, he left to take care of himself.

Chapter Thirty-Nine

Adeline couldn't remember when she'd been more furious and scared in her life. Boolie had to be the most obnoxious human being on earth, and she detested the way he sat motionless, staring at her for long stretches of time. He refused to answer her questions, saying, "Keep talking, lovely, and you'll be gagged again as fast as you can blink." She was terrified for her men, and she had no idea what Boolie planned to do with her. She stopped asking questions so he wouldn't stuff that nasty rag back into her mouth.

Glaring at him as he looked her up and down, she tried to formulate a plan, but it wasn't working. She came up with nothing.

What felt like hours after her capture, another one of Boolie's men rushed into the room. "Here's what's happening..." he started.

"Outside!" Boolie barked. Apparently, he didn't want to share information with Adeline. She wondered if that came from a warped sense of pride. Boolie might be worried about looking bad in case there was news he didn't like.

Through the closed door, Adeline could hear their hushed voices and was gratified to sense frustration and anger coming from Boolie, even though she couldn't make out the words. *That has to be good*, she surmised. Looking around at her cluttered surroundings, Adeline saw something she liked a few feet away. *A writing desk! Perhaps there is a letter knife or a metal-tipped pen that I can grab and use as a weapon.*

Adeline began to rock and scoot her chair toward the desk. If she found something, she had no idea how she'd grab it, but doing nothing felt like losing, and she desperately needed to accomplish something. Inch by inch, she scooted toward the desk, stopping several times to listen for evidence that Boolie was still conversing on the other side of the heavy door. He was. In fact, he repeatedly raised his voice in anger and then seemed to catch himself and lowered his voice again.

Adeline was so close now she could see writing instruments lying haphazardly atop the writing surface. *Messy clod*, she thought.

And then she spied it. Behind a crumpled piece of paper, there *was* a small knife just lying there for the taking! *Hallelujah!* It was the most beautiful sight she'd seen all day. *I'll grab it with my teeth if I have to. I just know that having some kind of weapon will be to my advantage.* In her excitement, she kicked her feet faster and harder... and toppled over with a thud, landing hard on her shoulder. "Ow!" she moaned in embarrassment as the door opened.

Boolie took in the sight of Adeline laying on her side with her skirt exposing her legs, and he laughed nastily at her predicament. "I can't leave ye for one minute, can I?" he snarled at her.

"Help me up!" she demanded.

"Or what?"

"Or you're no gentleman!"

Boolie guffawed at her then. "I ain't never been called a gentleman, and there's no reason to start now. Besides, I rather like this view of ye." He saw where she was heading in her traverse across the room and narrowed his eyes. "Ye was planning on stealing from me, weren't ye?" He strode past her, snatched up a pen from the desk, and tossed it into the drawer. He also grabbed the knife and dropped it into his pocket. Regarding her thoughtfully, he said, "I'll set you to rights, miss, but ye'll owe me something for it."

"What?"

"A kiss."

"I'd rather kiss a pig."

"Now that's something I can arrange. Have ye heard of my fine establishment, The Boar's Head? Men love to watch what ol' Spartacus can do wi' a woman."

Adeline decided further conversation would be futile and gritted her teeth. Lying sideways on the floor seemed preferable to anything Boolie was likely to come up with.

Chapter Forty

Jasper felt almost cruel eating a meal while Royal lay in bed, barely awake. They were both clean and dry at last after Jasper took it upon himself to bathe and dress Royal. After getting his head stitched and bandaged, Royal had begun to come around, but the light seemed to bother his eyes, so he tended to keep them tightly closed. He'd vomited a couple more times and shook his head almost imperceptibly when anyone offered him something to eat or drink. The only things he'd said so far to Jasper were, "Thank you" and "Addie?" Royal looked absolutely dreadful, so as soon as Jasper finished wolfing down some food, he kicked off his dry pair of boots, climbed into the bed with Royal, and wrapped his shivering husband in his arms.

Jasper knew he needed to find Adeline, but he also knew that if he didn't sleep for at least a few minutes, he'd keel over. He'd been awake at this point for over thirty straight hours, and he felt like a wreck and worried that his judgment might not be at its best from sleep deprivation. He detested the idea of trusting someone like Boolie Bollinger, but they'd been told that Boolie would get in touch. So, for now, they needed to wait to hear from him. In his heart, Jasper longed to rip San Francisco apart to find Adeline, but his brain argued that it would be a stupid, dangerous thing to do. And so, he succumbed to the inevitable, wrapped snugly around Royal—who'd finally stopped shaking—and fell asleep.

A couple of hours later, Jasper awoke when someone gently shook him by the shoulder. Doc Louis was there looking at him with concern. "There is a messenger here to see you," he told Jasper. "I'm sorry to wake you, but it's obviously important."

Jasper jolted upright, jostling Royal, who groaned. "Oh, sorry, Roy," he said in a soft voice and gently rubbed Royal's arm. Royal, however, also sat up unsteadily and squinted his eyes at Doc Louis.

"What do you know?" croaked Royal.

Jasper kept an arm around Royal's body from behind and squeezed him gently. "Glad you're finally back with us," he murmured into Royal's neck. Then he climbed out of bed and stood as Royal slowly maneuvered around to sit on the bed with his feet on the floor. He swayed a bit and then steadied himself.

Doc Louis bent over and looked closely into Royal's eyes and then smiled broadly at him. "You'll do just fine, young man. You must have a skull made of diamond. It's so hard, it can withstand a bullet." He chuckled and then looked at Jasper. "Shall I send in the messenger now?"

"Yes." Jasper scrubbed a hand over his face and through his hair, hoping to make himself look more awake than he felt.

Doc Louis opened the door to a filthy young boy who appeared to be around eight years old. He had a piece of paper in his hand that he extended to Jasper and announced, "He told me to get yer answer. In writing."

"Who told you?"

Looking at the floor nervously, the kid answered, "Some man. I dunno who he was. Paid me a dollar to deliver this and said I'd get more when I brung back yers."

"Where was he when he asked you to make this delivery?"

"He said if I answered any questions like that, he'd knock my teeth so far down my throat I'd eat them for supper, so I can't say."

"What if I paid you ten dollars? Would you tell me anything about this man?"

The boy's eyes lit up at the promise of what Jasper assumed was more money than he'd ever dreamed of, and just as quickly, his enthusiasm dimmed. He got a tearful look in his eye and said, "I don't want him to hurt me, mister. He seemed like a bad man!"

"Was he wearing a straw hat?"

Furrowing his brow, the boy nodded.

"Do you live in Sydney-Town?"

The boy shook his head but added as he looked away, "Not too far from there."

Regarding the plate of food that Royal had refused, Jasper picked up a slice of buttered bread and handed it to the boy, saying, "I'll write my answer while you wait."

Jasper unfolded the paper, which was actually of such nice quality, it surprised him. Inside, the note said:

> *I want $10,000 in gold by to-*
> *night. If you pay that, you'll get*
> *your woman back. If not, when*
> *I'm done with her she'll go to*
> *work for me in one of my broth-*
> *els, and I'll be able to earn that*
> *for her in no time. Think of*
> *all the men who will have her!*
> *My next messenger will take the*
> *money. Be ready.*

Jasper felt like his skin was crawling as he showed the note to Royal. Royal squinted at it as if the words swam around the page. Finally, he nodded at Jasper, who sat to write his answer:

We will have your gold. Send your man.

Jasper refolded the note and handed it to the boy, saying, "Stay away from those men, son. They're nothing but trouble. Find yourself a job, work hard, and make something of yourself, but *not* in Sydney-Town. We could even find you a job here if you'd like."

As soon as the boy pocketed the note, he sneered at Jasper, saying, "I got a job, and he pays me plenty!" He spat nastily on the floor and scooted out the door. Jasper waited a moment and then followed after him.

When he got to the hotel lobby, he grabbed one of his watchmen and quietly ordered him, "Follow that boy discretely and see where he goes. He's our only clue right now to Adeline's whereabouts. Be careful. In fact... take someone else with you, and do it *right now.*"

"Yes sir, Mr. Langley," the man replied sharply and was out the door in a flash.

Jasper stood for a moment in thought and then headed to the kitchen, where he found Chef Guillaume deep in a discussion about the dinner menu with his staff. Seeing Jasper, Guillaume stopped what he was doing and went to him with deep concern in his eyes. "How is Royal?" he asked.

"Better, thanks. Doc Louis says he has a hard head." Jasper made an attempt at smiling, but it only seemed to work on one side of his mouth. "Do you possibly have any soup we could give him? His throat seems terribly uncomfortable, so solid food isn't working."

"*Ah, mais oui!* I should have considered that. *Je m'excuse!*"

"It's fine, Guillaume. You didn't know." Jasper's expression was grim despite his comforting words.

"And is there any word on Madame Adeline?"

"We just got a ransom note, and I sent some men to follow the messenger. I'd have gone myself, but I can barely stand; I'm so tired, I doubt I'd be much use to her."

"*Vite, vite.* Go back upstairs, and I will send someone up with hot soup in a few moments. Get some rest so you can recover and help. It's a very good soup, so I'll send enough for both of you. *Maintenant, partez tout de suite.*" Guillaume shooed at Jasper with his hands. "I see how you are struggling."

Two hours later, the exhausted watchmen returned with bad news.

"I'm so sorry, sir. We watched that little shit try to lose us all over San Francisco. He took every back alley, ducked in and out of doors where he could have handed that note off to a thousand different people, but then we finally saw him right out in the open in the middle of Montgomery Street. He handed off three pieces of folded paper to three men, and they scattered in different directions. Took off running. We knew we'd been duped, but we tried anyway to chase after two of the men. They were fast and knew that part of the city better than we did. We lost them both within minutes. We'll accept it if you want to fire us." He hung his head.

"I'll do nothing of the sort. Thank you for doing your best. Your jobs are safe. We'll just have to outsmart Boolie. Somehow." Jasper thought for a moment and said, "Please go tell all of the watchmen to meet me in the saloon in fifteen minutes. I'll alert the partners, and we'll have a meeting." He took off to find the other men who were no doubt eating or sleeping. They had to be just as exhausted as he was.

Ten minutes later, however, when Jasper entered the saloon, it was to find at least fifty men seated around the room and talking softly. "Sorry, men," he called out. "The saloon is closed today." Then he looked and realized that neither Séamus, Timothy, or any of their regular employees were behind the bar.

A man he recognized as a regular patron stood and explained, "We're not here for liquor or entertainment today. We heard about what the Ducks are trying to do to you and came to offer our assistance. If we can help find Miss Adeline for you, it will be our pleasure. Those shifty-eyed bastards have to stop terrorizing our city and return your woman. That's just way, way too much to stomach." He looked around and asked, "Right, men?"

A chorus went up in angry agreement. The noise abated then, however, when they were greeted with the sight of Royal making his heavy-footed progress into the room. Normally glowing with happiness and vigor, this Royal looked broken. He had a heavy bandage covering a lot of his head, and his eyes looked both pained and haunted. With a resolute expression on his face and a voice that cracked with emotion, he addressed the crowded room. "Much appreciated, gentlemen." He nodded and found a chair near where Jasper stood, gaping at him. "Carry on, Jas," he said softly.

Jasper knew better than to order Royal back to bed. He looked around the saloon and had to fight back tears; he was so moved. As he gathered his thoughts, at least fifteen more men drifted in to help the cause. And one woman. Madame Beaufort sailed gracefully down the stairs and positioned herself in the chair next to Royal. She patted him on the arm, smiling sweetly.

Finally, once they were nearly one hundred men strong—all armed with pistols and knives—they carried out a strategic planning meeting. The first decision they made was to make the meeting look like a regular day in the saloon in case they were infiltrated by one of Boolie's spies. So, out came the bottles of whiskey and beer, and everyone was on strict orders to refrain from drinking too much. Suspicious glares went around the room then, and all the men were asked to vouch for each other. So far, everyone in attendance was legitimate, but Jasper knew that sooner or later, Boolie's messenger would arrive. He positioned a lookout at the door and tried to appear to be drowning his sorrows in drink rather than plotting.

And very soon, that messenger did arrive—not one of Boolie's men or a child this time. This messenger was a woman —no doubt one of Boolie's prostitutes. She might have been attractive had she not been sporting a black eye. Jasper figured that in itself was a warning—letting Jasper know how "nicely" Boolie treated anyone who disobeyed. She asked for Jasper by name and handed him another written note:

> *You thought you could follow my boy. Your foolishness is going to cost you. The price is now $15,000. Pay me now or your woman will be on the next ship to China. It leaves in two hours. The buyer is anxious to have her aboard.*

Jasper read the note with a clenched jaw. He grabbed some ink and a pen from behind the bar and wrote:

> *Meet me yourself at the corner of Montgomery and Broadway. Forgive me if I don't trust your "deliveryman." That's a lot of gold, and I'll need to see that Adeline is safe with my own eyes before I hand it over. If she is unharmed, I will make it $20,000. I will be there in an hour.*

The woman wordlessly snatched the paper from Jasper's hand and stalked away. Before she could make it through the door, however, Jasper stopped her, saying, "Miss, we could give you a decent job here at The Discovery, you know. You wouldn't have to prostitute yourself, and no one would lay a hand on you in anger... ever." The woman whipped her head around momentarily, and Jasper caught a brief look of disbelief and longing in her eyes before she ducked her head and sped through the door. He figured that was the last he would see of her.

Turning back to his crowd of assembled men, he said, "Now that we all know where and when, it's time to get into position. Please be careful. We don't want any of you getting hurt. Once again, thank you all from the bottom of my heart."

The men filed out in groups of two, three, and four. Many of them stopped to shake Jasper's hand, mutter reassurances, or nod to him in solidarity as they passed by. Jasper knew these were good, solid men, and they were sincere in their commitment to get Adeline back safely. He also knew that if they were smart—and lucky—this might be the beginning of the end of the rampage of the Sydney Ducks.

Turning to Royal, Jasper was surprised to see a small smile gracing the man's face. "You ought to go back to bed now. We'll take it from here."

"Not on your life." Royal stood, tall and straight, with a newfound strength. "I'm coming too."

"But..."

"No, Jas. I'll be fine. My aim might be a little off because I'm seeing double, but if I have to shoot at Boolie, I'll get to kill him twice that way."

Jasper shook his head with a grin. "I love your spirit. And everything else about you."

"Me too. Let's go."

Jasper hoisted a heavy-looking sack that Royal eyed, asking, "Are you sure you want to carry that much gold anywhere near Sydney-Town?"

Chuckling, Jasper explained, "There's only a thin layer of gold. The rest is dirt."

Leaving a small team behind to guard the hotel—mostly made up of armed kitchen workers—the six partners took off for the rendezvous with Boolie. Doc Louis and Madame Beaufort brought up the rear, both armed with concealed pistols and a little something else. One could never be too careful.

Chapter Forty-One

The area of San Francisco near the base of Goat Hill teemed with activity any time of day, so it didn't seem unusual to the casual observer that there were men milling about. Some were laughing at a joke, some conducting business, shopping, or simply exchanging information. More than a few were sitting or lying on the ground, apparently sleeping off whatever they'd overindulged in. It was a normal sight in San Francisco.

Jasper took up his station at the appointed corner, and his partners were all cleverly positioned out of sight nearby. He tried to breathe normally, but his heart nearly beat out of his chest. He wished fervently that he'd asked Royal to stay by his side for moral support, but he also knew there was too much possibility of further harm to him in his weakened state. Jasper hoped that Boolie's greed would bring the man to the corner without any foolishness.

Time felt sluggish. Minutes dragged. No Boolie. No Adeline. Jasper's hope began to dwindle. *Perhaps Boolie's seen through our plan,* he worried over and over. *Don't give up hope. She's fine. She's fine,* became his mantra. *She has to be fine.*

At nearly fifteen minutes past the appointed hour, the same young boy from earlier sauntered up to Jasper with a cocky look on his face. "I'm here to make sure you have the gold," he announced with great bravado. "Show me."

Jasper untied the bag and opened it. He watched as the boy's eyes went wide at the glittering contents. Jasper reached in and grabbed a generous pinch that he placed in the kid's grubby palm, saying, "Get out of here and tell Boolie to stop sending children and women to do his dirty work. He's not much of a man, is he?"

The boy scowled at him, then spun around and ran down the street. He had no way of knowing that eyes followed him along his route, for men from The Discovery were positioned all over Sydney-Town, watching and waiting for Boolie's messenger to appear.

The boy doubled back several times, expecting to find someone in pursuit, but there was no one. Finally, sure he was safe, the boy ducked into the back of a sturdy building. It was uncharacteristically clean and well cared for, devoid of a sign proclaiming it to be a saloon, cat house, or any other den of iniquity so common in the area, for it was actually Boolie's house.

Assured that no one had followed the boy, and heartened by the pinch of gold dust his messenger brought him, Boolie poked his head out of the house. He looked suspiciously from side to side before proceeding in a circuitous route toward the appointed corner where Jasper stood waiting.

Unfortunately, Boolie was not accompanied by Adeline.

Eyes followed Boolie as he trudged down the street, limping slightly and looking nervous. His shoulders squared as he reached the rendezvous point.

Face to face at last, Jasper frowned at Boolie and demanded, "Where is she? I told you I'm not paying until I see her unharmed!" Jasper shifted his bag from one hand to the other, trying to make it look heavier than it truly was.

Smirking, Boolie—whose face looked a tad greenish— replied in an oily tone. "I don't trust ye any more than ye trust me, pretty boy. Ye'll have to come wi' me to get yer woman. She's safe enough. She looks good, but she's about as pleasant as a crocodile, that one." He turned away again, clearly expecting Jasper to follow him like an obedient dog.

As Boolie started walking, Jasper noticed the man's slight limp. Something clearly hadn't gone according to his plans. Smiling to himself, he fell into step behind Boolie, giving the impression that he was following the man's orders.

Slowly and surreptitiously, men fell into step behind them. Ranks closed in on all sides, but carefully and out of Boolie's eyesight.

Suddenly, a beautiful, elegantly dressed woman rushed forward, right in Boolie's path. She collided with him and landed on the ground with her skirt exposing most of her lower body. She let out a steady stream of what had to be furious curse words in French even though Jasper was sure she had "helped" her skirts into position as she took her tumble.

Boolie stopped dead and gaped at the woman's shapely body. He was a man, after all, and this was certainly not an everyday occurrence in broad daylight. With his jaw unhinged a bit, it provided the perfect opportunity for Doc Louis and Isaac to slip up behind him. Doc Louis shoved an ether-soaked rag over Boolie's face at the same time Isaac clobbered Boolie over the head with the butt of his pistol. Boolie dropped to the ground like a rock. Doc Louis held the rag in place as he waited for Séamus and Timothy to arrive with the same old cart they'd used to transport Walter and Royal to The Discovery.

Helpful men closed ranks around them protectively as, swiftly and efficiently, they loaded Boolie into the cart. They covered him with a bunch of old sacks, leaving the ether-soaked rag over his mouth and nose.

Jasper helped Madame Beaufort to her feet and told her, "Thank you for your invaluable assistance, ma'am." He gave her a courtly bow then rushed off to follow the path the various neighborhood watchers pointed out. *She has to be there,* he prayed to himself. *She just has to be.*

As Jasper rushed off to where he hoped he would find Adeline, Royal, Walter, and a small army of their men fell into step around him with their guns drawn. Jasper gave Royal a doubletake and then grabbed his arm affectionately. "We'll find her," he promised. Men all along their path directed them and joined in beside them.

The other group—led by Isaac, Séamus, and Timothy—rolled the Boolie-laden cart down to the waterfront. Volunteers rallied around them with their guns drawn, fanning out to protect them on their way. However, if there had been any of Boolie's Ducks lurking in the area, they scattered like rats in the face of the guns and furious attitudes.

After they wheeled their cart to the pier, they quickly tied Boolie up with a heavy rope. They dumped him unceremoniously into a rowboat, and two men rowed him out to a ship that was just getting ready to pull up anchor. The captain of the ship was more than delighted to accept a new "crewman," and when he realized that he didn't even need to come up with a sum of money, he was elated. Within minutes, Boolie Bollinger was sailing away to Shanghai whether he wanted to or not.

"See how you like it, you rotten bastard!" hollered Isaac at the departing ship.

Blocks away, Jasper, Royal, and the others followed their spies to the house Boolie had recently vacated. With guns at the ready, they surrounded the premises with caution. Listening carefully at first, they heard nothing, and then all hell broke loose. A woman screamed, and several sets of feet thundered downstairs inside the building. The doors in front and back of the building flew open, and wild-eyed Ducks raced out into the ambush of guns trained at them. A few got away, but the men were able to tackle three of them as Jasper, Royal, and

Walter ran into the building. Giving a cursory look around the ground floor, they found no one, but Walter asked, "Do you smell smoke?"

The air was clouding, so they headed to the stairs. The frantic woman screamed again from above them on the second floor. "Addie!" Royal shouted hoarsely as he and the others ran up the stairs. There were a few rooms off a long hallway. Most of the rooms were open, but they came to one that was closed and locked. Black smoke billowed out in smelly plumes from under the door. Frantically, they kicked and rammed their shoulders against the heavy door while the smoke got heavier and heavier, and the screams from inside grew more frantic.

"Addie! We're here! Hang on!" Royal hollered back at her.

"He has a gun!" she cried.

"What?" Royal looked at Jasper, who looked equally confused. "Why is there a man inside with the fire burning?"

Getting nowhere pounding and ramming the heavy door, Walter ordered them to stand back. He pointed his pistol at the door handle and fired point-blank. The noise was deafening, but the door exploded, and they were finally able to shove it open. The sight that greeted them was a strange one. A man lay bleeding on the floor just inside the room, and Adeline sat across from them, tied to a fancy chair. Apparently, Water had shot Addie's captor when he blew a hole in the door.

"Is he dead?" Walter asked with a wobble in his voice. No one paid him any attention, so he kicked the man's weapon away from him and tried not to faint.

Royal had run to Adeline and was attempting to free her from her bonds, while Jasper fought the fire in the corner of the room. A mattress lay smoldering and smoking with a big gash in the middle. An overturned oil lamp lay beside it— obviously the source of the fuel and the flame. There was a lot more smoke than fire at this point, but the threat of disaster was always present in this kind of situation.

Jasper turned the smoking mattress and began stomping on it. Then he spied a knife lying on the floor. It looked like it had been the instrument that ripped the hole in the mattress in the first place. "Royal! Use this!" He kicked the knife toward Royal and Adeline, who was coughing her head off. "Walter! Call down for some water! We need to put this out before it burns down the building and causes another big fire!"

Shaking himself into action, Walter ran down and organized a bucket brigade. Within moments, the fire was no longer a threat, Adeline was freed from her confines, and they were safe at last.

When they got themselves outside, Royal, Jasper, and Adeline clung to each other. They couldn't get close enough together, it seemed. Adeline—most uncharacteristically—was sobbing.

"Everything is alright now, Adeline. You're safe. We're safe. It's all fine," Jasper crooned over and over to her.

"I thought one of you was dead!" she sobbed at last. "I was so scared and so angry with that horrible, conceited monster! Where is he?" She looked around wildly. "I'd like to kill him myself!"

"He's gone," Royal assured her. "You don't have to worry about him anymore. Look around you, Addie. These men are all friends, and they came to help us save you. Everyone is fine, just like Jasper said. Let's go home now."

On the way back to The Discovery, Adeline asked, "What happened to your head, Royal? Why are you all bandaged? You don't look very well."

"Don't worry about me, darling, I have a hard head. It was just a little run-in with a bullet in the middle of the harbor. Jasper here is the big hero of the day. He saved me from drowning." He looked adoringly at Jasper as Adeline gaped at him.

"*A bullet?* Royal! Jasper, you're incredible. I need to hear the whole story."

To redirect the attention off himself, Jasper asked, "Do you know what happened to Boolie? By the time he reached us, he was limping and looking sick. I was afraid he might not show up, and when he finally did, I wondered if he'd been delayed by an accident."

Adeline finally looked pleased about something when she explained, "He left me alone for a moment, so I tried to get to a weapon off his writing desk. In doing so, I tipped myself over. He thought that was hilarious and left me like that for quite a long time. Then I guess he got tired of looking at me that way, so when he approached me to right the chair, I kicked him right where you told me men feel pain the most."

"You kicked him in the nuts?"

"I must have done a good job of it. He vomited, but I was afraid he was going to kill me for it. Then his messenger showed up with word that you had the money. He gave orders to the man Walter shot to create a distraction if anyone showed up, and he left. He wasn't in very good shape when he walked out of that room." She gave them a satisfied smile. "How are the rest of the men? Is everyone alright?"

"Everyone will live. Just bumps, bruises, and a few stitches," Royal assured her. "You must be starving and exhausted, Addie."

And so it went. All the way back to The Discovery, they filled each other in on the parts of the story they knew. More and more of their men joined them on the road back, filling in even more information. The only person's fate no one seemed to know about was Captain Greely's because nobody cared to check on whether he still lay on the dock, made it back to the Wind Gypsy, or ended up Shanghaied while he lay unconscious. In the grand scheme of things, it didn't seem very important.

Chapter Forty-Two

After refreshing baths, a solid meal, and a long, long sleep, Jasper and Royal woke to the sun pouring in on them through the curtains. They were all naked and wrapped tightly around each other. Adeline was the last to wake, and she hummed with pleasure as she felt the hands of her men stroking her body.

"Good morning, my lovely men," she chuckled. She kissed them both soundly and smiled as they kissed each other, leaning across her body. She felt surrounded and protected by them and added, "I have never loved you both more than I love you right at this very moment, and I want to show you just how much you mean to me."

Adeline wiggled out from between them and encouraged them to lie side-by-side. She knelt between their legs and alternated kissing one and then the other. In between kisses, she whispered endearments to them. Jasper and Royal stroked her body wherever they could reach as she played with them. She kissed their mouths, nibbled their ears, licked their throats, and trailed long sweeping, wet kisses down their chests and abdomens. Her hands were never still, and she spent a lot of effort stroking their massive erections, purring her approval.

"Adeline, are you trying to tease us to death?" Jasper asked with a pained laugh.

"Oh? You need more?" Immediately, she raised her body up over Jasper and impaled herself onto his cock. She rammed herself to the hilt as he cried out in ecstasy.

"Yes! That's it. Oh, Adeline..." His eyes squeezed shut as he delighted in the feel of her warm body encasing him like a hot, wet vise. His eyes flew open again when he heard Royal hiss in pleasure.

Adeline had shifted around so that she could remain on Jasper, and at the same time, she'd leaned over to engulf Royal in her mouth. It was messy and uncoordinated—and thoroughly erotic—until she worked out a rhythm of rocking back and forth. Royal scooted around to make himself more accessible and seemed to be enjoying the view as much as the sensation. When Adeline licked her fingers and thrust one of them into Royal's backside while she sucked him, Royal's eyes rolled back in his head. Jasper thought this must be the most beautiful sight in the world.

Jasper reached one hand to Adeline's clit and probed her backside with the other. She gasped in surprise when he breached her bottom but quickly recovered and merely sped up her sucking Royal and fucking Jasper. It was like a giant free-for-all of pleasure. All friction and wetness, sighs and moans.

Faster and faster, she sucked, probed, and bounced while Jasper manipulated her clit and toyed with her bottom. Royal reached for her breasts, caressing and pinching her nipples until she thought she might go mad with pleasure. That wonderful rush feeling began to grow from somewhere deep within her until the feeling expanded and flourished. Golden light suffused her vision behind her eyelids, and the warmth for her two men in her heart made her explode with the sheer joy of being alive and being in love with her two perfect men. Pleasure like she'd never experienced before crashed through her, and she shook from head to toe.

Royal and Jasper felt it too as they released their seed into her precious body. Crying out with the delight of infinite love, they shouted and wept with happiness.

Chapter Forty-Three

Life at The Discovery settled back into a normal—for them —pattern. The hotel prospered, the restaurant did well, the saloon drew crowds every night, and the casino continued to make all the partners rich. Adeline and Isaac entertained dancers with their music, and both of them received invitations to give recitals at the National Theatre. Now they were not only loved for their wonderful music, they'd also become something of local legends after their troubles with the Sydney Ducks. Everyone wanted to get a glimpse of them.

As successful as they were, however, running their establishment was beginning to get old for most of the proprietors. The men who crossed the country from coast to coast to build The Discovery were men of action and vision. The personalities of adventurers and entrepreneurs don't often coincide with staying put in one place and doing the same thing for a long time. They were becoming restless and needed a new challenge. No one was ready to quit, but plenty of "what if..." conversations were beginning to take place during their meetings. It started out as a hint of a whisper but gradually turned into an ongoing conversation.

For their part, however, Timothy and Séamus shrugged off their partners' ennui. They loved what they did and made plans to bring their families over from Ireland. The Discovery seemed like a great place to keep at least some of them employed.

The volunteers who rushed to save Adeline came back again and again to visit and talk about crime and violence in San Francisco. Their meetings blossomed into regular discussions and a more organized effort to save the city. The group grew to over seven hundred members, all concerned citizens who'd had it with the incompetent local government, rampant corruption, and the reign of terror by the Sydney Ducks.

In 1851, the disgruntled city residents elected a brand-new Vigilance Committee. The appointed members took care of justice their own way—decisively and efficiently, without bribery to influence them. They rounded up the worst of the Sydney Ducks and tried several of them for their crimes, mostly murder and arson. Four were publicly hung, fourteen were deported back to Australia, and another fourteen were driven out of the state. Of the four who were hanged, one unfortunately turned out to be the wrong man with the same name as the real criminal, but the actual perpetrator was soon discovered and brought to justice. Fifteen more Sydney Ducks were rounded up, and one was publicly whipped. To the great relief of the San Franciscans, this put an end to the gang for good.

Nearly losing one another made Adeline, Jasper, and Royal appreciate their marriage more than ever. Jasper had already been painfully aware of how fleeting life can be after he lost Isabella in the blink of an eye, but now his comprehension of how blessed he was to have found deep, abiding love again simply floored him. Their devotion to one another took on a new level of tenderness and sweetness, and they tried to relish every possible minute they had together.

Royal had witnessed Jasper's devastation and never wanted someone so dear to him to feel that kind of pain again. And for him, the threat of losing Adeline was inconceivably heartbreaking. That stab of terror he'd felt when they discovered she'd been taken would resurface now and then at odd moments, and he had to tamp it down so he could function normally. Sometimes, he would wake in the middle of the night shaking and sweating. *It's over*, he told himself repeatedly. *Over. Now buck up and be a man.*

Adeline told her husbands, "I was beyond terrified that my future would be ugly and barren if I were ripped away from being able to express my love for you. I realized that the hell I feared was that existence. But that hell was vanquished."

On a magnificent day in early 1852, as they lay wrapped around each other after hours of tender lovemaking, Adeline sat up in bed. She needed to see both of their faces. "I have something wonderful to tell you," she said with a beatific smile. Seeing that she had their full attention, she announced, "I'm expecting a child."

Jasper cried with happiness, and Royal laughed with joy. They both hugged her, kissed her, hugged and kissed each other, and hugged and kissed her some more, both declaring that it was the best news they'd ever heard.

"We need to build a house and move out of this hotel," Jasper declared in a no-nonsense tone.

"I agree. This is no place to raise children," chimed Royal. "We need to build a house with room for the children to play..."

"One at a time, Royal," she interrupted with a laugh.

"I need to write home to my parents and let them know they'll be grandparents!" Royal said cheerfully.

"Writing home is a great idea," Jasper added. "My mother will be happy to hear it, I believe."

"Why do you think it took you so long to conceive, Addie?" Royal asked. "My mother seemed to be expecting all the time. In fact, I wouldn't be surprised if I have six more brothers than I had when I left." He laughed then and added, "Maybe she's even managed to have a couple of girls by now."

"I don't know why, but it was the same for my mother, I believe. They were married for five years before she had me, and then she never had more children." Adeline suddenly looked sad. "It was probably lucky she didn't have more children considering how sick she became. My father barely knew what to do with me."

Six months later, they moved into a beautiful house on Rincon Hill. It had been designed by Walter and appointed fantastically by Isaac and a crew of builders the two of them had hired. The house was a showcase that made them all proud.

Building the house on the hill was a great project for them for a while, but for most of the partners, the restlessness still hung in the air and clouded their vision like San Francisco fog.

A month after moving into the house, Adeline was blessed with a beautiful baby girl who looked incredibly like Jasper. She had black fuzz on her head and startling blue eyes. They decided to name her Marigold Hart Dawson-Langley, and she was so loved by her three parents and her four "uncles" she was rarely out of someone's arms.

A month after Marigold was born, a letter arrived from New York. Jasper's jaw dropped when he read it. "What?" he gasped.

"What is it, Jas?" asked Royal.

Looking up from the page, Jasper blinked at them a couple of times as if needing to clear his vision and explained, "My father has decided to sell his textile factories, and he wants to move west. He's sorry he was so harsh with me for leaving and thinks that coming west will be good for my parents and good for our family. He wants to retire here in San Francisco because he says the weather sounds too healthy to pass up, and he and Mother miss me too much."

"Well, I'll be..." Royal mused in a soft voice. "Does he still want you to go into business with him? Maybe start up something new?"

"No. He made it perfectly clear that he had unrealistic expectations of me and wants to repair the rift he caused by trying to control my future. He says he's proud of what I've accomplished on my own. He did add, however, that he would not be averse to investing in something I'm working on." He looked at them solemnly and added, "What he doesn't realize is that none of what we've accomplished would have been possible without you. I love you both so dearly."

"Does he know about your marital status?" Adeline inquired.

"Mmm... not exactly," Jasper hedged.

"Well, we'll break him in," Royal asserted with more confidence than any of them actually felt. This was going to be a touchy topic to handle for an older gentleman who hadn't seen the lifestyle in the West for himself yet.

Jasper shrugged and reached for Marigold. "He'll certainly love this little one, no matter what, won't he, my precious treasure?" He kissed Marigold softly on her cheek and watched her little hands flail around. "You're so perfect; you'd melt the heart of an ogre. My father loves children."

Chapter Forty-Four

Ayear and a half later, Mr. and Mrs. Langley still had not been able to leave New York. It was taking longer than expected to sell off the factories and their home. New laws divided everyone's opinions and left folks wondering about their futures. Some people were sure the country depended on slavery for economic strength. Others were just as certain that slavery needed to be abolished. Mr. Langley abhorred everything about the slave trade in principle, but he couldn't deny that the material for his business came from them. This painful dilemma made him want to leave more than ever.

They also missed their son tremendously.

Finally, in November 1854, he sold the last of his businesses, and as soon as they could, they purchased tickets on a ship that sped them down to Panama. Late in January of 1855, they boarded the first commercial railroad, which took them across the Isthmus of Panama in comfort and safety in a single day.

The train journey was nothing like the trek earlier travelers had to take through the disease-, snake-, and insect-infested jungle by mule and dugout canoe. Whereas once the journey routinely killed off many hopeful travelers in horrible, painful ways, now travelers like the Langleys enjoyed the breathtaking scenery of the surrounding jungle from the comfort of a railroad car, captivated by colorful birds and exotic species of plants.

Once across the country, Jasper's parents booked passage on what was now a regularly scheduled steamship line and sailed swiftly north to San Francisco. Any discomfort they'd put up with along the way could never compare to the horrors faced by the earlier travelers.

The family was to be reunited at last.

As soon as Jasper got word that his parents would be arriving, he and the other partners began building them a house. It was also on Rincon Hill—the most prestigious address at that time in San Francisco.

They had such a great time building once again that they decided to form their own building business. They signed The Discovery over to Séamus and Timothy and maintained a silent partner investment in the property, thus allowing the Irishmen to continue running it. It was, by now, filled with the relatives of both Irishmen and running smoothly in their hands.

Even as the zeal for prospecting for gold dwindled away, immigrants continued to flock to the city from all over the world. San Francisco grew and grew, and many well-heeled newcomers needed houses.

Royal, Jasper, Walter, and Isaac created their new company, which they called Roja Wais. Building beautiful mansions stimulated them in a way they had not felt for well over a year, so they were all happy. Walter, of course, drew up the architectural plans and oversaw the construction. Royal pitched in to help Isaac with building projects, and soon discovered he had a wonderful knack for carpentry. Jasper ran the business side of things. Meeting with customers and looking at possible building sites gave him the challenge and the variety he needed. He also honed the wheeling and dealing skills he'd developed as a miner and constantly looked for the best deal on materials.

To Séamus and Timothy's great regret, Chef Guillaume decided to quit the restaurant at The Discovery and chose instead to work for Jasper, Adeline, and Royal in their new house as their private chef. He was tired of working so hard and looked at his smaller workload as almost a vacation. He'd done a good job of training his staff at the hotel, however, so the Irishmen still had an impressive kitchen turning out lovely meals.

Timothy and Séamus converted the dance hall at The Discovery into more gambling, and Adeline's piano was, at last, moved to her house where she and Isaac continued their music lessons for children—only one day a week at this point. Her responsibilities with her own babies didn't leave her with time to give nightly entertainment, so she was delighted with the change.

The day the senior Langleys arrived by steamship, it seemed that the entire city came out to see who might disembark. Greeting arriving ships was a favorite pastime of the San Franciscans. Men often saw it as a way to scope out prospective wives, prospective employees, and in a few less scrupulous cases, an easy mark for pickpocketing or other swindling. The ship arrivals took on a circus atmosphere with much shouting and carrying on.

Jasper could barely hold still as he waited with his partners for his parents to walk down the gangway. He stood on the dock with Walter, Isaac, and Royal, who all smiled knowingly at his nervousness. Adeline elected to stay home with the babies, rightly thinking that a more subdued greeting would be less traumatic for infants and a youngster. Finally, Jasper shoved his arm into the air and waved his hand frantically, calling, "Father! Mother! Over here!"

His eyes grew misty at the sight of them. There was nothing like having children of his own to make his parents more important to him at last. He understood, finally, their deep-seated desire to assure a perfect life for their son. What he'd felt was stifling control had always come from a place of love. Maybe it was off the mark in some ways, but it was never intended to be mean—he was convinced of that.

Jasper shoved his way through the throng of gawkers until he got to his parents and grabbed them into a tight bearhug. His mother looked shocked and his father taken aback, but they settled into his embrace and kissed his cheeks. They'd never exactly been known for public displays of affection, but people all around them behaved accordingly—so, why not?

"It's wonderful to see you both!" he exclaimed over and over and then prodded them toward his friends. "Come and meet the men. Adeline is at home with the children, but she's beside herself with delight that you're here."

Shaking hands all around, Mr. Langley took in the rough, calloused palms and general sawdusty appearance of the partners and declared, "How nice for you all to come and meet the boss's family. I'm sure you have better things to do."

A bit of Jasper's excitement evaporated with that statement. "No, Father, you misunderstand. We have all been putting the finishing touches on the house we built for you and Mother. Clothing etiquette in San Francisco is much more relaxed than you're used to, and we all felt it was more important to have the house finished than to dress formally for your arrival. I apologize if that offends you. These are all my *business partners*, and my..." He suddenly thought that calling Royal his husband at this juncture might be a bit premature, so he stopped talking.

"You aren't moving us in with you?" Mrs. Langley inquired with raised eyebrows. "Whyever not? I thought you'd written that your new house is large with plenty of extra room."

"Oh, don't worry. You'll be close enough. We're filling our house up pretty quickly with children anyway and thought you'd prefer your privacy, and we, er... I was able to purchase a prime lot for you. It has a beautiful view, and the house is well-appointed like nothing you've ever seen, Mother. I'm sure you'll enjoy it." Looking around, he added, "Let's get your trunks loaded into the wagon and get you situated. You must be tired after your journey. Later tonight, we can have everyone together for a lovely supper."

Later that evening, they convened at the mansion they affectionately called Hart House. All six men were at last cleaned up and in tailored suits for the occasion, looking like urbane and handsome gentlemen—despite their calloused hands. Séamus and Timothy only planned to stop in and stay for a while before the would politely excuse themselves. The Discovery needed them on hand in the evenings.

To her tremendous credit in Jasper's mother's eyes, Adeline had produced a handsome set of identical twin boys they named August and Earnest—or Augie and Ernie—shortly before the grandparents arrived. The boys looked a tiny bit like their sister Marigold but very obviously favored Royal with his golden hair and facial structure. This would not be all that obvious to Mrs. Langley at first—she was just so thrilled to have three lovely grandchildren to spoil at last.

Having twins shocked Adeline until Royal admitted that he was the only non-twin of all his siblings. It was just one more way he'd felt out of place on the dairy farm.

Sweet little Marigold took an immediate delight in meeting her grandfather and insisted that he hold her on his lap so she could babble at him about her day, the dog she got to pet, and how badly she wanted a pretty brown-and-white puppy. She enchanted him instantly, and the man looked besotted with her. As the time grew later, Marigold began punctuating her one-sided conversation with some huge yawns, and the nanny came in and whisked her off to bed. As she left the room, Marigold waved her chubby little hand at her grandfather.

While her husband had been charmed by Marigold's chatter, Mrs. Langley carried on without hardly breathing about the adventure they'd been on to get to San Francisco. She moaned about some mild *mal de mer* and excess humidity but mostly extolled the beauty of the scenery they'd passed through.

Mr. Langley interjected, "My lovely wife calls the discomfort mild, and for her, it was. However, seasickness made *me* feel like I would die one moment and then afraid I wouldn't the next." He laughed heartily at his own joke.

His humor was met only with polite smiles from those who remembered their own journeys to the West.

"But the birds in Panama!" exclaimed Mrs. Langley. "Oh, you should have seen them with their incredibly colorful plumage. It was a delight for the eyes."

Before the meal service began, they said goodnight to the Irishmen, and Séamus explained with a cocky grin, "We need to get back to The Discovery before we *discover* it's been looted in our absence."

Jasper's mother seemed to pale at that statement.

Isaac and Walter remained for supper with the family. In truth, they ate most of their meals there out of habit and camaraderie. They pitched in to help pay the chef's wages.

Chef Guillaume outdid himself once again by preparing a meal that was more magnificent than anything the Langleys had ever experienced. They were privately impressed.

Adeline had to excuse herself toward the end of the meal when they heard the twins crying. Even though they had a nanny, Adeline preferred to feed the babies herself.

"Your wife is quite lovely, son," Mrs. Langley said approvingly. "She seems very well-mannered as well."

Jasper squelched a snort when he thought of the very unladylike ideas Adeline was fond of expounding in private. Just last night, she'd played one of her "games" with the men that she liked to call "Sword Swallowing." It turned into a competition for how deep... His mind trailed off when he realized he was getting stiff thinking about his lovers. Clearing his throat, he answered, "Thank you, Mother. So... ahem... Adeline and

Isaac are extremely talented musicians, and they planned some entertainment for you tonight—if you're not too tired from your travels."

"Oh, how lovely," she responded. Regarding Isaac, she asked politely, "Where do you live? Do you also have a house nearby?"

Isaac shook his head and said, "No, ma'am. Not yet. Walter and I are looking for the right property, but so far, we're still living at The Discovery."

Mrs. Langley seemed to think that was a somewhat odd reply, but she smoothed her furrowed brow and turned her attention to Royal. "And you, sir? Do you live at the hotel as well? I suppose it makes sense for a single man to be at a hotel."

The room was silent for a few seconds until Royal straightened his spine and answered with a polite smile, "No. I live here."

Jasper didn't know how to broach this topic, so he sat in silence for a moment longer. He could see the confusion on his mother's face, and she finally turned her attention to him, "Why does Mr. Dawson live with you and Adeline? Is he actually your valet or butler? You seem awfully comfortable and informal with him if that is the case, and that's not exactly how one ought to treat an employee."

Jasper sucked in a deep breath and tried to not snap at her for an honest—though rude—question, so he sat up straight and looked her in the eye. "As I have already explained, Mother, Royal is not employed by me. He is my partner, my best friend in the entire world, and he is my... I mean *our* husband."

"Your *what?*" his father cried as Mrs. Langley gaped at him. "Are you depraved?"

"On the contrary, Father. I love Royal the same way I love Adeline. And they love each other equally as well. We tried to deny it at first, but this is what works for us. We're happy, and no one else cares at all."

"We came all the way across the country to *this?*" Mr. Langley stood and reached his hand to his wife, saying, "Come along. I won't stay here one more minute."

Mrs. Langley was not as quick to stand—she was too nonplussed. In fact, her jaw dropped in a very unladylike manner.

Walter stood as well and took this opportunity to interject his opinion. Skewering Mr. Langley with a fierce look, he growled, "Sit down, man, and listen to me. You have absolutely no idea what these people have gone through or how they are beloved and *respected* in San Francisco. No one—pardon me, ma'am—gives a *damn* about who anyone falls in love with or lives with around here. They have *far* more important things to worry about." He glared at Jasper's father until the man took his seat. Relaxing back into his own chair, Walter continued, "These two men nearly died crossing the country on that wagon train, and rather than moaning about their hardships, they bucked up and became men about it. Countless people with big dreams of making a great life for themselves in the West *died every single day* around us, and that makes you appreciate life, I can tell you. Jasper and Royal supported each other and were unfailingly generous to every single person whose lives they touched. Jasper lost his lovely Isabella, but he made it through because Royal helped him. And Royal had so many close calls with things like poisonous snakes and killer frostbite—and who was there to support him? Jasper! It's no wonder they formed a bond. Lots of men in the West sleep together to take the edge off,"—here Mrs. Langley whispered "Heavens!"—"...but they had more between them than that. How can you call that depraved? They are two of the finest men—outside of Isaac here—that I've had the great pleasure of considering my *brothers.*"

Mr. Langley began to open his mouth to speak as Walter took a drink. "I'm not finished, sir. Hold your tongue before you say or do anything that might burn a bridge that you can never rebuild."

Mr. Langley closed his mouth but looked perturbed at being told to do so.

"After we all nearly died crossing the Sierra Nevada—again saved from freezing to death because of Jasper's thoughtfulness and generosity—we made it big in the gold fields. How? By hard—*damned* hard—work the likes of which most of the lazy prospectors didn't even try to accomplish. They heard the rumors and thought the streets were lined with gold—so all they had to do was bend over and pick it up, and poof! Millionaire. Not so. We worked our asses off! All around us, men died of scurvy and malnutrition, and some were murdered in cold blood for a measly sack of gold. It was once again our strong bond that helped us stay safe. Stay *alive.* There were men from all walks of life at those gold fields. Doctors, Harvard professors, Negroes, Indians, military men, farmers, and former prisoners—all scratching away to fill their pockets with gold. Most went broke. Many died. We saw it all. Every cursed day.

"Jasper made several treacherous trips to San Francisco by himself to bring us supplies and see what further opportunities there would be for us if and when the gold ran out. There were no roads back then, I might add. He didn't need to come back. He could have taken our gold and run off, but we trusted him! Royal was the one who made sure we all pulled our weight while Jasper was gone, and Isaac kept our spirits up with his fiddle music. It's a beautiful thing when you know you can count on your partners to do what's best.

"And then we built The Discovery, and they met Adeline Hart." Walter's expression softened at the memory. "It was a special, special day when that beautiful, half-starved, and grief-stricken woman showed up. Her own father—who *died* as soon as their ship landed—*used* her to pay his passage to

California. Treated her like a slave, if you ask me! And she still had it in her big heart to love him. I don't know what all happened on that voyage because it's Adeline's business, but she sure looked like she had some secrets. Can you imagine being the only woman aboard a ship with a crew of lecherous sailors?" He gave Mrs. Langley a hard stare, and she blanched.

Jasper interjected, "I can tell you that she was attacked, but she was not raped, so please don't think that about her." He would not say more on that topic.

Walter continued, "So, what does this exquisite beauty do when she arrives in a city full of outlaws, roughnecks, and heaven-knows-what kind of men from all over the world? She puts on her prettiest dress and entertains them on the *piano* for hours every night. Every single night we could see men so touched by her, they cried! She treated each of them with respect and never said a rude word. She's a treasure, I tell you. Half the men in this city would have given their left arm to marry her, and the other half their right arm.

"It was no wonder she fell in love with Jasper and Royal and they with her. Together they are whole. When Adeline was kidnapped, I thought these two men were going to die of grief. And even in the midst of their crisis, Royal took a bullet and nearly drowned trying to rescue his friends. He's *that* kind of a man.

"Don't even try to believe that there is anything false or im-moral about three people who love each other the way these do. We should all be so lucky. And that's what you need to chew on before you make any rude comments to the wonderful man you raised. Be proud of him as much as we are. Be happy that he's with two of the finest people you'll ever meet.

"And remember when you think of the lovely little *adventure* you took by steamer ship and rail for a *month and a half*, that Adeline served as a cook aboard a ship that took *half a year* to get here, and she was probably scared for her life the entire time. And when she got here, San Francisco was largely a hovel. There were starving, disease-ridden people in the muddy streets, tents and filthy, rickety lean-tos for so-called buildings—not a freshly built, beautiful house ready for you to move into. Adeline never once complained or looked askance at anything or anyone. She was happy to be here, hoping it would please her father. So, when you think to judge anyone for behavior you don't care to understand, try standing in the shoes of the people who have bravely held onto their dreams and built this city from *nothing*. You have no right to criticize the way they love."

"I see," was all Mr. Langley said as he nodded his head thoughtfully.

Isaac also had to add a few things and explained, "Up until just recently, there were simply no laws in the city, and unless you killed someone, nobody really cared. That laissez-faire attitude has spilled into everyday life as well. I'm sure it will change gradually, but you'll get used to it when you see what's going on. The city residents were far more concerned with day-to-day survival than idle gossip. They're a resilient crowd who have rebuilt the city *six times* now after major fires because the gang that kidnapped Adeline committed arson over and over—killing countless people." Under his breath, he added, "Ruthless scoundrels. I'm glad some of them hung."

"Thank you, Isaac and Walter," Royal spoke up at last. "That was a ringing endorsement and really only scratched the surface of what Adeline has been through." He turned to the Langleys and said solemnly, "I love your son and Adeline more than I ever expected I could. When we all agreed to marry, it was the happiest moment of my life, and I intend to spend the rest of my life making certain they know it. The children are and will continue to be loved by all of us equally, in case you wondered."

At that moment, Adeline swept back into the room in her lovely silken gown, looking like the goddess she was. "I'm back. Sorry for the interruption. Did I miss anything interesting?" When she was met with silence, she faced her mother-in-law and said, "You must meet my friend Olivia. She also crossed Panama but under extremely less comfortable conditions. The poor thing lost her parents to cholera, and her brothers deserted her as soon as their ship arrived in San Francisco. Can you imagine? I'm sure she would love to hear about how things have improved since her journey. She's married now to a delightful man who is a banker, so all is well."

"Yes, well..." Mrs. Langley began. "I'm sure that will be a very illuminating conversation." She blinked a couple of times and added, "You have a lovely gown, Adeline. Is there a dressmaker in this city?"

Adeline's laughter trilled as she answered, "Oh, my yes. Madame Beaufort is most talented and a terribly interesting conversationalist. I shall make it a priority to introduce you to her if you would like."

Jasper coughed, and Royal squelched a tiny snort.

"So, Father, would you like to retire to the parlor for a cigar and a brandy? I'm sure Mother would like to see more of the babies." He smiled kindly at his mother, who looked relieved and happy at last. "After that, we'll all hear some music."

With her eyes sparkling, Adeline added, "Yes! Isaac and I have had the best time preparing a Beethoven sonata just for your arrival, and we're anxious to play it for you. Perhaps you're familiar—it's called *Spring*." She laughed then and added, "We even had the piano tuned finally."

When Isaac and Adeline played, their listeners were justifiably transfixed. Never had the Langleys expected true virtuosity and musicality from anyone in this wild, largely untamed part of the world.

And that was that. If the Langleys had any leftover prejudice, they were finally wise enough to keep it to themselves. Walter's golden words had eased their minds, and Adeline and Isaac calmed their hearts with glorious music. Their loved ones would love whomever they loved, and life would go on.

Mr. Langley noticed that whenever his wife had a dress fitting, she came home in a good mood with some fairly outlandish ideas. He loved them.

The End

Musings and Acknowledgements

It is important to point out that although I have made a serious attempt at producing a true account of the California Gold Rush, the fact is, the conditions were actually far worse than I have portrayed in this story. I just didn't want to depress everyone who read the story with uber-realism. I've also taken historic events, such as the many San Francisco fires, and fudged somewhat on dates so that the narrative flowed in a logical pattern that allowed the story to unfold. For example, the fire I described actually happened on June 14, 1850. Also, Henri Herz was really there a month before I had him entertain the residents. His part of the story is as accurate otherwise as I could come up with, as is the story about Sam Brannan. Their interactions with my characters were, of course, fictional. I could find no written reports of the actual marriage ceremonies Brannan performed, only that he did them because he made money that way. He was terribly fond of money and came up with numerous ingenious ways to get folks to part with it. He was on the outs with the Mormon church for quite a while until he finally paid his tithe. Judges in San Francisco at that time were as corrupt as can be.

My intent with this book was to provide entertainment within the realm that existed during the Gold Rush era. It was never to write a history textbook, so taking some creative license here and there seemed appropriate.

Crossing the country by Prairie Schooner was never for the faint of heart, and countless lives were lost in the process. We all owe a debt to the courageous souls who risked everything to settle the American West. I can barely imagine their level of hardships. Lost lives, lost dreams, lost loves. It goes on and on tragically.

Researching this era was both fascinating and frustrating because many, many accounts contradicted each other. I just had to choose which seemed to have the stronger ring of truth. For instance, there is a scholastic article online that cites California's admission to the U.S. on April 1, 1850, when all others say September 9. In truth, San Francisco did not even become a true city until May of 1850, so the earlier date of statehood is doubtful. I found inaccuracies in the information presented by none other than The History Channel as well. Oy!

Sydney-Town was also known as Sydney Valley. I just chose one and went with it. Later, that area became known as the Barbary Coast.

I only barely touched on the rampant racism of that era. If I offended anyone by skirting around it or by mentioning it... well... I did what I felt was best. To ignore it completely would be false, but to dwell on it would have turned this story into something completely different. Remember—this is first and foremost a work of fiction. I used the history of the time as a backdrop fraught with many, many hardships.

As a native Californian, the Gold Rush history has always fascinated me, but when I found out that my own family had its roots smack dab in it, the book simply had to be written. But what an undertaking this has been! I discovered quickly that I could rarely write more than a paragraph before having to do some research or fact-checking. Language that was appropriate to the era became a tremendous challenge as well as a fantastic, amusing education. For example, "randy" sounds to us like an old-time word, but was actually used well after the time period of this story. The word of choice then was actually "horny" that we are more familiar with today. I guess a good word doesn't go out of fashion too quickly.

San Francisco has never been my hometown, but I did go to college near there and loved visiting the city as often as possible.

Throughout this wonderful education process, I discovered that some of the oral history my family was fond of passing along when I was a kid was partially (pardon me) a crock of shit. Research doesn't always yield the answers you expect, but you just have to live with whatever truths you uncover. My own however-many-greats-grandfather arrived late to the Gold Rush party in 1852 and built a hotel right where The Discovery was fictitiously erected. I couldn't resist. The similarity ends there except for the fact that he had a son named Royal, and I knew immediately I had to use that wonderful name. Obviously, I never met my Uncle Royal, so I can't claim that *my* Royal's personality was based on him. Ultimately, the family settled in southern California, north of where I grew up. I will add for interest's sake that my Uncle Royal was one of nine children, and my grandmother was one of eighteen. No twins. Staggering, isn't it? My great aunt wrote about their mother, characterizing her as a hard-working woman who never said "I can't." She was also quite beautiful, judging from old photos.

I have wanted to write a historical romance for years, but I guess it was in my best interests to learn to build up my writing confidence before tackling such a project. The timing for this was finally appropriate, and I am so happy that I accomplished it. Now I'm hooked, and I'm ready to write a sequel.

Thank you to my patient readers, who waited a lot longer than normal for me to publish a book, but I just had to do this one right. As I've mentioned, the research made the book slow to finish.

Thank you to my helpful researchers. My beta reader Susan was a picky fact-checker who called me on a few bloopers, and for that, I am tremendously grateful. I treasure her friendship, and her dedication to helping me write coherently is incomparable.

One of my readers, Judy Neurauter, researched names of the mid-nineteenth century and ended up winning the naming contests I held for *both* the ship as well as the main female character. I adore the name Wind Gypsy, and it was a landslide winner when we had the vote via my newsletter. She not only came up with Adeline Hart's name that everyone loved, but I also used her second-place winning name, Isabella Carrington. So, thank you to Judy for her diligence and talent! I hope I brought Izzie and Addie to life enough for her.

Huge thanks have to go to my husband. He enthusiastically researched everything there is to know about life in early California, crossing the country, and prospecting for gold. The man could get a Ph.D. in it at this point. I must admit that several times I had to stop him and say, "That part is already written, and it's okay." But some of the stuff was just too good to pass up, so I went back and rewrote certain scenes to make them more accurate or interesting. This is another reason I'm interested in writing a sequel, though. All of this research should not go to waste. Sadly, not all of what we uncovered had a place in the story, but it is all fascinating. So, the time spent researching was enjoyable.

One frustrating outcome of tackling this research lay in the face of Google's new policies. It was often completely impossible to research some specific event. If we entered a date, place, and specific names, the results that showed up were often material that was either from companies that pay for ad space or for newspapers that required buying a subscription and then may or may not have had the information. Gone are the days,

I'm afraid, of easy Googling, and I did finally end up subscribing to the *San Francisco Chronicle* that seemed to offer the most information from their archives. Some city records also must have been lost due to the series of fires in San Francisco, so it's not ALL Google's fault. Anyway, we did our best. I could have lived at the library, I suppose, but the time that would have taken was prohibitive, and it may not have yielded any better results. My lack of footnotes in the book attests to the fact that what I have recounted is mentioned in many, many sources.

One of my favorite sources of information was *The Timelines of Slang*. I could look through that for hours and be entertained. So, thank you to Jonathan Green for compiling that amazing collection.

Thank you to my wonderful friends who have cheered me along through this process and listened to me rhapsodize about my progress or frustrations. Some are fellow authors, and others are simply the people who make life amazing.

Thank you to Dar Albert of Wicked Smart Designs for coming up with the incredibly beautiful cover. It was as if she read my mind and then did an even better job.

Thank you to my wonderful editor Amy Maranville who makes this process fun even when she ever-so-gently tells me that I don't need *everything* I've written to stay in the book. Thank you to Amy for weeding my idea garden and for helping me make sense of all of it.

And thank you to my fantastic proofreader Mattie Davenport who has been with me since my very first book. She is the last word in what gets published, so her responsibilities are huge and tremendously appreciated. She also makes this process fun, and if it weren't fun... I'd just stop doing it and look for something else to obsess over and let rule my life!

Thank you to all of the pioneers and the Forty-Niners whose fascinating, often tragic, stories grab our imagination and won't let go. Their innovation and diligence helped to form California, especially San Francisco.

The early live-and-let-live attitudes of the settlers are thought by many to have spilled over into the colorful San Francisco culture we know today. Certainly, their tolerance toward the gay community was a result of the very prevalent bachelor marriages that I wrote about. Laws changed over time that made things more difficult, and that all came when more and more women settled in the city with their families. With the women and families, churches also sprang up and began to color local ethics. There was a certain resurgence of what was determined to be "proper morality" that swept through the city, but eventually, that was also wiped out again, and, as we all know, gay marriage is once again par for the course. Too bad it took so long to get back on track.

One thing the women did do, however, was eradicate the prostitute trade that was rampant at that time. Those wives simply could not stand the idea of a prostitute earning even a small bit of respect, and to see them parade around in polite company was intolerable.

Thank you, dear reader, for taking the time to read my books. I hope you love them as much as I do. And if you do, please leave a review. All authors appreciate an honest opinion, and it doesn't need to be long.

If you'd like to stay in touch, please sign up for my newsletter. https://landing.mailerlite.com/webforms/landing/m6f3i7 I generally mail one out once a month.

Also, I love to hear from readers. info@ariellatalix.com

Books by Ariella Talix

Porter the Importer: Prequel to The Drummonds Series

The story of the Drummond family begins with Molly Drummond and Porter Delaney in this prequel novella. Find out how Porter became the Importer and how Molly started her naughty boutique. Fall in love with Porter and the Drummonds.

Make Believe: The Drummonds- Book One

Lily Drummond's emotional love story with Finn Reilly is romantic suspense with plenty of humor and cute dogs. A page-turner! It's a Canterbury Tales-like saga with a host of interesting characters.

The Artist: The Drummonds- Book Two

This is David Drummond's story with Amelia Hernandez. It takes place mostly in Paris, and it will pull at your heartstrings. Imagination and beauty from page to page. A sizzling, sexy love story and much, much more.

Save Her: Lovers in Louisville- Book One

This series is a spin-off from The Drummonds. Your favorite characters appear again in supporting roles. *Save Her* is full of suspense and a couple you will adore. Åse Halvorsen is a beautiful jewelry designer, and Gunnar Dahl is a famous mystery writer with a secret.

Saving Him: Lovers in Louisville- Book Two

Sibylla Eliana Xenopoulos (Sibley) was Åse's roommate and best friend in college. She returns to Louisville for a great opportunity and finds love with Gunnar's buddy Leo Spanos. Their chemistry is off the charts, but danger lurks in the shadows.

Savor This: Lovers in Louisville- Book Three

In this passionate and unpredictable story, Halden Dahl, Gunnar's younger brother, is a successful glass artist and total ladies' man. Handsome and talented with an ego as big as all outdoors, has he finally met his match?

The Rule of 3

Since no one actually lives in Louisville in this book, it became a standalone spin-off from the popular "Lovers in Louisville" series. Tanner Lassiter, Zoë Deliban, and a new character, Eli Whittaker, all make for a delightful book about ambition, loyalty, and the deepest, most enduring kind of love. It's a second-chance, billionaire, small-town, MMF love story.

Just Curious

This standalone MMF story is about Willa, a gorgeous and highly successful writer who falls for her billionaire neighbor Jackson and his life-long friend Casey. An old acquaintance causes them trouble, and the seriousness of it escalates to a dangerous level. The setting is mostly in southern California, but they do some globe-trotting as well.

Compelling Urges

A loose spin-off from *Just Curious*, this MMF story is also set in San Diego County. Bodhi Monaghan, Cooper Houston, and Ivy Chambers navigate some troubled waters before they can manage their life together as a triad. Doubts and trust issues plague them as well as a strange and interesting character who is bent on claiming or possibly ruining Bodhi.

The Golden Rush

This is an MMF romance set during the 1849 California Gold Rush. Six men travel across the country, creating an unbreakable bond of friendship, and find themselves in the right place at the right time. Jasper Langley and Royal Dawson eventually meet Adeline Hart, and both fall head over heels for her. It is a moving tale of perseverance, compassion, and sheer grit.

Fiddle and Fire

The sequel to *The Golden Rush* will be out in 2022.